Flame

Flame

STEPHANIE PERRY MOORE

ISBN 0-7394-2522-6

Printed in the United States of America

For my youngest daughter

Sheldyn Ashli,

As I cradle
you in my arms,
I witness a flaming glow
in your precious eyes
that is full of love for me.
It's my deepest desire
that everyone
who reads this book
will carry
that same torch of love
for Jesus Christ.

Contents

Acknowledgments

As I finish this book on Christmas Eve, I long to relax with my family by a roaring fire. In order to enjoy the flame, several things have to happen. The same is true for the writing of this book. Here is a special thank you to all who aided in building the manuscript to a blaze.

To my parents, Franklin and Shirley Perry: You are like my FIREPLACE. You two have held the substance of my dreams close to your hearts for years. Without your love, nurture, and support, I would never have had the courage to realize my goals. The FLAME that holds my character burns bright because of you both.

To my mentors, Matthew Parker and Eugene Seals and everyone at Moody Press: You all are my LOGS. Because of your vision to help African-American writers get published, I had a positive vehicle to assist me in completing many novels. Although sometimes I almost lost faith that this could happen and wanted to give up, you knew, as does any unburning wood sitting in the fire, that eventually it will ignite. And in God's time that is exactly what has happened. Through your encouragement, I kept writing and now I have five novels published. The Flame that holds opportunity now runs ramped up my chimney of success because of your strong desire to help others.

To my friend Marla Clark: A RACK is what you are. You have the extremely tough job of supporting and lifting my big dreams. Discouragement and gloom can't fit in the fireplace of your business because you only mount up God's truth. The Flame that holds encouragement is never dim in my life, for you are always showing me the bright side to everything.

To my daughters, Sydni Derek and Sheldyn Ashli: You two lil' angels are the PAPER. Just as a fire sometimes needs a boost to aid in its catching, so too do I sometimes need a boost to help me fill the empty page. Being your mommy ignites my inspiration to achieve. The Flame that holds procrastination burns out, as I long to make you both proud.

To my husband, Derrick Moore: You are my MATCH. Not only do you heat up my life with your wanted presence, but because of your leadership my desire for God is sparked. Even though things get quite hot sometimes, I realize I need your charge. I thank you for providing for our family. This has afforded me the opportunity to stay home. When not being a wife and mother, you gave me the time to flare up my pen. The Flame that holds love is constantly glowing in my life because of how I truly feel for you.

To the reader, saved and unsaved: you are the SCREEN. This novel was devised to warm your heart. As you view what lies before you, may the words God's given me to share embody your soul. The Flame that holds determination remained alive, for I strongly believed you needed to read this.

And most importantly, to my Savior, Jesus Christ: you are the FIRE! Because the Holy Spirit lives inside of a sinful me, I am a light. It's so good to know that I follow You in darkness, I'll easily find my way. The Flame that holds grace is daily bestowed upon me. It is my earnest prayer, that every living soul will have a burning passion to know You—an awesome God.

1 Melted

On my twenty-second birthday, I sat alone in my apartment, staring at a stale cupcake with one candle in it. Given the many things I'd already been blessed with, it seemed like I had nothing to make a wish for. Eventually, as the candle's flicker grew dim, something came to mind. I wanted, longed for, and needed male companionship. Before I could blow out the flame, the phone rang, interrupting my moment.

"I'm engaged! Bacall, I got engaged yesterday," my sister, Brooks, blabbed into the receiver with glee. "Say something, will ya?"

"Ah, so you're getting hitched . . . cool," I responded with little excitement.

"Why are you acting like this?"

"Acting like what? Just 'cause I ain't turning flips doesn't mean I'm not happy for you and Karrington. I'm just dealin' with some things. Anyway, y'all been dating since your sophomore year at Alabama. Shoot, you've been out of college for a year. I kinda think it's time."

Brooks, my only sibling, is two years older than I am. We're not opposites. We just differ in how we play the game. She follows the rules and I break 'em.

"So, what did the Rev say?"

"Well, you know how Dad is. He warned Karri to take care of me . . . said if he didn't, he'd have to answer to my two fathers—him and God. Mom was ecstatic! She and I are meeting later today to start planning for my wedding next Christmas Eve."

Yeah, I knew my mother was pleased. She is Ms. Society Queen. For years, Mom has had a file full of wedding ideas for us. She's been dying to pull it out and get started on the wedding of the century. Who knew if she would ever get to use the file on me?

I'm from Montgomery, Alabama. Not the largest city in the state, but being that it is the capital, a lot of influential people live there. My folks fare among the most notable.

My father is a Baptist preacher whose ministry is known worldwide. He has an awesome vision: television, radio, concerts, pulpits . . . you name it, the Reverend Brad D. Lee has done it. He's still doing it. Shoot, Daddy just recently built a recording and television studio. He also wears the hat of president of God's Town Records. Although my dad has hefty standards, to which I don't always measure up, I'm definitely a Daddy's girl.

My mother certainly doesn't sit idly in the background. She's the anchorwoman for KTWB news in Montgomery. Because of her Civil Rights footage, she's a renowned journalist. She's an occasional *Dateline* correspondent, covering stories from the South. My mom is always busy. If I had to define our sometimes-strained relationship, I would say she's my mother, not my friend.

"What are you thinking about? You're so quiet," my sister probed.

"Quit badgering me," I huffed. "I'm here! What more do you want?"

"Don't take this the wrong way," Brooks began, "but . . . you need a man. Bacall, you're a college senior. You've never had a boyfriend. College isn't just about getting an education, you know. Sis, you're a beautiful girl. Aren't there any guys at Auburn who interest you?"

"Not every girl is in school to snag a guy and get an M.R.S. degree. Maybe I'm not trying to follow your path. Now, don't *you* take this the wrong way, but plan your wedding . . . not mine! Good-bye."

I hated hanging up on her, but sometimes she could be annoying. Now, with her news, I was officially depressed. Brooks was getting married . . . wow! True enough, I did know it was inevitable. Even a fool could tell that it only made sense for my sister and her beau to make their love permanent. When they're together, there's no denying they're perfectly matched.

It's not like I wasn't glad for Brooks. I was just sad for me. Contrary to what I told her, I longed to walk down the aisle on Dad's arm and say "I do" to my Prince Charming. Being that I didn't have a guy, I just kept telling myself I didn't need one. Yet, I desperately wanted companionship.

Later that day, after I sat for hours mourning my birthday, I prayed. "Father, thank You for allowing my sister to fall in love with an awesome Christian guy. May You continually bless them and keep them together. Please, Lord, don't let Mama take over the wedding plans and not give Brooks a chance to make any decisions. I pray for their counseling sessions with Dad. I pray Reverend Lee understands his role as advisor, not as Brooks's father, and that he won't dictate how they should live their lives."

I paused for a second and decided to open up further to

the God I'd made my own since I was eight. Only He could fully comprehend my deepest desire. But I didn't know how to pray such a selfish prayer. A prayer for a mate.

Continuing, I said, "Now, a small request. OK, maybe it's not so small. Please send me a guy, Lord. Not just any guy, but one who's handsome, popular, charming, lovable . . . ." I rattled off the list quickly. "There's more, but I'm sure You know who to send. In Jesus' name, amen."

As I got off my knees, my roommate, Wesli Ezell, startled me. The two of us had shared an apartment for three years. She's from Jacksonville, Florida, and hopes one day to return home as a doctor.

"Hey, Callie," Wesli said playfully. "Get dressed, girlfriend. Alma and everybody will be over in a few to go to 'Skegee. Your turn to drive."

It was our first weekend back at school. Auburn had a big game against Mississippi State University. We won. You'd think that, since we won, Auburn would be live instead of Tuskegee. However, all that was going on in Auburn was a bunch of lame frat parties.

So, most of the black students either had private apartment sets or headed fifteen minutes down the road to the college where something was always going on. My crew and I were no exception. The eight of us were almost always the first ones down there from Auburn. Always loud and ready to party.

Two of my friends, LaKisha and Portia, had boyfriends who attended Tuskegee. Sophie's so-called guy, Goode, went to Auburn with us. But shoot, he stayed in 'Skegee so much, you'd think he had a girlfriend there. That's why Sophie loved to go with us so that she could keep an eye on him.

The rest of us were what you'd call very, very available. We were five young black women with our claws sharpened, ready to hook onto a good black man.

That night, we all wore jeans and some type of midriff

top. I had on a red off-the-shoulder shirt. I chose it because it showed off the tan I obtained during our family summer vacation to Charleston. My friends said the tan, which made my milk chocolate skin look like sweet, dark chocolate, was all that. I never admitted it, but I too was digging my new, smooth, darker complexion.

Finally, after all the primping, we reached the historical town. On a normal day, I could drive through beautiful Tuskegee in ten minutes or less. However, thanks to the party, when we hit the city limits, it took us almost an hour to move through the college city and find a place to park.

Wesli and I lagged behind while the rest of the crew rushed to the gym door. The two of us kept hogging the rear-view mirror as if those last-minute changes would make us irresistible to any man who laid eyes upon us. A dumb thought, huh? But you couldn't tell us that.

When we finally reached the front of the line, Wesli whispered, "Oh, Callie, check out the guy working the door."

She raised her finger and pointed to the six-foot honey-suckle-tone, baldheaded, two-hundred-pound hunk sitting at the table next to the entrance. My eyes lit up and my heart instantly melted. Absolutely gorgeous didn't begin to describe this dude. He seemed like my Prince Charming, my Knight in Shining Armor, my Dream Man, my Mr. Right, the guy I'd saved myself for. Well, maybe this cutie wouldn't fit that last description on my list because for that he'd have to possess a lot more than good looks. He'd have to have character.

Alma overheard us. "Yeah, Wesli, he's kinda cute!"

"Kinda cute?" Portia jumped in. "No, girrrl . . . that man is fine! If I weren't tied to Butch, I'd be on him."

My friends laughed, but I was mesmerized. I could tell

by the sly glances he shot our way that he knew we were sizing him up. Yet he was cooler than Snoopy with shades.

Then he looked up at us and said, “You ladies look lovely this evening.” His strong, mellow voice sounded like Billy Dee Williams.

“Thanks!” we replied in unison.

Then Jade, the forceful one, asked, “Well, since we look so good, do we get in free?”

“Free?” his strong voice questioned. “Give a brother a break! We’re trying to raise money for the school.”

Suddenly, he looked directly at me and stared. I can say that I definitely felt the chemistry at that strong glance. Embarrassed, I dropped my head. The next thing I knew, his strong hand softly lifted my chin. As my head slowly rose, I finally found myself staring into his eyes. Oh, what a captivating sight.

“How ’bout I let the eight of you ladies in for the price of four?” he offered as he dropped his hand from my face.

We all said thanks, then my girlfriends broke my deadlock stare by pushing me through the door. It was clear that I was hesitant to move from his side.

Portia hollered, “Well, it’s obvious that Bacall thinks he’s kinda cute . . . and then some!”

I didn’t say anything, but I was thinking that Portia was right on.

There was nothing spectacular about the step show that started the party. The ladies of Delta Sigma Theta were “oo-ooping.” The A.K.A.s were “skee-weeing.” The Kappas were bopping those crimson canes, while their sweethearts chanted, “Too sweet, too sweet!” The Alphas were saying, “A Phi A.” Naturally, the Omegas were barking and sportin’ their gold boots. And the Sigmas and Zetas were huddled together doing their thang. Yep, it was a typical entertaining

Greek show.

When the dancing began, I searched the room, but I couldn't spot my mystery man. I did all that I could, but he could not be found. Why was I looking for him, anyway? I didn't know—except that I was totally captivated. Never before had I experienced love at first sight. *Well,* I thought, *there's a first time for everything.*

Finally, I spotted him walking across the stage. His debonair strut made me singe as he held the microphone with one hand and caressed it with the other.

"Ladies and gentlemen . . . for those of you who don't know me, I'm Rory Kerry . . . your student body president."

My roommate hit my leg hard, letting me know that she too thought he had it going on.

"The SGA thanks all of you for coming out this evening. I worked the door and found that not only are our students in attendance, but we've got people from Alabama State, Troy State, Morehouse, and Clark. And . . . I can't forget the lovely group I met from Auburn. I know you all came to party. We'll start that in a few minutes. But the judges are still debating over the winner of our step show. So, to fill the time, I'll sing a number with my band, Rise," Rory announced.

My eyes widened as he began to breathe a beautiful melody of song. His voice was smoother than the finest wine and sweeter than a honeycomb. I'd been around professional singers all my life, and I'd never heard a melody sung more lovely.

I knew my dad needed to hear him. With his label deal at Yo Town Records, my father could sign eight new artists under his sub-gospel label, God's Town Records.

The standing ovation brought my attention back to Rory, who was gracefully gliding off the stage. As someone else began to announce the step-show winners, I left my seat to find the man with the magic voice.

When I stepped into the hallway, I caught a glimpse of

Rory standing against the stairs, though all I could actually see was his back. I walked closer to the creature who'd managed to intrigue me, and finally saw his face. He was leaning against the rail, in an obvious disagreement with some girl. Her voice was loud enough for me to hear her words.

"No . . . no! It's not over. How can you just walk away from our relationship?"

Tons of questions swept through my mind. *Who is this chick? Is she Rory's lady? Why is she so mad?*

Their conversation grew louder. People in the hall began to crowd around to witness the scene. Like the others, I couldn't resist listening to the heated discussion.

"We can get through this problem." The girl was almost screaming now. "Don't you think you can desert me. Uh-uh . . . not without some drama," she threatened. Suddenly, she dashed toward Rory with her fist aimed at his precious face.

He stretched his arm out to defend against her attack. "Calm down, Ashley! Believe me . . . this is not the way to keep us together. There's nothing you can do. I'm through, and I'm through yellin'."

She jerked away from his grasp. "Keep your hands off me and don't tell me to calm down."

As she continued to throw angry words at him like daggers, Rory was as laid-back as a dead man in a coffin. I was starting to admire him even more. Not many men could handle a woman's fury with such ease.

Finally, he shook his head at her raging outburst and strolled away.

He walked outside, and like a puppy dog, I followed. As my legs trotted after him, once again my head wondered why.

I caught up with him at the same table where we'd met earlier that evening. His dejected look reeled me in even more.

"Rory," I called out softly in my kindest voice. I was

determined to be the opposite of the voice he'd just heard.

"Yeah," he gasped with frustration. He looked up at me.

"Well, I see this is a bad time for a chat. You've obviously got that girl on your mind. Sorry." I turned around to walk back into the gym.

He rushed from the table and grabbed my arm, stopping me. Although the pull was forceful, I didn't feel overpowered. Instead, I felt needed.

"I don't have that girl on my mind."

I stared into his eyes.

"Come over here. I'd love to talk to you."

Even though I still had questions, I decided to do as he requested.

My impulse was right again. He did need the company. And I was just the person to steer him away from the chaos.

He guided me down a lonesome path to the lighted football field, where we sat in the stands. We were quiet for several minutes before Rory spoke.

"I'm really sorry you had to see that," he said softly.

"That's OK. It didn't seem like it was your fault."

He shook his head. "I'm too old to be going through this kind of stuff. I'm a senior, for goodness' sake. I shouldn't have all this drama in my life."

"Have you been at Tuskegee for four years?" I asked.

He nodded. "Almost five, actually."

I was dumfounded as to why we'd never met.

"I'll be graduating this year," he said. "The first in my family to get a college degree."

"Really? Where are you from?"

"Atlanta. It's just me and my mom."

Rory went on to tell me that his parents never married and that he had no siblings. He beamed with pride when he spoke of his mother, sharing with me that she was at the top of his list of favorite people.

"She gave up everything to raise me," he told me.

Rory said that apart from school and his mother, music was his life. With his seven-member band, Rise, he managed to make a little cash performing.

"With most of that money, I've created a mini-recording studio in the house that I'm renting."

"Wow!"

He chuckled. "Don't be too impressed. I share the house with a roommate, and it's really more of a shack than a house."

We laughed together.

"What's your name, beautiful?" he asked, looking at me intensely.

I was surprised by his question. We had been talking for at least an hour, and I hadn't told him anything about myself.

"I'm sorry. How could I be so rude and not introduce myself properly?"

"Don't apologize. I didn't introduce myself, either," my honeycomb guy replied. "Hello, lovely lady. I'm Rory Danton Kerry. And your name is?"

I laughed and said, "Well, fine gentleman, my name is Bacall. I am pleased to make your acquaintance."

"No," Rory whispered sweetly in my ear. "The pleasure is definitely mine." He took my hands into his.

I shivered. I wasn't sure if it was his words or the forty-nine-degree temperature that made the chill run through my body.

However, being cold was the last thing on my mind. I felt secure with Rory that early autumn night. Having my hands in his felt like I had my palms over a fire. His grip was warm, snug, and cozy.

"You're shaking," Rory said with a look of concern on his face. "We've got to head back so I can get you inside."

"I hate to move. I'm enjoying being with you."

He looked at me and smiled. He didn't just look and turn away. He stared. His glare didn't make me feel uneasy, though. It made me feel radiant. In fairness, there was a full moon and its light shined right onto my face. Maybe that's the real reason I felt all aglow. Whatever, I didn't want the growing emotion of love to leave.

As the night's chill became more intense, Rory placed his jacket over my shoulders. Then he stood and pulled me from the bleachers. Hand in hand, we walked back toward the path. Suddenly, he stopped.

"How would you like to ride?"

I frowned, then smiled when he leaned over for me to jump onto his back. We laughed together as he galloped like a pony.

All kinds of feelings and thoughts rushed through me. We'd only met a few hours ago, but I felt like Rory was the kind of man who would attend to my every need. I was impressed with him. My heart was moving very fast toward his. I couldn't stop the momentum. I didn't want to.

When we reached the gym, Rory slowly lowered me onto the ground. Before he opened the door, he gazed into my eyes.

"Lady Bacall, I really like you. I'm forever in your debt for rescuing me out of my gloom."

I laughed, then smiled, and silently thanked God. Earlier I had prayed for a guy, and behold . . . my request was granted. Rory Kerry didn't know it, but I knew he was sent into my life from above. And I knew, as long as we pleased God in heaven, we'd have no problems.

Inside the gym, Rory stopped by the SGA table.

"Just checking on the money," he said to the young ladies

sitting at the table.

One of the girls handed Rory a sheet, and he smiled as he scanned the numbers. "By the way, who won the step show?"

The girl beamed. "Delta Sigma Theta, of course," she said and pointed to her red T-shirt with the white Greek letters.

I smiled. My sister was a Delta, and she would have been pleased to know that her sorors at Tuskegee turned it out with the first-place prize.

The dance was almost over, yet the gym was still crowded. Rory took my hand and led me toward the dance floor. I felt like Cinderella. All eyes were on me.

As we moved to the center of the room, I overheard two girls jabbering as we passed by them.

"Look at her! Who's Rory with, anyway?" one girl questioned.

The other replied, "Some chick who thinks she's cute!"

Suddenly, Rory stopped and turned toward the ladies. "You're right. She is cute. She's that . . . and much, much more."

Then we turned away, leaving the girls standing with their mouths wide open.

As Rory put his arms around me, I said, "You didn't have to defend me."

"Yes, I did," he said with a serious stare as we slow danced to "If Only for One Night," by Luther Vandross. "I could never let anyone offend a lady. I just apologize for my tacky schoolmates."

In his arms, I sighed. "Today's my birthday, and no one remembered. I thought it was going to be just another day, but . . . but you've made it meaningful. You made it beautiful."

His eyes widened. "Wow, your birthday." Then he kissed me softly on the cheek. "Happy birthday, Lady Bacall."

Throughout the rest of the song, I didn't utter a sound. I just stayed in his arms, mesmerized by his touch. He held me just right. Not too tight and definitely not too loose. His body felt almost too good against mine. All kinds of feelings were brewing inside of me. And I knew that I had to be careful not to let those feelings lead me into trouble.

We danced through the final song, then Rory slowly walked me through the crowd to my car. I was glad my girlfriends gave us space, lingering behind so that I could have more time with my new man.

When we reached my car, my heart was sad with the thought that the wonderful evening had come to an end. I unlocked my door with the remote, and Rory opened it and helped me inside. He leaned into my window and gently stroked my lips with his. I was not prepared for his quick, soft kiss, but neither did I regret it.

"Happy birthday," he uttered, pulling his lips from mine.

I jotted my phone number on a piece of paper. As I handed it to him, I said, "Tonight was really special to me. I hope that, unlike Luther's song, we'll be together more than just one night."

"Lady Bacall, now that you've entered my world, I wouldn't want to live without you in it." Rory spoke softly as his hand moved slowly through my hair.

Like a marshmallow roasting over an open fire, I melted!

2

Sizzling

I have to admit, I thought of the intriguing guy I'd met often in those first few weeks. Whether in the shower reaching for the soap, or in the classroom listening to the professor, no place was safe from Rory Kerry entering my mind. He was a fascinating character to me.

I so hoped he'd call. Just ring my phone. Tell me something sweet. Make me fall even deeper into his web.

Every time my mind wandered, I'd shake myself out of the dream world. I looked at the obvious. From just our one encounter, I knew that Rory was gorgeous, popular, and smart. What would he want with me when he could have his pick? That was probably why over two weeks had passed and I hadn't heard from him.

Actually, it was probably a good thing. I didn't even know his beliefs. Did he know Christ? Was he a Christian? I thought of my father's words. "Only say what is. Don't speculate on what may be because only our Father in heaven knows what is to come."

I was sorta glad now that I hadn't asked for his number. Didn't want to be tempted to call him. After all, if you take the chase out of dating, then there is no need for a guy to run to the finish line.

Wesli and I decided to spend our Saturday at the local mall. Since there was no home football game, there was not much else to do in Auburn. Didn't even have much to study being that school had just started.

We were browsing through the big department store when I saw him. I froze like water on a once-cascading waterfall. I didn't know what to do. I wasn't even sure if he'd remember me. It had been three weeks.

I pulled Wesli's jacket sleeve and pointed to Rory. Wesli gasped when she saw him.

"Should I go to him?" I asked with knots twisted tight in my stomach.

She answered with a smile. "Well, Callie . . . it doesn't look like you have to make a move. Appears that Mr. Everything is headed over here." She paused until Rory stood in front of us. "I'm gonna cruise the store. See ya!"

We remained silent until Wesli was out of hearing range. "Hello, gorgeous," Rory finally said. "I was riding through Auburn hoping to find the lady who'd captured my heart. Believe it or not, I lost your number."

His story was rather suspect, but like a sucker, I bought it anyway. True or not, the thought of him riding around town searching for me made my day. Heck, it made my entire week!

"Hi, Rory . . . how've you been?" I gasped, unable to hide my excitement.

"I'm a lot better now that I've found you." He looked me up and down. "Look at you; you are even more beautiful than I remember."

I blushed. The butterflies in my stomach grew even more active, and I felt my knees shaking.

"You OK?" He grabbed my arm as if to make sure I didn't fall over.

"Thanks . . . but I'm fine," I replied, trying to hide my embarrassment.

His smile was wide. "I've had 20/20 vision all my life, and my eyes aren't failing me now 'cause I can see . . . you are fine!"

Every word he spoke seemed to be straight from a romance novel. Someone had trained this guy well. But I was determined to enjoy his sweet remarks for as long as I could.

"So, I see you're here with a girlfriend," Rory said, looking around. "Did she drive? You drive? Are there others with you?" Rory tossed out question after question.

"It's just my roommate and me, killing a Saturday spending our folks' money," I chuckled. "And Wesli drove."

He looked like he wanted to ask me another question but was hesitant. Finally, he spoke. "You think I can give you a ride home? Or . . . I could follow you guys back to your house."

I'm sure it was my frown that made him pause.

"Wait," he said. "I have another idea. May I take you and your friend out to dinner?"

It's not like I thought he'd do something crazy to me, but I didn't really know him. So the thought of Wes tagging along was comforting.

As if on cue, Wesli returned. "Hey, Callie, you ready to go?" She asked me the question but was looking at Rory.

"Yeah, but Rory just offered to take us out to dinner."

"Oh, did you now?" Wesli laughed.

He smiled. "It would be an honor."

Wesli said, "Well, what are we waiting for?"

We agreed to meet Rory at *Sunset,* the local tavern.

Wesli and Rory hit it off like a smash song. While they chatted about the pros and cons of historically black or predominately white colleges, I sat back and listened—which was easy because it was difficult to slide a word into the conversation. But I didn't much mind. My silence gave me more time to read the fine print on the guy I'd grown so fond of.

"Actually, one of the things that Tuskegee has done for me is given me confidence in my music," Rory said to Wesli. "I know with what I've learned in my head and what I've been given in my heart—I'll be a star."

A star. Although he was studying electrical engineering, it wasn't hard to imagine him realizing his dream.

As soon as he told us about his hopes, Wesli said, "You have met the right lady. Bacall's daddy owns a big studio in Montgomery. Tell him, girl! Doesn't your father have a lot of record deals . . . deals for acts . . . something?"

I kicked Wesli under the table. I wasn't ready to divulge information about my father. The last thing I wanted was for Rory to be attracted to me because of what my father could give him. If I deemed him worthy, he'd be introduced to my parents later.

Getting the cue from my thump, Wesli giggled. "That would be the ultimate blessing, huh?"

Rory laughed with Wesli and I sighed with relief. He thought she was kidding.

We chatted through the rest of the dinner, then Rory followed us to our place. As soon as I walked through the door, I turned on the television. My mother had phoned earlier that morning to let me know she'd be filling in for Bob Bowles, the weekend anchorman. I never missed seeing her through the weekdays and definitely wanted to see her tonight. Even though Brooks was the one following in my mother's footsteps, I was her biggest fan.

Wesli went into her bedroom, while Rory sat in the living

room with me. He tried to chat, but my eyes were glued to the TV screen.

"Guess I better get going." Rory stood after we'd been watching the news for a few minutes. "Seems like I'm boring you so much that the weekend news is more appealing." He sounded a tad dejected.

"I'm so sorry," I said, taking his hand. "It's not you. I'm really into . . ."

"The Montgomery News." He laughed. "Yeah, right. Don't spare my feelings. The only interesting thing about that broadcast is the beautiful anchorwoman. Now for an older woman, she has it going on."

I simply smiled.

"But for real," Rory continued, "I should get going. I'll call you later, and we can continue what's been a great day for me."

❦ ❦ ❦

"I got home OK," Rory told me over the phone later that evening.

Boy, was I excited to receive his call because I finally had the answer to my important question. When I had walked him to his old white minivan earlier, I had taken a deep breath, then asked, "Rory, do you believe in God?"

He stared at me for a long moment before he nodded slightly. "Yeah, I do. I accepted Jesus when I was just ten. But I have to admit, as I've gotten older, I haven't grown in God the way I wanted to." He paused. "That was an interesting question. I can't say that anyone's ever asked me that before."

I smiled. "That's because you've never met anyone like me before."

He laughed. "You got that right." Then his laugh disappeared. "Seriously, though, I really want to grow more spiritually."

He leaned over, kissed me on the cheek, then drove away.

"Hey, Lady Bacall," he whispered now, interrupting my thoughts. "You know a lot about me, but what do I really know about you . . . my mystery lady?"

"I don't know what kind of juicy details you want from me," I said with a smile in my voice.

"Anything you want to tell me."

I wanted to melt at his words. "Well, let's see, I'm from Montgomery. My folks have been married for twenty-five years. I have an older sister. And I still don't know what I want to be when I . . . grow . . . up."

"I hope it's that you want to be with me." He laughed.

"What do you mean?" I teased, trying to keep him on his toes. "I don't know you that well!"

"I can fix that. How 'bout we get together again tomorrow? I sing in the Tuskegee University Gospel Choir, and tomorrow we're singing at a church in 'The Gomp,'"

I laughed. "What do you know about The Gomp?"

"Everyone who's down and lives in Alabama knows Montgomery's nickname," he answered. "Hopefully, I'll be back around three. Would it be OK if I took you to dinner and a movie? I could be at your place by five."

With a pillowed voice I said, "Sounds wonderful, Rory."

"Good. Sleep tight, Lady Bacall. May God bless your dreams."

When I hung up, my heart was happy. I'd never had a gentleman wish me sweet slumber.

I knelt to pray. "You are the Almighty. You know my needs and You meet them. You are my Shepherd. You never leave me with a want, Father. I'm so grateful that I met Rory. I can't begin to describe all the beautiful emotions he has stirred up inside of me. I'm not quite certain where this relationship will go or how long it will last. You alone know what the future holds. However, Lord, I do trust You to protect and guard all these crazy emotions. I'm a little scared my heart may break. But I know as long as I remember to keep You in the center of this relationship, whatever happens . . . will be for my good. I know that only if I'm out of Your will Satan can enter in and destroy all this greatness."

I kept my eyes closed and meditated on the words I'd just spoken from my heart. Then I climbed into bed and dreamt about the new man in my life.

❦ ❦ ❦

Church the next day was as uplifting as always. My dad was in the pulpit bringing God's Word to life. I knew his words would lead many to salvation.

Brooks and I were sitting in the choir. Her fiancé, Karrington, was positioned down in front, facing us, as usual.

See, Karrington was not only the choir director but also one of my father's most promising artists. Actually, Karri didn't sing, though he wrote some of the most powerful songs. But instead of singing, Karri talked over the choir and the music in a very inspiring way. The guy is so talented.

Looking over at my sister, I realized how sorry I was for hanging up on her when she called with the news of her engagement. I had apologized earlier, and my big sister was as gracious as she always is.

"That's OK, sweetie. I understand," Brooks had said to me. "I shouldn't be butting into your life." We hugged and she continued. "But there is one thing I want you to remember. When God is ready, he'll send you your man."

"Y'all know . . . uh-huh . . . that I wasn't here last week." My father's voice brought me back to the present. "I preached over in Texas for the Trinity Broadcast Network. Today I wanted to make a special announcement, though I'm sure the word has probably already gotten to ya. You may have heard through the grapevine that I'm about to add a new member to my family. Now, if you haven't heard, I want you to know that ain't nobody havin' no babies." He waited for the low chuckles throughout the congregation to die down. "Now, y'all know that God has blessed me with two special girls." He turned to Karrington. "Come here, Karri." Karrington stood and joined my father at the pulpit. "This joker right here asked my older daughter, Brooks, to be his wife. Now, he did get permission. That's right, he . . ." My dad talked on.

I couldn't believe he was telling the whole story to the church. Talk about exposing a private moment.

I glanced at my sister. She was smiling, so I guess she didn't mind. I, on the other hand, would have been furious. That's Daddy, though. To him, his church is his family.

"So I said, sure you can have her hand," Reverend Lee continued. "Now I just gotta give Bacall away. Then maybe my pockets won't be so empty."

As Daddy gave Karrington a big hug, the congregation whistled, cheered, and said, "Amen." Then my father walked over to the piano and took a seat.

"Some of y'all remember, when the girls were small, I used to have them sit beside me and we'd sing. Young ladies, appease your earthly daddy and let's try stealing back a few precious moments."

He banged on the piano keys, making a harmonious chord, and Brooks and I proudly joined him. I took a quick glance at my mother's beaming face before we began singing. We sang *Amazing Grace*, the way we had when Brooks and I were little. And for a moment, I was lost in time.

Just after the sermon, my dad proclaimed, "First Baptist, y'all know I love surprises. I feel when you work hard for the Lord, He rewards you. When I got back from Texas, Deacon Smith called me and said, 'Pastor, we have surpassed the new wing building funds targeted amount.' Now, give me just a little time to say thanks to y'all for going beyond the call of duty. Sit back as I enlist the help of the Tuskegee Gospel Choir."

The church's back doors suddenly opened. The choir marched in, adorned in maroon and gold robes.

I sat frozen in my seat, even though I wanted to get up and hide. I didn't want Rory to see me. Not that it made a big difference, but I wasn't quite ready to introduce him to my family.

Since I had nowhere to go, I remained in my seat. As the dynamic choir started singing, I forgot about my desire to flee. I was feeling the music in my soul and so was everyone else in the church, if their raised voices and stomping feet were any indication. Rory sang the solo in two of their three songs.

Looking at my dad's face, I could tell he was more than impressed with Rory's performance. My father had never been known to sit on talent. And Rory sounded even better singing gospel than he did the first time I'd heard him singing with his band. I leaned back in my seat and smiled. This was going to be interesting.

After church, I was scrambling, trying to get out before Rory saw me. My mother and sister cornered me and insisted I come home to the celebration dinner given in honor of the newly engaged couple. I already had a previous commitment with Rory, and I did not want to break it. Not that I didn't want to toast with Brooks—but let's face it, she already had a man.

How can I get out of this? I wondered. *How can I not let them down? How can I make them understand without divulging everything?* I had all the questions and no answers, so I finally agreed to go, thinking I could leave a message on

Rory's machine.

Before I could get out of the church, someone took hold of my arm. I didn't even have to look. The gentle touch was familiar. Turning, I confirmed what I knew.

"Hey, beautiful, where are you going in such a hurry?"

I shook my head wordlessly.

"I guess a better question is . . . what are you doing here?" he interrogated.

"Hi, Rory," I said with surprise in my voice. "What am I doing here? Uh . . . I worship here. This has been my church . . . all my life."

"Gosh, I guess you've been blessed. Having *the* Brad D. Lee as your pastor. I truly admire that man. I've watched him for years. Got all his albums with the Changed Souls Choir. So, being a member of his church means you probably know him pretty well, huh?"

I hesitated. "Uh, you could say that. He's my—"

He grabbed my arm before I could complete my sentence and pulled me into a corner. "Actually, it's funny I ran into you. Please don't get offended," he said, lowering his eyes. "But I . . . I can't make dinner. See, Reverend Lee likes my voice and . . ." He stopped.

"What are you trying to tell me?"

"He asked me to . . . This is hard to say."

"Rory," I said with frustration, "spit it out!"

"He wants me to meet his daughter." Rory said the words quickly.

"What?" I yelled.

"I know, I know. Believe me, if it wasn't my career, I wouldn't even consider it. It's the last thing I want to do. But Bacall, I promise you, my meeting her will in no way alter what I feel for you. I realize that dating her could probably get me a record deal because she is the man's daughter. But that's not what I want, nor what I'm after."

He looked sincere. I knew he was concerned about my

reaction. Who could blame him for wanting to make good career connections?

He continued. "I didn't know how to gracefully turn him down. I really respect Reverend Lee, and I get the feeling he thinks highly of me, too. I didn't feel like there'd be too much harm in going to his house and being sociable. But don't worry. She's probably some ugly duckling, anyway, with Daddy trying to fix her up and all."

"You mean, you didn't see her sing with him today?" I wanted to make absolutely certain he wasn't pulling my leg.

"Naw . . . we were downstairs. I heard Reverend Lee singing with them, though. Now, the sistahs can blow. I'd love to sing with his daughter. But believe me, Bacall, that would be the extent of our relationship."

Rory placed his hands in mine, then took a deep breath. The look he gave me assured me that he wished he didn't have to postpone our date.

"If you have a problem with this, I'll talk to Reverend Lee and see if we can reschedule."

I was relieved. All this time, I was worried about him liking me just for my connection with, as he put it, *the* Brad D. Lee. Now I knew that would have never been an issue. Rory didn't know who I was, yet he liked me for who he thought I was. Kind of complicated, but I prefer to think of it as simply a great foundation on which to build a solid relationship.

"I have no problem with you going over to Reverend Lee's home and meeting his daughter. As a matter of fact, I'm sure you'll have a lovely time. She's probably all that and a bag of chips," I laughed. "See, I'm—"

Rory abruptly let go of my hand, and I wondered if I'd said something wrong. My eyes widened with surprise when I heard my dad behind me.

"I see you waste no time. You guys better get going. Mrs. Lee is gonna be mad if you're late. Right, dear?"

My mother just smiled. I knew she was waiting for me to introduce them to the guy beside me. For the first time, I had no objections to doing that. But, before I got the chance, Rory stuck his foot in his mouth.

"Oh, sir, she's not coming. I wouldn't think of bringing . . . ."

My mother cut in. "What do you mean, she's not coming? Bacall, honey, we just went through this."

"Ah, man, I get it," Rory said as if a light bulb went off in his head. "Mrs. Lee, I recognize you now. I see why Bacall wanted to watch the news so bad last night. She had to see her pastor's wife."

"You watched the show?" my mother asked, suprisingly shocked.

My dad frowned. "Last night?"

"Sir," Rory began clarifying, "I know you wanted me to meet your daughter, but truth is, I'm already seeing someone. This lovely young lady and I have been working on a special friendship for a few weeks. Therefore, sir . . . I know it may cost me an opportunity to work with you, but Bacall and I had plans that I just can't break."

"Son, are you OK?" my father asked seriously. "This *is* my daughter. But from this 'last night' business, I may not want you with my daughter. We'll talk at the house, Bacall. Bring him . . . so I can thoroughly check this fella out." My father pulled my mom away before she could ask a million questions.

Rory stared at me with his mouth open. I knew he'd be seething with anger since I deceived him. But suddenly, his frown turned into a smile.

He took my hand and led me from the church.

"I'm sorry, Rory . . ."

Before I could continue, he laughed. "Lady Bacall, you are amazing . . . or should I say a tasty bag of something? I know your motives were pure. You didn't know me, so

there's no way I could blame you for protecting yourself. You and I have something cookin' and I'm starting to like the smell of what's brewin'."

He hugged me. At that point, our relationship reminded me of two slices of bacon heating up in a cast-iron skillet. Yes, indeed, we were sizzling!

Heat

Around October, my dean told me that I could graduate early because they revamped the Bachelor of Arts degree, so my forty-two academic credits would be enough. Of course, I was ecstatic. Going to summer school the past two years had paid off in a big way. Those two quarters made this year's winter and spring quarters unnecessary.

My folks were glad to hear the news. But after the initial excitement, I realized that I had no direction. I wasn't prepared to be an adult in the real world. Sure, I'd possess a degree. But, let's face it, I had no on-the-job training—no experience in the music field.

Also, I had no clue as to what I wanted to do. Before college, I wanted to teach music. But that dream faded quickly as the hardheaded students in my classes at Auburn allowed me to see that spending my life teaching knuckleheads wasn't really my heart.

But on Thanksgiving Day, I was given a gift from God . . . and my dad. Out of the blue, my father offered me a job in his record company. I'd be the vice president of God's Town Records—second in command only to my father.

Besides the fact that I'm the boss's daughter, there were many other reasons why having me at the helm was a smart business move for my father. First, there was the salary. The job was slated to pay sixty thousand plus a bonus of 2 percent on record sales. Dad offered me half, thirty grand a year and a 1 percent bonus. Second, I would be in place to carry out my father's instructions.

By the time my father explained everything to me, the lower money and reduction in power made the opportunity less appealing. But, hey, being that no one else was ringing my phone, I accepted Daddy's call to be his right-hand girl.

"What?" I asked Rory bashfully as he stared at me intensely.

"It's just amazing to me." He pulled me from the recording switchboard onto his lap. "We've been dating now for three months, and every time I look at you, I get more crazy about you."

I smiled. We had been inseparable. Rory had become as familiar as my right hand. I did nothing without considering him first. I was scared to say it out loud, but I knew it was love.

"Everything is so perfect. The only thing I can't figure," Rory continued, "is why your dad hasn't signed me yet."

I sighed. "You know, sweetheart, you don't need to focus on that. So he didn't feel you were ready for a solo gospel career yet. Just concentrate on this project. I promise, we're gonna blow him away with this duo thang. We've got a cool sound. We'll be the next BeBe and CeCe Winans. Well, except we're not related."

"Not yet, anyway!" Rory kissed me on the cheek.

The sounds we made as we sang together were splendid

harmony. Our melody sounded heavenly. Even more special than our voices was the message of each song. We were singing God's Word. I could never use my voice for any greater honor.

While Rory laid his vocal tracks, I pondered his earlier question. Though I didn't admit it to my guy, I shared his concern. Even though Daddy already had a male solo artist, Holy G., signed to God's Town Records, Holy G. couldn't even be Rory's backup singer. Think I'm biased? Then why was my father paying for Holy G.'s voice lessons? So go figure. It really bothered me that Dad didn't want Rory as a part of his eight-package deal. With Rory's raw and rare talent, I knew my dad was crazy to let him go.

"So, how'd it sound?" Rory questioned with excitement.

"Great, sir, as always," I said honestly. "No need to do a retake."

"I want to retake you into my arms." Grabbing my hands, he pulled me from my seat. Before I knew it, he had me thrown across the knobs on the board. His passionate kiss made me forget everything.

As Rory worked his hand up my shirt, I let out a loud sigh. This was the first time he'd touched me in such a way, and it seemed like my ethics had gone slap out the window.

Just that quickly, I had dropped from singing God's Word to lust-filled sinning. Rory's touch felt so good, so warm, so right. The way my body responded, I knew I wanted him, though I knew the *want* was wrong.

I definitely couldn't take his kisses in my ear. Wet and wild they were. The tingling sensation made me pull away with a smile, though I still wondered where we were going.

"Don't move, baby. Don't move one muscle." His voice was husky. "I've longed to plant my lips all over your chocolate, silky skin. I want to bring a shining smile to your face as you enjoy my every touch. Thoughts of you have dominated my dreams. Don't deny me what is mine." Rory caressed my tight frame.

A part of me wanted to tell him to get off me, or tell him that he was going too fast. But that part was so small that those words never reached my lips.

We continued the devilish play. I was too close to the fire to pull back. Like a child who longs to touch a hot stove, I never once entertained the thought of getting burned.

Next I started returning his caresses. His Lady Bacall took to seducing him like a pro. I knew he wasn't aware of my inexperience. I hadn't felt comfortable enough to tell him that I'd never been intimately touched. However, I was determined not to let my greenness show, which wasn't hard, because what I felt for Rory was so explosive that the unfamiliar movements came to me naturally.

As our desire for each other grew, we fell to the floor. Caught up in the moment, we forgot something. Neither of us gave thought to locking the door to Studio B. And, as fate would have it, feet walked through the door.

I pushed Rory aside and sprang to my feet, adjusting my clothes. As my eyes met my father's, shame and anger stared back at me.

But I wasn't a kid anymore. I truly felt I could stand up to him. He had held the reins of my life for years. It was now time for Daddy to let go and allow me to run on my own path.

I braced myself, determined to counter whatever sermon my father wanted to give. But I wasn't prepared for what he had to say. The words he spoke weren't his. They were words of the Lord.

My father's voice was calm as he said, "Train up a child in the way he should go, and when he is old, he will not depart from it. Bacall, you're twenty-two now. Although you have been difficult, you've never been disobedient. Many a thing I want to say, but I feel heaven holding my tongue."

How could I lash out? How could I scream back? How could I rant and rave, when such conviction made me see truth? At a loss for words, I merely stood there.

Finally, Rory spoke. "Uh, sir," he said, lifting himself from the floor, "if I may . . . say something?"

My father turned his back. The anger I felt earlier over my dad busting in on me had quickly turned to sadness. The despair in his face, voice, and actions gripped my heart with shame.

"Not now, Son! Not now." My dad shook his head and walked out of the studio.

I grabbed Rory's arm as he moved to follow my dad. I knew it wouldn't be wise for the two of them to talk right then. Besides, there were no words to say. No magic dust to make it all better.

Regaining my composure, I adjusted my clothes. But I couldn't contain the shame any longer. A tear trickled down my face.

"Come here, baby." Rory reached for me. "I'm so sorry. I should have known this was not the place . . . for . . . you know." He tried to comfort me, but his words made me realize he didn't comprehend the problem.

Of course, this wasn't the right place. There was no right place! My anger turned toward him.

I jerked away from his arms. "Rory, the problem is not that we were on the floor, 'bout to get busy in my dad's studio with the door unlocked. I shouldn't have been in that position with you anywhere. Not only is my father not pleased, but God is disappointed as well. Don't you care what the Lord thinks?"

"Bacall, I told you before that I'm not where I should be on a lot of things. Come on; I'm no virgin."

"Yeah," I yelled. My voice shook with emotion. "But I am, Rory. And I plan to stay that way for a long time."

The seconds that passed seemed like days. Neither of us

looked at the other. Finally, I broke the trance.

"I'm going up to the main house. I need some time. Please see yourself out."

On the entire walk to the house, then to my room, I cried. I wasn't a fool. I knew eventually Rory would have expected more than a hug and a peck. However, I never really gave the consequences much thought. I mean, never in my life had I felt so much for a guy, been so deeply in love that I could cast aside my beliefs.

All I could do was look toward heaven and plead, "Lord, I'm sorry. Forgive me . . . please."

Two weeks after graduation, on Christmas Eve, I was moving off campus back home. Rory and I hadn't spoken since the night in the studio. He had not contacted me, and I did not bother to get in touch with him. Guess you could say we were being stubborn. Or maybe we were facing the music, and we realized we weren't a hit.

"So you're through with him?" Brooks asked as she helped me load boxes in the trunk.

I wanted to tell her that I was, but I wasn't. "No! I'm not through with him," I said in anger. "I'm just torn. That's all. Things were getting a little too heated between us, so I cooled our relationship down."

"Bacall, the way you've been moping around here, I'd say you really miss this guy. Maybe you need to call him," Brooks said. "Seeing how caught up in this guy you seem to be, I hope things work out the way you want them to. But if you stay involved with Rory, make sure you know him . . . really know him before things get too serious. And remember, as you follow your heart, always first seek His Spirit." Brooks pointed toward the sky before she wrapped her arms around me and gave me an encouraging hug. "He can't be that bad. Any guy with the last name Kerry can't be too far off."

"I keep forgetting, you've got a Karri, too," I said with a slight smile, trying to hold back the tears. "Thanks for understanding. I'm sorry I snapped."

We finished unloading my car, and Brooks left me alone to unpack my things in my bedroom. I was glad to be through with school. However, moving home made me realize there was quite a bit about Auburn University I would forever miss. Most of all, I regretted leaving Wesli. Something told me that our close friendship would never be the same. Placing a picture on the nightstand of the two of us embracing at my graduation, I thought of what she said to me that night.

"You've been more than my friend. You've been my rock. How will I stand without you?" Wesli questioned with sweet sadness.

"Girlfriend, you know I love you. God just gave you a different journey than He gave me. I will miss you like crazy, but I'm grateful that for four years the Lord allowed our paths to cross. And you know as long as we lift each other up in prayer wherever we are, we'll be together in spirit." I paused as Wesli's eyes filled with tears. "Don't cry. I'm just—"

"I know," Wesli cut in, "a phone call away."

I sat down on my bed and moved my attention to Rory. I wondered what he was doing on this Christmas Eve. Was I in his thoughts at all? Oh, how I wished Wesli wasn't in Florida. If she were here, we would dissect the whole situation.

The ringing of the phone interrupted my thoughts.

"What?"

"Goodness, Callie! What's your problem?" Wesli asked. "Sounds like I'm bothering you."

I was excited for the first time that day. "Girrrl, don't trip. Do you have ESP.? I needed to talk to you, too."

"I have some real problems," Wesli started explaining.

She became more hysterical with every word.

I panicked. "What's wrong?"

"I . . . I can't get into this over the phone. You gotta come to the apartment . . . now."

"You're still at the apartment?" Now I was really worried. Wesli should have been in Florida by now.

"That should tell you something's really wrong. Can you come over here now?"

"It's Christmas Eve, honey. You know how my family is. We've got all kinds of stuff planned—dinner, singing carols—you know the deal. Besides, I just left Auburn."

"I wouldn't ask if I didn't need to talk really, really bad." Wesli sounded as if she was going to cry. "Please come. Will ya?"

I said, "Wes . . . for you, I will. Hold on, I'll be there soon."

I ran downstairs from my bedroom with my coat in my hand. My mother was sitting in the living room, looking over some notes.

"Mom, I'm not going to be able to go with you guys tonight."

She looked up with surprise in her eyes.

"It's Wesli," I continued, then told her about the call.

"Oh, honey. Go. I understand. We'll miss you, but I hope Wesli is all right."

I hugged her. "Thanks, Mom. I'll be back as soon as I can."

I headed toward the front door, but just as my hand touched the doorknob, my father's voice stopped me.

"Bacall, I need to talk to you."

I sighed and turned to him. "Dad," I said, trying to be polite, though I knew I sounded rushed, "I'm on my way to Auburn. Wesli needs my help. Can we talk when I return?"

"This won't take long," he quickly responded. "Come . . . have a seat in my study."

As I walked behind him, I shook with nervousness. What was this talk about? I reviewed the options in my mind. Business meetings were going to start at the beginning of the year, so I knew this didn't have anything to do with God's Town Records.

Then I thought of Rory. My father hadn't brought up the incident in the studio. Yep, that had to be what Daddy wanted to discuss.

After getting comfortable in the chair, I said, "OK, Dad. I know you want to discuss what you witnessed between Rory and me. Well, I am sure it will please you to know that I realize I was wrong. So there is no need for you to lecture me about him. Love ya . . . gotta go." I stood.

"Sit down," he said simply.

Thoughts of Wesli in despair caused me to let out a sigh. I wasn't trying to be rude, but I knew whatever this talk was about could wait. My friend was having a crisis, and it really irked me that my father didn't understand that. But I followed his directions and returned to my chair.

In his pastoral, authoritative voice, Reverend Lee said, "I will get straight to the point. You know . . . I've been in prayer about you and your life. I've asked the Lord for wisdom on how I should guide you."

Looking away from his direct stare, I wondered when my dad would get to the point. Unfortunately, there was no way to rush him. Although I was grown, I had never disrespected my dad. So I looked back at him and smiled.

"For reasons not necessarily beneficial to you, I offered you the job of VP. I still feel that you will do great in that role. But I believe the offer may have been a bit premature. You aren't quite ready."

I was shocked by his words. This was not the talk I expected. "But Dad, I can do it. Please give me a chance.

Don't pull it from me before I start the gig," I shouted.

"Calm down, Child," my father said sternly. "I'm not taking it away from you. You just need training. Training that you cannot get here."

I blinked in confusion. It sounded like my father still wanted me to have the position, but I didn't know what this would mean. It only took a few seconds for my father to answer the questions in my mind.

"I'm sending you to Los Angeles. You'll be an intern at Yo Town Records."

It was starting to make sense. Yo Town was the parent company for Dad's God's Town company.

"You'll be leaving next week. We'll talk about how long you'll be staying once you get there."

I sat frozen on the edge of my chair as my father explained the details. The longer he talked, the more it made sense to me. By the time thirty minutes had passed, I accepted my fate—not that I had any choice.

When my father stood, I followed, knowing that I could finally leave. He walked me to the door.

"I have only one warning for you," my father began with his arm around my shoulder. "At God's Town, the focus is on God. But at Yo Town, it's on the world. No matter where you are, Bacall, watch where you keep your focus. Remember, we seek God. Never let Satan cloud your vision."

"Yes, Daddy." I kissed him on the cheek and smiled as I headed out the door.

I drove a little too fast on my way to Auburn. Wesli's anguished voice was still in my head and made me put the pedal to the metal. I didn't know what could be wrong with Wesli. It bothered me that she left me hanging with no details. Wes knew that was a pet peeve of mine. Shoot, she vowed never to leave me on the edge. I don't do too well when left to speculate. I always assume the worse.

As I reached the city limits, I turned my attention from Wesli to what my father had said. I had mixed emotions about it. Even though I knew deep down that I didn't possess what it would take to run God's Town, I had been looking forward to the challenge. Now I'd have to prove to a stranger that I could cut it, and then this person would report to my dad, letting him know if and when I was ready. Oh, what a task. I had just finished final exams and here came yet another test.

Well, there was one good thing about going away. Tuskegee and Rory Kerry would be miles away. Maybe the distance would help lessen my feelings for the guy who had charmed my heart and help me refocus my mind on Christ.

Weeks before, I had bought Rory a Christmas present, even though we hadn't seen each other since the incident in the studio. He had a mini-recording studio in the basement of the house he rented. But all the equipment was used—some of it on the brink of total collapse. So I bought Rory speakers.

I still wanted to give him the gift, but I wasn't sure if I wanted to do that in person. If I sent them in the mail, then I wouldn't be forced to deal with the hard stuff. *I still have time to decide,* I thought as I neared my old stomping grounds. After all, I had a week before I had to leave.

I pulled into the apartment complex and searched for Wesli's car. I panicked when I didn't see her red Volvo. Looking up at our apartment window, I didn't see any lights. What if I'd gotten to the apartment too late?

I thought about driving around to try to track her down. But instead I parked, hoping Wesli had left a note inside.

I jumped from my car and ran toward the building. I tripped on the curb, nearly falling. I didn't know whether the fast pace of my heart was caused by my near fall or my panic for Wesli.

It didn't take long to reach the apartment, and when I opened the door, the first thing I saw was the flicker of candlelight. Boy, was I relieved to see that tiny glow.

I was glad I still had my key; I was going to turn it in soon. When I stepped inside, I blinked in confusion. There wasn't simply one candle, but tons of them burning throughout our place. Just as I was about to scream for Wesli, Rory stepped into view. He was holding a white lily bouquet. The guy was more handsome than I'd remembered. My heart, which had been steady for a moment, was racing once again.

"You don't have to look for Wesli," Rory said as if reading my mind. "Wesli is in Florida and she's fine. We hated playing this trick on you, but frankly, I was desperate. Hope you won't hold this against us." Stepping forward, he gently uttered, "These are for you, my lady."

I inhaled the fresh scent of the lilies and smiled. I was still silent, not knowing what to say.

"Wesli wanted me to tell you to phone her tomorrow," he said softly. Then he took my hand and led me to the dining room table where plates were already set up.

"What is all this?" I whispered.

"A little something that I catered for us."

I was silent as Rory filled my plate with angel-hair pasta. Then, he filled the glasses with cider. He finally sat down, took my hand, and said grace.

When I looked up, his eyes shined through the glow of the candlelight.

"I've missed you, Bacall. That's why I did this. I didn't want us to be apart any longer."

I beamed inside. Even though I was dealing with a lot of things, I missed our relationship.

We talked through dinner, though we kept the conversation

light—away from what had happened between the two of us. I told him about graduation, and he told me about what had been going on with his band.

After a while, Rory rose from the table and walked over to the corner where he had set up a boom box he'd brought along. "I got you a couple of Christmas presents," he said.

I smiled as I thought about the gift I had for him.

"First, I want to give you the gift of song. Here are the lyrics." He handed me a sheet of paper. "I wrote this last week, so it's kinda rough. But this is how I feel."

"'Too Long a Break,'" I read the top of the page aloud.

"That's the title I came up with 'cause I've been waiting too long for you to call me. I understand you needed time. I'm not even trying to rush you now. I just hope the break is over."

"I'm glad you didn't wait any longer for my call. It's so good to see you."

I read the lyric sheet. Once he started singing, I was even more overwhelmed. The sound was sweet and sultry. I was so moved that I couldn't even comprehend the words.

By the time he sang the last note, I couldn't hold back. Seeing my tears, he held me. He held me tight and with such feeling, I cried some more.

"Bacall, what's wrong?" Rory asked.

"Don't worry, these are tears of joy . . . and sorrow. Joy because I have found I do care about you and want to work through our problems. But I also feel sorrow, because just when we're in sync straightening out the trouble, I have to go away."

He pulled back and looked into my eyes. "Go away? What are you talking about?"

"I'm moving to Los Angeles next week." I told him about my dad's latest plans. The more I explained, the more dejected my guy looked. Seeing Rory's expression made me want to run straight to my father and beg him to let me stay.

"Well, I can't control or worry about what's gonna happen tomorrow, next week, or even next month. But baby, I got you wrapped in my arms right now, and I *can* control making the rest of this night enjoyable for us both."

I smiled at his words, and my smile widened when he handed me a neatly decorated, skinny box. Opening it, I was amazed to find a gorgeous fourteen-karat gold watch with a ruby in place of the twelve. I gasped, then looked at Rory.

He grinned. "Turn it over," he said.

It was engraved on the back. "Thinking of you every minute. Love, R. Kerry."

"Oh, Rory, this is beautiful." I hugged him. "Thank you so much."

"Anything for my girl."

I pulled back. "I have something for you, too. We can get together tomorrow and I'll get it to you. Ouch!" I yelled out as I bent down to grab my ankle. "I must have hurt it earlier this evening. Don't laugh, but I almost fell outside. That's how worried you and Miss 'Con Artist' Ezell had me."

"Sit," Doctor Rory said, pulling some ointment from his bag. "I've been nursing a sore shoulder. This stuff will fix you up. Let me know if I put too much pressure on you."

Rory rubbed my ankle in silence. I could tell by the way he looked at me, then dropped his eyes, that he had more to say. Yet it appeared he didn't know how to tell me what was on his mind.

After a moment, he said, "I've had time to replay the night in the studio. I'm sorry for moving too fast. I never realized you were saving yourself." He paused and looked into my eyes. "Just know, when you're ready . . . I want to be the one you give yourself to."

While the Ben Gay worked on my ankle, Rory's touch worked down my resistance. His words were like a torch of passion, and I gave in. We kissed for what seemed like hours. Then his hands began to roam over my body as we lay across the couch. I panted as my body temperature rose with the intense heat.

4

Ignites

While I was flying to Los Angeles, I remembered that intimate Christmas Eve night. Even though a week had passed, my actions consumed my thoughts. Part of me was glad I stopped Rory. The other part of me regretted not letting love take over.

"Father," I uttered humbly as I talked to God, "why is it so tough to restrain my flesh? I didn't tell him, but I love him, Lord. I love Rory, and the love feels good. You know what to do to keep me from slipping into sin. You ship me clear across the country. It's like I'm sailing away from temptation. If I sound mad, forgive me, 'cause I dare not question Your plan for my life. I don't know. Maybe I'm just a little torn. I do hope, though, that Rory doesn't forget me while I'm miles away. I guess this will be a good test to see just how strong a bond we share."

The "fasten seat belt" sign came on and moments later, the plane took a dramatic dip.

I continued to pray. "Father, it would be great if the pilot could get a grip on this plane." I took a deep breath and looked toward heaven. "I know You have control over landing this jet, and also where my relationship with Rory will land."

After my prayer, I relaxed. I felt bad for not focusing more on God. Yeah, I pulled away from Rory's kisses that night. I told him I wanted to stand for Christ in everything I did. But I'm old enough to know that actions are what count. Rory and I had never even prayed together. Had never mentioned picking up the Bible. Shoot, lately the songs we'd sung together weren't even gospel.

"Lord, I hope You help us refocus and keep things right. Even though things aren't perfect yet, I thank You for sending me a fellow who warms my heart." I finished praying just as the plane safely landed.

When I exited the plane, I was greeted by a familiar face—Mr. Blain Price. Short, stocky, "all 'bout business" Blain Price. Blain was a Martin Lawrence look-alike. In fact, people often mistook him for the famous celebrity. There was no doubt he was a powerful and spunky man.

He was the road manager for the hot musical group, Kidz No Mo. The four-guy group was world famous for their harmony and blended sound. They kinda had a gospel flavor happening over an R & B beat.

The reason their gospel part was so real is because they started in the church. Four years ago, when Kidz No Mo started, they came to my dad's studio. He only agreed to work with them 'cause they were singing gospel. Somehow, somewhere along the way, that changed. However, they were able to keep part of their old sound and warm spirits.

My father had a tough time accepting their decision to go mainstream. But, he moved past it and continued praying for the group. Their strong relationship remained intact.

Even though the guys were from Mississippi, they claimed Reverend Lee as their pastor. Kidz No Mo visited our church and home regularly. When they came, Blain came, too. The two of us always hung out, and I tried to make each of his visits special.

Two years ago, when I was a sophomore, Blain sent a plane ticket for me to visit him in Los Angeles. It was my first time to the gorgeous city by the sea. Boy, did I feel the waves, and I'm not just talking about the ocean. I felt a lot of pressure from Blain. We were friends, so I didn't think there'd be any harm in visiting. My sister told me she thought he liked me romantically. But I never believed it.

Shucks, I didn't even tell my folks I was going to L.A. I didn't have to check in every weekend, so I just kinda up and went.

At first, he offered me his bedroom and said he would sleep in the family room on the pullout. That arrangement was fine with me. After all, we'd been friends for years, he knew my parents, and he was like an older brother to me.

But then this guy, ten years my senior, started coming on to me. The first night I was there, Blain made his way back to the bedroom where I was sleeping. He must've thought I was the pillow 'cause he tried to lay all over me. I was furious.

I was more than uncomfortable with his unwanted advances I felt like a cat trapped in a shoe box, trying desperately to meow my way out. However, Blain wasn't letting me loose from his grip.

The next morning, when he'd gone to work, I packed my things and returned home on a standby ticket. When Blain got home that night and saw my note, he called. I didn't return his calls at first, but finally I did, and after many long talks, we cleared up the situation. Eventually, I began to feel comfortable in his presence again, and we were able to resume our relationship. We'd overcome that challenge with our friendship intact, which was a good thing because Blain knew my deepest secret. I, like Rory, had dreams of being a big R & B singer. I rarely told people because I sensed that not many would support me. I even thought my dad would disown me, though I suspected that Reverend Lee knew my dreams without me ever saying a word. That might be the reason he sent me to L.A. It was a way for him to have me finally experience firsthand a world I'd always secretly admired.

I was surprised to see Blain at the airport waiting for me. I hadn't spoken to him since the summer. He had been out of the country on tour with Kidz No Mo, and I didn't expect them back in the States 'till March. But I was elated to see him at the terminal, smiling, and holding a rose.

"'Call . . . come here, girl, and give me a hug. And close your mouth. It's really me," he joked.

As I hugged him, I felt the first bit of comfort in my new surroundings. I didn't realize until that moment that I was hesitant about moving forward. Reality hit me. I was a college graduate. Ready or not, it was time for me to make my mark in the world.

"Boy, am I glad to see you," I finally blurted out. "I'm kinda nervous 'bout this assignment. But seeing you, I know I'll be OK."

We walked to the baggage claim, and Blain chatted about the apartment the company had found for me. I looked toward heaven and thought to myself, *What an awesome God!* He always knew what to do for me. The Lord always brought sunshine to my cloudy situations. How could the whole world not want to follow Him?

I smiled at Blain as he continued talking. I was ready to take my first steps into my new world.

My first day at Yo Town Records could be summed up

in one word . . . interesting. I was introduced to most of the staff by Kelly Evans, the vice president. This king of songwriting took it upon himself to make certain I was comfortable.

Although I was coming to the record company as an intern, I instantly received VIP status. Mr. Evans made a point of telling all the employees to take special care of me.

"We've got to make sure that Miss Bacall has everything she needs. You know who her father is, right?"

After a while, his tactics bothered me. I could tell by the rolled eyes and smirks that came my way that many people didn't like the preferential treatment I was getting.

I could deal with the fact that some of my peers appeared not to like me. I just figured, after they got to know me, they'd see I was cool. However, when Mr. Evans introduced me to my boss, the Artist and Repertoire Director, I knew my time at Yo Town would be tough.

Her name was Raven Gibbons, a twenty-eight-year-old control freak. She was like a gorgeous angel on the outside, but a demon within. I'll never forget her nice, sweet words when Mr. Evans introduced us, compared to her harsh, bitter words once he was gone.

"Kelly, baby," she started, stroking his back, "don't worry about your precious intern. I'll take her under my wing and teach her how things really work around here. Now get going and let me and my new assistant get to work. Don't worry. She'll be fine . . . just fine."

The Minute he shut the door her attitude changed from roses to weeds.

"Sit down. I'll tell you my rules." Her brashness surprised me. "Look, Miss Lee, I wanted someone else in this job, but upper management told me I had to hire you. I detest kids who climb ahead in life by riding their parents' coattails. I'm where I am because of hard work and dedication." She glared at me. "I guess you wouldn't know anything about that. Just make sure you don't cross me. Calling the shots is my job. Following orders is yours. And I expect no tattling. If this is too much for you, bail to another department now."

I took a deep breath. Then I boldly said, "Ms. Gibbons, I've never had any problems following orders from a superior." I stopped, letting my words sink in. I wanted to let her know that she wouldn't be working with a lightweight. "Three weeks ago, I graduated from a major university in less than four years. I came away with a 3.69 grade point average. Needless to say, hard work does not and will not deter me from my goal. I'm not some brat with a silver spoon in my mouth."

She didn't blink an eye, so I continued, "Like me or hate me, the work will get done. But I won't kiss your tail. If I have a problem with the way you're treating me, I'll discuss it with you. And if you have a problem with my performance, I hope you'll tell me. No one can solve our differences but us. I'm sorry I'm not who you selected for this position, however; I intend to make sure you are satisfied."

The wrinkles across Ms. Gibbons's forehead faded. With one brow raised, she stood. She extended her hand and grinned slightly.

"Perhaps I underestimated you," she said as she took my hand. "Welcome aboard. Well, enough of this small talk. Let's create a star. Oh, and call me Raven."

I sighed with relief. I'd passed the first test and I was ready to get to work.

As the A & R director, Raven was in charge of finding and making great talent. At this music empire, the artists ranged from jazz singers to rappers. The main focus now was on getting a male rhythm-and-blues singer. All afternoon we listened to one tape after another. The ones who had the look couldn't sing. The few who had dynamic voices possessed limited physical appeal. We left for the day with no prospects. It looked like this was going to be a tough task.

But as I headed home that evening, I still felt great. Overall, my first day left me feeling like a winner.

❦ ❦ ❦

The first day had been so hectic that I was happy to finally be in the quiet two-bedroom apartment the company had prepared for me. Boy, did I miss me some Rory Kerry. I had been in L.A. for two days and hadn't had a moment to call him.

Last night, I spent the evening with Blain. We cruised Melrose Boulevard restaurant hopping. We ventured to four of Blain's favorite spots. One place for appetizers. Another location for the entree. Next, it was on to a cozy outdoor restaurant for dessert, then a coffee house for cappuccinos. I got a chance to fill him in on the man who melted my heart. Then Blain caught me up on his life by dropping a bomb that blew my mind.

"'Call, this is tough," Blain started before he took another sip of his cappuccino. "I'm glad you found someone you love. It takes a load off of me."

He paused, and I frowned. "What do you mean?"

"Now I can tell you that I'm married." Blain's words were barely a whisper.

I sprang from my seat as if I were bouncing from a trampoline and rushed to his side. I hugged him. Truly, I was happy he'd taken a bride. Although thirty-two wasn't too old to be single these days, at least I'd no longer have the worry that my buddy would grow old and lonely.

"That's fantastic! I'm dying to meet your wife," I yelled with excitement. "Guess you haven't had time for a honeymoon with the tour and all? Well, you must take her someplace special. I'm so excited for you—"

He cut me off. "I've been married for eight years now,

'Call." He paused and dropped his eyes. "Valerie and I have two girls."

It took a few moments, but his words made my head spin. *What did he just say? How could this be?*

Although we'd never been intimate, at that moment I felt violated. As if our entire four-year friendship had been built on sticks of lies instead of bricks of truth.

"'Call, let me explain."

He tried to tell me some garbage about how for years he didn't truly love his wife.

I held up my hands. "Blain, save the lame explanations. Obviously, you never cared for me either if you could lie to me like that."

At all times, Blain was aware of my life's details. Yet he didn't deem me worthy enough to bring me into his reality.

Silence filled the car as he drove me home. At my apartment building, he walked me to the front door. When I opened it, I turned before he could step inside.

"You can go now, Blain," I said without emotion.

He opened his mouth as if he was going to say something, but then just shook his head. I closed the door behind him, but my head was still filled with what he'd told me. Not only had he wanted me to lose my virginity to him, he also wanted to commit adultery. I was repulsed by the thought.

How could any man be so cruel to his wife and me? Simple answer. Only a man who didn't fear God could do it. I knew then that I had to pray for Blain. He needed the Lord, and even in the midst of my anger I committed myself to seeing him get saved.

After my first day at work, I knew I had to speak to Rory. I called him the moment I got home, and for hours, there was no answer. Where could he be?

I tossed in the bed and looked at the clock. It was almost two in the morning and I had to get some sleep, but I decided to give Rory one last try.

The phone rang five times, and I expected to hear the answering machine again. But, this time, my love's voice came over the line. Not a tape, but the real deal.

"I was beginning to think you weren't going to answer."

"Bacall!"

I smiled at the way he said my name. He missed me.

"I've been waiting for you to call," he continued with enthusiasm. "How's it going? How was your first day? Tell me everything."

I leaned back against the headboard and filled him in on my two days in Los Angeles. When I looked at the clock, I couldn't believe that fifty minutes had passed. I had to get to sleep.

Reluctantly, I said, "Rory, I hate to hang up, but I've got to go if I'm going to get up in time for work. I really miss you."

"I miss you, too."

"I'm a little worried about what you'll be doing there without me," I said only half-joking.

"You don't have to worry about that," he said softly. "Chances are, I'll only be thinking and dreaming about you."

I hung up the phone and went to sleep with his words on my mind and a smile on my face.

The routine of work, then going home, became natural. So much so that the first week flew by. Raven never eased up on me. I didn't have any problem with the pressure because I produced every time. But even with our full-fledged efforts of checking nightclubs, backup singers, and audition tapes, we still hadn't found the male singer Raven was searching for. She was really starting to sweat it.

I'd been at Yo Town for almost two weeks when Raven came to my desk in tears. Well, as close to tears as Raven could get.

"Bacall, what am I gonna do? I can't find this boy wonder anywhere." I sat silently as she continued. "We're being eaten alive in this category by all the other record companies." She sniffed.

I handed her a tissue from the holder on my desk.

"Everything else is in place. Kelly and the other staff songwriters have a few tunes lined up for an album. All they need from me is to deliver the dude, and I can't even do that. I could lose my job over this."

As I reached for another tissue, my hand bumped the picture frame on my desk. Rory's photo fell onto her lap. I tried to grab it before she had a chance to be nosy, but Raven's reflexes were quicker than mine.

"He is fine! Who is this, Bacall?"

"His name is Rory," I stated. "He's my man."

"This is what I'm looking for—this is the image I need to put on the cover of the CD. Look at him. He's rugged, yet has a teddy-bear smile. Oh, yeah," she said, nodding. "A guy with a look like this would land me a promotion." She paused. Suddenly, her tears were gone. "Girl, you've got good taste, but how do you plan to keep a tiger like this tamed when you're here and he's there?" She chuckled.

Raven placed the photo down and strutted out of my office. She rudely brushed up against the mail girl who was coming into my office. I couldn't believe Raven didn't apologize, and I shook my head in disappointment.

"Oh, don't worry," the girl said. "I know all too well what to expect from Ms. Gibbons. She don't bother me none. I know she look down on me. But her ugly ways won't git her far. Word is, she already havin' trouble keepin' her man."

"Her man?" I asked in disbelief.

"Yeah, Mr. Evans on the top floor been tryin' to put out that flame for months now." She whispered, handed me my mail, then darted out of the office.

Before I got too wrapped up in the news of Raven and Kelly being an item, I browsed through my mail. There was a card from my parents and more letters from people at Yo Town welcoming me. Finally, I saw a package from Rory.

Tearing it open, I found a CD and a letter.

Dear Bacall:

As I sat tonight, thinking about you and how much I miss being with you, this song came to my mind. I hope you like it.

Love, Rory

My lips spread into a wide smile as I looked at the lyric sheet and put the CD into the player on my desk.

"Miles away, I know it's hard for us to take it.
Miles away, I know it's rough, but we're gonna make it.
Someday, some way. For now, I'll love you miles away."

He sang the words beautifully. It was special, just perfect. Simply his keyboard and his voice. I was so overwhelmed that I played it again.

Raven darted into my office. "That voice—it's so good!"

"Isn't it? Listen to him sing to me."

"To you?" Raven uttered in a perplexed tone. "Who *is* that?"

"My boyfriend. He wrote this song for me. Guess my tiger is still in his cage of love," I said sarcastically.

Raven held up the picture of Rory and pointed to the tape. "This guy . . . is that singer?"

Call me naive. I didn't fully understand where she was going with that question until after I answered.

"Yep. That's him. My precious Rory is the man with the magical voice."

"I want him!" Raven demanded. "He's the total package I've been searching for. Everything about this guy is hot."

My mouth dropped and I sensed trouble.

"He wouldn't even have to try to set a fire. Um . . . um . . . um . . . He ignites!"

Bright

"I don't care what you want, Raven!" I shouted. "Rory is not going to be your guinea pig."

The conversation about my boyfriend becoming the new male artist turned into a heated debate. And we had been going at it for more than thirty minutes.

Raven changed her demanding tactics and started pleading. "What are you worried about? Having a star for a man could be awesome."

I shook my head, but that didn't stop Raven.

"It's obvious this dude is talented. Don't stand in the way of his big break. At the very least, set up a meeting for me with him."

"I can't do that. Rory wants to sing professionally, but he wants a career in gospel. My father is interested in him, and he could sign with God's Town Records anytime now."

"But has he signed yet?"

I shook my head.

"Then he's fair game. As long as he isn't committed to

any label, we can legally pursue him."

She waited for me to say something, but I remained silent. Finally, Raven said, "I won't pressure you anymore tonight. Think about it, and we'll discuss it tomorrow." She turned and headed toward the door. But before she walked out, she said, "I do hope you'll keep in mind what's best for your guy and not just what's best for you."

Three weeks had passed since I arrived in Los Angeles. Raven was still pressuring me to contact Rory. I couldn't believe she kept asking. After a few days, she demanded to know my reasons.

"It's not in my job description to put you in touch with my boyfriend." I tried to control my emotions. "I don't have to explain my position or my reasons. No disrespect intended, but do what you need to do to get over it already."

It appeared that I had finally said the perfect words. She stopped asking me about Rory. Of course, I was more than thrilled to finally be rid of that problem. However, over the next few days, I realized that Raven had not only stopped pursuing Rory, she stopped looking for a new singer altogether. I wondered why we weren't sorting through more tapes. But I dared not question her. I could hear her sarcastically telling me that it was not in my job description to decide what type of artist we should spend the day looking for.

The beginning of my fourth week started with a slow workday. I hadn't been graced yet with Miss Raven's presence. Usually, before I could fix my morning cup of tea, she would be in my office with a list of items for me to tackle. This day, however, Ms. Gibbons was nowhere in sight.

Couldn't complain, though. The free time gave me a chance to catch up with my sister. The two of us hadn't spoken since I'd arrived in Los Angeles. Since I hadn't gotten around to getting an answering machine at my apartment, Brooks left me several messages at the office—none of which I had the time or guts to return. Sometimes my sister had too much of a conscience for me. I felt guilty enough keeping Rory in the dark about Raven's interest in him. Though I had my reasons for doing so, I knew Brooks would probably make me doubt myself.

I finally returned my sister's call.

"Hey, girl, what's up?" I said, trying to put cheer in my voice.

"I was calling to tell you that Karri and I are coming to L.A.," Brooks said stiffly.

"That's great, Sis. When are y'all coming? I know you're staying with me."

"See, that's the thing, Bacall," Brooks replied, sounding more upset with every word. "I was planning on staying with you. But when you can't even call me back, after I left four messages, I wonder if I even want to be in your company."

I rolled my eyes. "Don't trip and don't exaggerate. I only got three calls from you—"

"I don't care if it was three or four," Brooks yelled, cutting me off. "You should have phoned me back after my first message! I understand you're busy, but one minute of your precious time wouldn't have ruined your day. Anyway, I'm coming tomorrow."

"Tomorrow?"

"Yeah, that's why I'm hot with you. I've been trying to make plans for weeks, and I've been limited in what I could come up with because you haven't responded." She lowered her voice. "So, tell me, I know it's last minute, but are you sure I can crash at your place?"

"You and Karrington can stay, Brooks," I told her. "I've got a two-bedroom apartment. Do you need me to pick you up?"

"No, thanks. Don't wanna put you out any more than necessary. We're renting a car so we'll be able to enjoy L.A. as well as put the finishing touches on Karri's album. He's gonna stay at a hotel."

We talked for a few more minutes. I gave her the address to my office, then hung up and took a deep breath. Yeah, I should have called her, but she wasn't the only one with problems. And she never even asked what was up with me. How selfish! I decided to deal with her attitude problem when she got into town.

As I cleared tapes from my desk, I came across a package Raven and I hadn't reviewed. The picture of this guy was gorgeous. He called himself, "D Train." His bio was amazing. So amazing that he was either lying or spectacular.

I played the tape and was impressed. His sound was slammin'. The voice and range on this guy was dynamic. He had even written a couple of the songs.

I had one problem. Some of his lyrics were foul. One tune I turned off within seconds because the words were so vulgar. But those few words didn't sway me from being excited about this fellow.

"I hope Raven is here." I took the tape and headed toward her office.

Betsy, Raven's secretary, stopped me at her door.

"Bacall, honey," she said sweetly, "Raven is tied up in a meeting."

I turned around, prepared to go back to my office, but Betsy continued. "She's meeting with an adorable black gentleman," she whispered, as if she were revealing a top secret. "The bigwigs have been in and out of her office all day. I suspect that he may be our new male soloist." Her cheeks were pink with excitement. "Bacall . . . he's really hot. And he seems nice, too, such southern charm."

"Who is this guy?" I asked, trying to control my anger.

She shrugged. "They're supposed to be out in a minute

and coming to your office."

"I don't understand. I'm Raven's assistant and I didn't know anything about her finding a potential artist. I thought she'd given up the search."

Betsy held up her hands. "I'm just telling you what I know."

"Who is this guy?" I repeated my question a bit loudly.

"Why are you yelling at me?" Betsy frowned. "I'd tell you if I knew. All I know is that this gentleman came in here, and never once in my boss's busy schedule today has she taken the time to formally introduce me to him."

I tapped my fingers against Betsy's desk, then shook my head and turned back to my office. What in the heavens was my boss up to?

It was almost time for me to leave for the day, and I still hadn't seen Raven or her mystery artist. She must have been so angry with me about the Rory incident that she deemed me unworthy to be on her team.

I pulled out my Bible and started studying. With the way my day was going, I needed some sound perspective. I turned to 2 Corinthians 10:5: "Bringing every thought into captivity to the obedience of Christ." I looked up and shook my head.

Here I was stressing and trying to control things, letting evil thoughts dominate my mind all afternoon. And now, the first Scripture I turned to said for me to submit my thoughts to Jesus. I knew that if I did that, anger wouldn't consume me.

I meditated for a while, then knelt to pray. Spending those moments with my heavenly Father made me not so anxious. As I got up, I heard my door open. I looked up and thought I was dreaming. I envisioned Rory at my door. A second later, I realized it wasn't a dream. It was most definitely my guy.

"Don't just stand there." He grinned. "Come over and hug me."

It was like time had taken me back to when we were last together. His bald head was just as tantalizing and sexy. His clothes were just as suave and debonair. His face was just as mesmerizing and alluring. And that smile, his smile, was just as overwhelming and irresistible.

I whispered, "Rory, what are you doing here?"

"I sent him a ticket," Raven announced as she entered my office and grabbed his hand.

It only took me a second to figure it out and become boiling mad. Without knowing any other details, I was hip to Ms. Raven's cheap game. The smirk on her face was irritating.

Harsh words floated in my head but were stopped from exiting my lips when I noticed Kelly Evans, accompanied by the president and CEO, Mr. Daniels, standing at my door. Mr. Daniels slapped Rory on his back as if he was their boy.

"Miss Lee," Mr. Daniels said, smiling at me, "I'm going to have to call your father and tell him what a great job you're doing. Because of you I'm told we may quite possibly have the next Marvin Gaye."

Kelly Evans added, "Well, we can't jump the gun too fast. Tomorrow will be the real test when we hear him sing. But I'm sure the voice will fit his dope image."

The two gentlemen huddled around Rory. As they laughed together, Raven the betrayer asked to speak to me in the hall. I would have been satisfied not speaking to her ever again in my life. I wanted to call home and tell my parents that I quit. But I knew they were counting on me to stay. I was sent here to learn a lesson, and I couldn't learn much back in Alabama.

My dad had tried to warn me. He told me this could be a cutthroat business. I just didn't think that fact would be confirmed in the first weeks of my new job.

When we were alone in the hall, I crossed my arms in front of me. "Yes, Raven, what do you want?" I sighed with sadness, not at all interested in her sorry explanations.

"Look, you told me to do whatever I needed to do to get over wanting Rory. The only thing that would satisfy me was if Rory turned me down himself. You wouldn't help me, so I found him myself."

"You found him yourself," I uttered in disbelief. "His number isn't even listed. What did you do? Review my phone records?"

"I didn't have to," Raven said. "You roared and boasted to quite a few people about your tiger back home."

She went on to explain that someone told her Rory was the president of the Student Government Association at Tuskegee University. She called the school and was put in touch with Rory.

My arms were still folded in front of me. I was glad I had found out what a slithering snake she was.

"I do want you to know that I asked Rory not to discuss my conversation with anyone, including you."

I frowned and she continued. "I told him, for confidentiality reasons, he had to keep this between the two of us."

That was the only good thing she told me. At least I couldn't be mad at my guy for keeping me in the dark. The only question now would be, how was he gonna feel when I told him what I'd kept from him?

"So, do you understand?"

"Why do you care? I have nothing—not one polite word—to say to you right now. You've accomplished what you set out to do. Now, please move from my door."

I stepped back through the doorway and exchanged good-byes with the executives. Oh, how I wished Raven would have followed them. But no such luck.

"Why don't we all go to dinner?" Raven asked. "That

way, you two can catch up and I can fill you in on my awesome plans for this fellow."

Before I could refuse, Rory declined her invitation.

"I don't think so. I haven't seen my lady in weeks and I want to spend some time with her." He put his arm around my shoulders.

It did my heart good to know he wanted to be with me instead of discussing business.

Raven wasn't happy, but she played it off. "Well, maybe tomorrow." She tried to smile. It was obvious that her intentions were to spend quite a bit of time with my guy. Thank goodness, his plans were different.

We picked up Chinese food and headed to my apartment. Having Rory next to me was like a dream. Just the day before, I had driven home from work wishing I could be near him. Close to him. Holding him. Longing to see his face. And now he sat in the passenger seat, not a foot away from me.

Though it was what I desired, it felt strange. Something was different. There was silence in the air. The distance between us seemed farther than the miles from California to Alabama. I knew it was my secret that created the problem.

"You're so quiet," I said to Rory as we drove down La Brea Avenue, a street that was so different from the ones in Alabama.

"I'm just amazed at what's happened to me in the last twenty-four hours. It's such a blessing!"

I took a deep breath. "How . . . how do you know it's a blessing?" I asked softly, hoping he wouldn't get upset with my question.

"Because, honey, I've wanted this all my life. I now have a chance to get my dream. If I never get this close again, I can say I was granted a chance to hang with the folks at Yo

Town Records. Don't know what tomorrow holds, but their interest in me today was real! That fact alone, my lady, is an answer to prayer."

When we got to my apartment, we put aside all the music stuff and relaxed. But I couldn't relax totally. I knew what I was hiding needed to come out. I wanted to tell Rory, but I was afraid.

I blocked all those thoughts from my mind as Rory showered me with words of affection. The wet kisses he placed all over my face were definitely a tasty treat. Heck, it made me not even want dessert.

"Is it so bad that I want you?" Rory asked huskily. "Is it terrible that right here, right now, I want us to go all the way?" We were locked in an embrace.

Here we were, faced again with the decision to satisfy the spirit or our flesh. I must admit, I wasn't feeling righteous.

"I can't," something inside me found the strength to say. "Rory, I want you, too . . . in every way. But . . ."

"But, what?" he dragged out in a whisper, then he filled my ear with his tongue.

"You can't do that, Rory," I moaned. "It's turning me on." I lifted myself from the plush queen-sized bed. "I haven't been completely honest with you. Trouble is . . . I don't know where to begin." I took a deep breath, then said, "Rory, I knew a few weeks ago that Raven was interested in you." I spoke softly.

The puzzled look on his gorgeous face let me know that I needed to explain.

"She heard your CD and wanted to get in touch with you, but I told her that you were interested in singing gospel." I continued to talk, trying to get the words out quickly, hoping he would understand my reasons. But I could tell by the look on his face that my reasons weren't good enough.

"I don't believe this junk you're telling me. Raven asked you to call me and you refused? Dang, Bacall. I thought you and I had something here. You know, me givin' and you givin'. But it seems like you want to pull all the strings."

"That's not it at all, Rory." I moved toward him.

"Naw!" he shouted. "Back up. You need to know that I make my own decisions. I'm my own man."

"I know that, Rory. I wasn't trying . . ."

He waved my words away as his eyes searched the room. "Where's the phone? I need to call a cab, 'cause I don't need to be with no woman who's gonna try to hold me back."

"It's not like that," I said, grabbing the phone. "I'm so sorry, Rory. I thought I was doing the right thing." Even though I apologized repeatedly like a broken record, he would not calm down. I desperately wanted him to stay so that we could work this out. So when he reached for the phone, I held it behind my back.

"That's fine . . . whatever," he yelled. "I don't have to use your phone." He snatched his jacket. "I'm getting out of here. I need to think."

In a final effort to plead my case, I sobbed, "But what about the fact that we were supposed to be a group? It wasn't supposed to a you or me thang. Us, Rory . . . us! Don't you care about our dream?"

He stomped out the front door.

I should have told him that I also wanted to protect him from Raven's schemes, but it seemed as if it was too late for explanations.

"Please, don't go, Rory," I pleaded. "Don't be mad." I followed him out the door. "I love you. Let me explain."

But he wasn't hearing anything I had to say. The man whom I felt the world for just walked away in a cold-hearted huff. And I couldn't blame anyone but me. I prayed that my selfishness wouldn't cost me Rory for good.

I slowly cleaned up my apartment, then climbed into bed. I prayed with distress in my soul. "Lord, not only do I owe Rory an apology, but I owe You one, too. I shouldn't have done what I did. I should have trusted You. I desire, Father, to be more holy, more spiritual, and more Christ-like. However, in every area, I seem to be failing. Help me, please." Then I closed my eyes and cried myself to sleep.

❦ ❦ ❦

"Miss Lee," the representative from Yo Town Records said over the speakerphone, "could you come down to our office on the third floor? There's someone here to see you."

Hearing that made me smile for the first time that day. I knew it was Brooks. Even though she was a tad upset, there was no question my sister would get over it. I realized, though, that she shouldn't have to get over it. I should never have given her a reason to be mad. Though I had man problems, men come and go. Girlfriends and sisters are forever. Brooks is both to me.

Fortunately, Brooks knew I needed grace. The moment she saw me, she extended her arms and wrapped me in love. After I greeted Karrington and he said good-bye to Brooks, my sister accompanied me to my office. She listened intently to my dilemma.

"I don't know what I'm going to do," I said when I finished telling her the whole story.

"Well, I think you're going to have to give him a little time. I understand what you were trying to do."

I sighed with relief. "Really?"

She nodded. "But I also understand what Rory is saying. You didn't trust him. That hurt him."

My hopeful sigh turned back into sadness.

Brooks leaned across the desk and took my hand. "Bacall, if this guy truly loves you . . . it'll be OK."

We had lunch together. Then Brooks dragged me to Bloomingdales to break my somber mood. But as hard as my sister tried, I just couldn't shake Rory, and the whole mess, from my mind. Getting caught up in my sister's wedding plans did cheer me up somewhat, though. Helping her make plans for a Christmas Eve candlelight ceremony sounded enchanting and took me away, if only for a few hours.

❦ ❦ ❦

"Hey, baby," Brooks stated with joy as she hugged her fiancé in the studio. "Sorry we took so long, but we had some catching up to do."

"Aw, don't sweat it. I've been working hard here all day. Glad you got out and enjoyed yourself. Look here, beautiful ladies," Karrington said, suddenly serious. "I need your voices to do dubs for me on the choir parts. The sound needs to be stronger." Brooks and I agreed. But his next words shocked me. "Bacall, your boy should be here any second. Rory's gonna sing, too."

I stared at Brooks, not knowing what to say. Surely Rory would walk right back out the door when he saw me. Even though I had just agreed to help Karrington, now I desperately wanted to decline. However, I knew the three of us were familiar with Karri's style and songs.

Karrington and Rory had collaborated on a few tunes last fall. They'd become buddies. Needless to say, when that happened back in November, Brooks and I were thrilled that her Karri and my Kerry were friends.

"No need to trip out, ladies," Karrington said as he watched the silent exchange between Brooks and me. "Rory was down here earlier and we discussed some thangs. I won't disclose what was said, but I will say . . ." Karri stopped when a sweet, masculine voice at the steel door interrupted him.

"Go ahead. Say what I told you, man. Tell her that I understand she was trying to protect me." Rory looked straight at me. "Tell her I'm not angry anymore. Tell her I need her. Tell her I can't sign a record deal without her in my corner. Tell Bacall that I love her."

I couldn't believe what he was saying. The words seemed too "storybook-like" to be true.

"I'm so sorry, Rory," I said as I rushed into his arms.

"I'm the one who's sorry, baby."

Then he kissed me. I realized at that moment that Rory Kerry did love me.

Rory and I excused ourselves and went into the hallway to talk.

"So when . . . when did you know?" I asked him intently, with happiness in my eyes.

"I knew I loved you," Rory answered, squeezing my hand, "when you left me back in Alabama. From that day till this one, I've wanted to hold your chocolate-brown, luscious body. Why do you think I wrote you that song? Baby, I created it because every time I sat at a keyboard, picked up my guitar, or tried to play the synthesizer, thoughts of you, my Lady Bacall, consumed me."

We sat on the floor, and he told me about the contract Raven offered. I was pleased that it was fair. The artist's advance and cocreative control portions were generous, especially for a first-time artist. But the pressure was on him to sign right away. The contract stipulated that his single would be released in three weeks if he signed now.

As excited as I was for him, I was equally saddened for myself. Visions of the two of us singing harmoniously on stage would never come to pass. I was also disappointed that he wouldn't be singing for God.

"So, what do you think?" he finally asked me.

I told him what I'd been thinking. "I'm sorry we won't be singing together, but I'm even more sorry you won't be singing for God."

Rory nodded. "The lyrics I sing may not be about God. But I know who gives me the strength to breathe, stand, and sing. Everything I do, I do because of the heavenly Father's grace in my life. And in everything I do, I will do my best for Him."

"Don't lose that perspective when you become a big star," I challenged.

He caressed my chin. "That's why I'm glad I've got you to keep me straight and remind me of what is important if I do blow up."

"You will," I replied as we both smiled.

We discussed his options. It appeared to be a no-brainer—he had to take the deal. After all, my father wasn't interested in signing him to God's Town Records right away. And taking this deal was what Rory wanted. How could I not support him? I was just thankful that after all the drama, Rory still wanted me to be a part of his dreams. I was going to be part of his future, and his future looked overwhelmingly bright.

6

Matches

To celebrate Rory's signing, Raven and Kelly took us out to dinner. It was a first-class evening—from the caviar to the stretch limousine, the company spared no expense. Kelly's excitement over Rory's project was mind-boggling. All through dinner, he chatted about the extensive plans to make Rory a major star.

All night, Raven beamed at Kelly. It appeared that their relationship was on the upswing. That was a good thing. Sometimes, Raven was a bit too friendly with my man, and my hope was that she'd concentrate fully on hers.

The next morning, Rory and I sat in Raven's office.

"I called this meeting between you guys," Raven began, "because we need to talk about Rory's image. We want to market the total package—the charming, hot hunk with the dynamic voice. In order to sell records, women have to want him."

I stroked Rory's hand and gazed into his eyes. "I don't think that will be a problem," I said. "This handsome guy of mine will win quite a few hearts. Just the way he's won mine."

Raven stared at me for a moment. "Well, Bacall, that might be a problem." I frowned and she continued. "Women need to fall for a male soloist . . . who is single."

"What?" I jumped from my seat. "Are you telling us to break up?"

The thought of releasing him because of fans he didn't have yet was too much to swallow. How could she think we'd agree to such a request?

"Rory, this is crazy," I said, turning to him. His look stunned me. He didn't seem bothered by the outlandish demand. Maybe his career was more important to him than our relationship.

Just as I was about to storm from Raven's office, Rory spoke to her. "I signed on to be your male singer, not to have my life dictated. I know we've just met, but if you'd known me longer, you would know that my lady means the world to me. That fact isn't changing for no one."

He rose from his seat and walked toward me. My heart wanted to cry out of sadness at the thought of losing him. Yet his comments allowed me to smile with joy. He took me into his arms, and at that moment, I wanted to be no place else.

"Okay, lovebirds, will you please sit down?" Raven asked.

I could tell by her tone that she wasn't finished and would continue to try to convince us. I wanted to tell Ms. Gibbons just what I thought. Although I didn't know everything about the record industry, I did know that giving up my relationship was not going to advance Rory's career. So anything Raven had to say along those lines would go unheeded.

But I could tell Rory felt differently because he let go of our embrace and led me back to my chair.

"I never said I wanted you guys to officially break up," Raven explained. "That is not my intention. After all, Bacall, you make our artist happy. We need you to keep him that way. However . . . "

Yeah, I knew something else was coming. I was hoping that since she was on track in her relationship, I wouldn't have to worry about my boss's sneaky ways any longer. Unfortunately, it appeared that as long as I dealt with this lady, I'd have to watch my back.

She continued. "All I'm asking is for you to give the appearance of a split. I mean . . . Rory can be married for all I care, but the world needs to think he's single. This is important for several reasons. Ladies need to fall in love with you, Rory, so that you can sell records. Also, the songs you'll be singing . . . women need to believe you're singing those songs to them. Not to some girlfriend you met back in college."

Raven turned and looked directly at me. "We're trying to make Rory a star. Be his lady, baby, sweetheart, whatever. Be all that in private. But in the eyes of the public, let him be free."

Before we could utter a word back, Raven stood. "Why don't you two mull this over? Then we can go on with the rest of the meeting." She left the room.

With this first point of the meeting hitting me so hard, I was in no rush to hear her other plans. This career of Rory's was starting to get scary. And even more terrifying was that this was only the beginning.

Rory and I sat silently, like trapped hostages with tape over our mouths. Neither of us wanted to address the issue, but we knew we had to.

Finally, I said, "Honey, are you for this thing?"

"I'm for being with you," he said quickly. "I want a record career . . . but . . . at what price? I don't know." He paused, then glanced at me through the corner of his eye. "What do you think?"

Great. Now, the ball was back to me and there was no

way I could score. Whatever answer I gave my beau would be the wrong one. I didn't want people to think Rory was unattached. But how could I truly love him and not do what was best for his career?

My father had warned me that R & B was a crazy business. Since the first day I arrived in Los Angeles, he had been proven right.

I didn't respond to Rory's question, and he squirmed in his chair.

"Honey," he finally began, "no matter what happens, I will always love you."

I nodded, wanting to believe his words.

He took my hands. "Even if everyone thinks I'm single and available, in your heart, you have to know that you'll always belong to me."

His words were sweet. But the bitter reality of what could happen made them taste like lemons. Still, I had been raised to make lemonade.

So I batted my eyes and took a deep breath. "Rory, I'll agree to it. But I've got to tell you one thing. If there comes a time when this crazy arrangement doesn't work for me, I'll tell you to really let me go."

He shook his head strongly. "I promise to make it work, baby. Hang in here with me. There's no way I can go through this record stuff without you by my side." He leaned over and hugged me. "I need you," he whispered in my ear.

"You've got my support, Rory," I said, holding him tightly. "I only hope it's enough to hold us together."

The rest of the day was bustling. Raven, Rory, and I sat in the boardroom through meeting after meeting. People from different departments were constantly hustling in and out: wardrobe, press, video, music. Everyone introduced themselves to Rory and explained what their role would be.

After a quick break for lunch, we returned to the boardroom. This time, the executives joined us to come up with Rory's stage name.

"How about R. Kerry?" Rory suggested, looking confident. "That's a name I always envisioned the world knowing me by . . . R. Kerry."

His suggestion was met with silence. Even I thought his suggestion sounded a little lame. It didn't have spunk. It wasn't catchy. But I wasn't going to be the one to crash his idea.

It was Kelly Evans who shot him down. "Naw, brother. That's not gonna cut it. An initial and a last name? It's not what we're looking for. We need something more powerful. A name that makes a statement."

As the meeting went on, we tossed around ideas. But soon I realized that this was going to be a challenge. The other suggested names sounded even weaker.

"What about using his real name?" I asked.

No one liked that choice, either.

By the time three hours had passed, we were filled with frustration. The chaos in the meeting room had given me a headache. People shouting ideas, as if theirs was the only right answer. Folks were getting attitudes when their suggestions were rejected. It was business, but it was rude and ruthless business.

What stuck out to me the most was that God was nowhere in the picture. At God's Town Records, my father prayed with his staff before every meeting. Not that Christians didn't have disagreements. But the way they handled problems was different.

I excused myself and went to the ladies' room. I went into a stall and prayed quietly. "Lord, like always, I need You. Please accept my apology for not involving You in this sooner. Rory and I need help. It's like a zoo in there. People screaming at each other like animals. I just want peace, Lord.

Peace for this whole endeavor. Also, Father, I pray that Rory doesn't lose perspective. He said he wouldn't, but as his career heats up, help him not sway from his commitment to You. To remember You in everything He does. I do thank You, Lord, for giving him an opportunity to realize his dream. I know only through Your grace and mercy is all this possible. I sense us straying a bit from You. Before we go too far south, please help us stop and wait for Your direction."

When I walked back into the boardroom, I was amazed. Things had calmed down.

Smiles dressed everyone's faces. It appeared they were in agreement. I took my seat.

"That's the name! That's perfect," Kelly Evans asserted with enthusiasm.

All those around the twenty-seat oval table were nodding in agreement. I was getting anxious because I still hadn't heard the actual name.

Finally, Kelly said, "Flame! Yeah, that describes you to a tee. You'll be an explosive artist. You'll set your audiences on fire. And your records will burn with passion. Flame . . . it makes a statement like Prince or Keith Sweat or the Temptations. The name is tight! It has flavor. It's what we need."

I looked over at my man and thought about his new name. Flame, I liked it indeed!

At last, the business day was done. Rory accompanied me to my place. I thought we'd have dinner, relax, and go over the day's events. I especially wanted to talk about his new name. But I was saddened to discover that he'd made other plans.

"What do you mean, you're not coming in?" I questioned with a tempting look in my eye, hoping to persuade him to change his mind.

"Oh, baby," Rory moaned. "Don't stare at me that way.

You're gonna make it difficult to leave."

I grabbed his neck and kissed him. "That's the point!"

Rory reluctantly stepped away from my arms.

"I have to go to the studio to work on the single. Then a few of the band members said they wanted to show me L.A. This will be a good way for me to get to know the fellas. It's business, baby."

I was disappointed. However, my Oscar-winning performance didn't let my boyfriend know I was dejected. I kissed him good-bye and told him to call me when he got back to his hotel.

In my empty apartment, I wondered where things were going? Were there going to be more brush-offs like this in the future? Would I be able to settle for second place night after night? I didn't have answers. Just lots of uncertainty.

About an hour later, Brooks came in all aglow. She had enjoyed the evening with her fiancé before he retired to his hotel. Karri and Rory were staying at the same place.

God is always aware of what I need. Having my sister walk through the door with videos and popcorn was a blessing. When Brooks saw my face, she pointed to the couch and made me sit down.

"What's wrong, Bacall?"

I told her about my day—what had happened in the office and especially what had happened that night.

"It feels like I'm changing," I said. "In my soul I want Rory to succeed, but . . . if he does, there may not be an us. I don't want to lose him. I love him so much." I paused and dropped my eyes. I couldn't look at her as I said the next words. "Somewhere deep inside, I think I want him to fail."

"Well . . ." My sister took a deep breath and held my hand. "That's understandable. You're scared his feelings will change with his success. But it's like I told you a few days ago, you're going to have to give him room. You don't want to control a man. You want him to come to you without a leash, without ties, without obligation. If Rory really loves you, you won't lose him. He'll be with you freely. And then, you'll know in your heart that with you is where he wants to be."

With tears in my eyes, I hugged my sister. I felt so much better. There was no doubt in my mind that on that night, Brooks was an angel sent by God.

❦ ❦ ❦

The day after Brooks and Karrington left, I found myself missing my sister. What made it worse was that with work, I wouldn't be able to travel home for the release of Karrington's album and listening party that would be held in a few weeks.

But I would be able to attend Rory's. His first single had been finished, and Yo Town Records made sure it had lots of airtime all across the country. The tune, "My Heart Burns for You," was receiving rave reviews everywhere.

The time had come to get Flame's act ready for a big-city tour. Our days were filled preparing for that. Most of the planning was complete—finding backup singers was the final piece. The two studio singers used on the record did not have the look the company wanted. I sang part of the three-chord harmony, but there were several reasons why I wasn't planning on making that my full-time job.

So we held auditions to find three perfect ladies. Not only would they have to be able to sing and dance, but they had to get along with Rory.

"I want Flame and his background singers to have chemistry," Kelly insisted.

Not too much chemistry, I thought to myself.

The day of the auditions, sixty-two women showed up, all wanting to be part of Matches—the name given to the background singers. In two hours we weeded them down to five. I took those five aside and taught them the parts. They all caught on quickly, but it was hard to keep their attention. Their eyes kept roving to the other side of the room where Rory was meeting with Raven and Kelly. By the way they were looking and lusting, it was clear that they had more on their minds than being a part of his singing team. One of the girls confirmed my worst thoughts.

"Yes, ladies, he is fine. And I want me some *him*," Aisha, the five-foot-five, honey-skinned girl stated. "Shoot, I might just have to have that mouthwaterin' chocolate malt tonight!"

The other girls laughed, but it took every ounce of restraint I had to keep from responding. These girls knew nothing about Rory. They didn't even know his real name. They only had knowledge of his newfound fame, and they were ready to surrender the most precious part about themselves. Go figure!

I headed back over to the other side of the room after I felt the girls knew the parts. The women were sent out of the room while we discussed them. I was asked my opinion, and I named the three best singers.

We tried one combination with the three of them singing, and Rory loved the sound. Unfortunately, Aisha was one of the three. Although I wasn't crazy about her, I couldn't deny her talent. As long as she kept her hands on the microphone, I rationalized, I could deal with where her eyes roamed.

The other two singers didn't appear to be angels, either. As they sang, they batted their eyes and puckered their lips toward Flame. He didn't seem fazed by the come-ons. My man's mind was on business.

The tough job of dismissing the other two candidates fell on me. The two ladies who got the ax were the sweetest, but their look and sound wasn't right for this project.

Rory practiced with the girls we selected. As I watched, I had to admit that the four of them would make the stage light up. The way they looked after four hours of practice together told me that they were just about ready to perform. Good thing—since they were going on the road in five days.

Finally, Kelly Evans announced a dinner break. Food was catered in so the break would be short. As I sat at the table, Rory came up to me with his serious face.

"Ms. Lee," he said in a professional tone, trying not to alert the others in the room about the true nature of our relationship, "I really need to go over some things with you. Could we eat over there?"

I was elated, but calmly replied, "Sure, Flame, that's no problem."

We scattered papers over the floor to give the appearance that we were discussing business.

"Do you know how much I love you?" he asked.

I nodded, warmed by his words.

"How does it look, baby?"

I was happy that Rory wanted my opinion. With a smile, I said, "It looks great. You're really working the stage. Audiences will be wowed by you."

I could tell my words made him feel good, but a moment later, the wide smile on his face turned to a serious stare.

"You know, God is so good. Even though I'm not where I need to be in my walk with Him, He has granted me this desire. Look at all those people over there." He motioned with his chin. "There are twenty folks scrambling to get a show ready for this hot new artist—Flame. I still can't believe that's me." He discreetly covered my hand with his. "Plus . . . the Lord allowed my special lady to help me in this. I'm so blessed."

"But soon you'll be leaving me and heading to the road." My tone was sad.

"If there was any way I could have you with me, I would."

There was no doubt that he was sincere.

In the middle of our special time together, Aisha sauntered over. She pranced between us, then quickly turned her back to me—all without saying a word.

Aisha leaned over and began talking to Rory. If she was supposed to be whispering, I couldn't tell. I heard every word she said.

"Uh, Flame, you said you liked my moves. Well, I'm available to come to your hotel room tonight and show you moves you've never seen. Show you some of my other talents, you know what I mean?" She smiled and waited for Rory to speak. When he didn't say anything, she continued. "I plan on making this tour very enjoyable for you."

I couldn't believe what I was hearing. She was throwing herself at Rory harder than a major league pitcher could throw a fastball. As bad as I wanted to snatch her, I couldn't. This wasn't my battle. Rory had to settle this one.

Rory paused for only a moment. "Aisha, please get your things and get out of here. Your services are no longer required."

Aisha's mouth opened wide in shock. "Flame . . . I—"

Rory held up his hand. "For the record, your voice is the only thing that would have kept you around. Displaying your other *talents* was never expected and definitely not wanted."

I was so proud of my man, and I stared at Aisha as she looked at Rory, then turned to me. I could see in her eyes that the message had registered, and she turned away.

As she walked toward the table where she'd been eating, I realized that we'd now have to rush to fill her slot. What a waste of the day! Raven wouldn't be happy.

"I have an idea," Rory began, as if reading my mind. "I need a new singer, right?" He didn't give me a chance to answer. "And I want my lady with me. You, Miss Lee, fit both criteria."

This time, it was my mouth that dropped wide open.

"Come on, Bacall. Solve my problems and say you'll join me. Even if not permanently, you could come just for this mini tour."

It was a simple request, but many thoughts flew through my mind. Would this be a good or bad thing? I hadn't even considered going on the road with him, but with what I'd seen all day, maybe I should. As I toyed with the idea, it began to feel strangely appealing, but at the same time, extremely dangerous. As dangerous as a child playing with matches.

Hot

My decision to sing background for Flame was made easier by everyone at Yo Town Records. They knew Rory wanted me by his side and they wanted whatever their artist wanted. So I was encouraged to give it a try. I was excited, though clouds of doubt lingered in my mind.

The only concern the executives at Yo Town had was how they could keep their word to my father. I was in L.A. to learn the business side of the record industry. Would being on tour help with that?

I wasn't eager to talk to my father about it, so Kelly Evans did. Surprisingly, it didn't take much to convince my daddy. He thought the on-the-road, hands-on experience would be valuable. I was glad my father felt that way. I was excited about learning what an artist went through under the pressure to perform.

Once everything for the tour was set, we had one final extensive meeting. This one was held in Kelly's office.

"Come in, come in," Kelly announced to Raven, Rory,

and me as we approached his office.

When we stepped inside, there was already a gentleman sitting in a chair, but his back was to us. As we moved closer, I got a whiff of his familiar scent and frowned.

"Well, Flame," Kelly's voice interrupted my thoughts, "you're ready for your first expedition as a solo artist. There is only one element to your success equation that's missing. That's having the best road manager in the business."

Suddenly, a huge knot developed in my throat. *No way,* I kept saying to myself. But even though I didn't want it to be true, I knew that I recognized his scent.

Kelly continued "Since Kidz No Mo is taking a break, Blain Price is available. We've asked him to give up his vacation and accompany you on the road," Kelly continued excitedly. "Blain's heard your material and accepted the job. I tell ya, Rory, with Blain Price and your talent, we are confident things will be great for you on your first time out."

I could have fainted. With everything going on, I hadn't even told Rory about my friendship with Blain. Not that it was anything worth telling.

Blain stood and strutted straight to me. He acted as if there was no rift between us.

"Bacall, my chocolate sundae, how ya doin'?" he uttered before kissing me on the cheek.

From the corner of my eye, I watched Rory. I had never seen my boyfriend jealous. The expression that rose in his eyes was one of deep confusion and slight rage. I could tell my guy wanted to remove Blain's arms from around me.

Blain was one of the best in the business because he had a way of reading people. He sensed Rory's discomfort and pulled away from me. Then he stuck out his hand to greet Flame.

"Come on, brother. Don't sweat the hug. Bacall is my girl, but I am aware that she is *really* yo' girl."

"I have an idea," Kelly said. "Blain, why don't you and

Rory go out to lunch together and then we'll all meet back here this afternoon."

"Sounds like a plan." Blain smiled.

I held my breath as I looked at Rory. When he finally smiled, I exhaled. I prayed they would get along.

My prayers were answered. Rory and Blain became fast friends, and when we went on the road, Blain made certain that Flame and his road crew received first-class treatment.

The ten-day tour was going better than anyone anticipated. We had already performed at some of the biggest clubs in seven major cities. First, we opened in Los Angeles. Then we took the show to San Francisco, Phoenix, Dallas, Detroit, Chicago, and New York. Now we were in Atlanta. Every club was unbelievably crowded, packed tighter than an overstuffed suitcase.

No matter where we went, Flame left a train of burning excitement. Rave reviews came from every direction.

Rory and I were especially surprised by his success. We didn't expect people to come out to see an artist they'd never heard of. It didn't take long to see that we were wrong.

Flame's song—"My Heart Burns for You"—had gone from nowhere on the R & B charts to number three. That brought the people out to see the singer they'd quickly come to adore. Needless to say, the company executives were extremely pleased with their new male artist.

All three of my prayers were coming true. First, Rory's career had taken off and was heading toward the sky. But at the same time, he had not lost his perspective. Through all of his success, he constantly said that if it had not been for the Lord, he would not be where he was. And finally, we were doing great as a couple.

Actually, our relationship was better than ever. When we weren't in rehearsal or performing, Rory and I were huddled together discussing our feelings and our faith. Although we weren't studying God's Word daily, we claimed Matthew 6:33, "Seek first the kingdom of God and His righteousness, and all these things shall be added to you." As we meditated on that passage, we saw evidence of it working in our lives. I could not remember a happier time in my life.

Toi Perriman and Camille Colon were the other two background singers. I didn't have problems with them, probably because all my free time was spent with my man, rather than with two females with nothing to do but talk about other people. Though I didn't have any problem with them, they managed to bicker every day. If Toi and Camille weren't arguing over makeup, they were getting into it over hair spray. I stayed out of their confusion. I knew neither one well enough to take sides.

Despite their ugly dispositions, they were both beautiful girls. Toi reminded me of caramel candy. Her skin was brown, rich, and smooth. Camille was as yellow as a ripe banana. Her long, jet-black hair graced her back like an even-flowing river.

Although the outer beauty they possessed seemed to dazzle every man we came in contact with, I didn't worry about their looks affecting my guy. I was truly secure with the bond Rory and I had tied and were strengthening. Boy, that knot of trust felt good.

Flame had just sung his third and final encore to the Atlanta crowd. As the days went on, Rory's performances became more dynamic. All of us on stage were feeling the spark Flame ignited in his fans.

I was pumped from the crowd's energy, but finally getting offstage was a relief. My body was exhausted. All I wanted to do was head to the hotel and hibernate.

As I headed to the dressing room, I overheard Toi arguing with a girl who was trying to get backstage. There was nothing new to this scene. Everywhere we went, girls were giving lame stories about how they knew Flame just so they could get backstage. Some of the tales were ridiculous. I listened to Toi, expecting to get a good laugh, but instead, my ears heard truth.

"Oh, you know Rory's girlfriend," Toi said sarcastically. "And she sings background? Yeah, right. I'm one of the singers, and I can tell you that Rory doesn't have a girlfriend. Sorry, missy! Sir, please escort this girl out."

I knew that had to be Wesli, even though I wasn't expecting her until tomorrow when we played at Tuskegee. Before the guard could remove my friend, I interceded.

"Sir, no need to do that. She's looking for me." Then I turned to Toi. "Everything she told you is true. Meet my old roommate, Wesli Ezell," I explained.

"Wait," she said, "you are Rory's—Flame's girlfriend?"

"Yes, Toi, Rory is my man."

"That's a trip," Toi said. "No wonder you two are always stuck together tighter than cheese on a grilled sandwich. Wait till I tell Camille."

"I'd appreciate it if you didn't say anything. It's my business. If Camille is to be told, it should be by me."

Toi stormed off, but I didn't care. I was so glad to see Wesli that my fellow singer's childish ways did not affect me.

"Girl, what are you doing here?" I asked as Wesli and I hugged.

"The girls and I decided to drive over tonight and give you support. You guys were fantastic," she gushed.

When I took Wesli backstage and told Rory about my college girlfriends being there, he invited all seven of my buddies backstage and introduced them to the band.

Since we were performing in Tuskegee the next day, the girls wanted me to ride back to Auburn with them.

"You've got to come with us," Wesli begged. "We've planned a slumber party."

I was excited. As I looked at my friends, my heart felt another one of God's blessings on my life.

But Rory and Blain were reluctant to let me leave the group.

"I don't know if this is a good idea," Rory said.

"Don't worry. I'll be fine." I turned to Blain. " I promise to be on time for rehearsal tomorrow."

It took a few minutes, but they finally agreed.

"Look here, special lady, don't go getting into trouble," Rory said. "I planned on riding down to 'Skegee with my head nestled safely in your lap. Now what am I gonna do?" he teased.

"Dream about me," I whispered as I nibbled on his ear. "Until your eyes meet mine again. I love you." I pulled away, then turned back to my man. "By the way, if you start to wonder what's on my mind . . . your performance tonight will be all I dream about. It was magical."

He kissed me again.

I looked into his eyes and smiled. "Let me get out of here before I can't leave."

Hanging with the crew gave me a chance to take off both my business and entertainer hats. I just let my hair, soul, and mind down.

The ladies asked me tons of questions about life on the road with my guy.

"What's it like to be Flame's girlfriend?"

"Girl, do you know how blessed you are?"

They were happy about the success Rory and I had achieved. But the subject of conversation wasn't about me all night long. I was glad to talk about what was going on with them. I learned that things were the same at my old school. There was still much drama and tons of assignments to complete.

We talked well into the night until exhaustion made us sleep.

Alma got up the next morning and cooked breakfast. And what a dish it was! She fixed cheese grits, scrambled eggs, and link sausages—all mixed together with ketchup. It looked like slop but tasted superb.

We chatted some more, but my thoughts kept wandering to Rory. Being away from him for a few hours gave me a deeper understanding of my feelings for him. I always knew I loved him, but now I realized how much I depended on his presence. Although I was having a great time with my friends, I missed him.

By noon, I had to start getting ready for the drive to Tuskegee. Wesli was taking me back. It was hard saying good-bye to my crew. The days of us simply hangin' out were gone forever, but I would always cherish the precious memories God gave us.

There was a football party at Auburn that evening, so they weren't sure if they would be able to make the concert that night. I didn't know when I'd see them again.

Wesli and I took the back way from Auburn to Tuskegee. It was supposed to be a shortcut that saved five minutes. Instead, the two-lane highway was backed up for miles because of a big-rig accident.

I glanced at my watch and squirmed. I was going to be late. Even though there was a good reason for my tardiness, this was not a good thing. After all, I had given my word.

"I'm so sorry," Wesli said.

"It's not your fault," I told her for the fiftieth time.

By the time I arrived at rehearsal, I was thirty-eight minutes late. I rushed to Blain.

"I'm sorry. There was an accident. Traffic was backed up—"

Blain held up his hand. "That's all right. These things happen. Just get over there. They've already started."

I sighed with relief. If Blain wasn't upset, no one else would be. When I walked onto the stage, the music stopped.

"I'm sorry," I said once again, feeling like I had uttered those words a million times. I took my place behind my microphone and was shocked by Rory's response. His glance at me was as cold as a solid block of ice, but I was confident that once we began singing, he'd be fine.

I was wrong. Halfway through the first song, Rory stopped.

"This doesn't sound right," he said angrily. He glared at me. "Bacall, I think it's you. You're off-key."

I shook my head. He was wrong, but I wasn't going to do to him what he was doing to me. "Sorry."

"You'll have to do better than that," he barked.

It was bad enough that he hurt my feelings, but to do it so publicly—I just didn't understand. I could hear Toi and Camille's snickers, but I took a deep breath and worked my way through the rest of rehearsal.

At the first break, I went over to Rory, who was going over notes with the keyboard players.

"Can I talk to you, please?"

Rory sighed. "Yeah, sure, whatever."

We stepped outside the room.

"What is your problem?" I asked. "I said I was sorry for being late, and I don't deserve your attitude."

"Oh, you think I'm upset about you being late?" He shook his head. "Uh-uh. Late has nothing to do with this. You see, all anyone could talk about last night was my *girlfriend,*" he hissed. "Get it, Bacall? The band was raggin' me about my girl. Now, I wonder . . . how did our private business become so public?" Rory's eyes of fire pierced my saddened soul. "Think about that question, 'cause I know you've got the answer."

I stood speechless as I watched him storm away. I felt

horrible, even though all I had done was confirm Wesli's story. Maybe that wasn't the best way. I should have known better than to open up to big-mouth Toi.

When I returned to rehearsal, Toi wouldn't even look at me. I had to work hard to stay focused, because all I wanted to do was pray that when I told Rory how our relationship came up in conversation, he'd understand.

As soon as practice was over, I rushed over to Rory. "I have something to tell you."

"Not now." He waved me away. "I don't have time."

As he stomped off away from me, my sadness turned to anger. He wasn't even giving me a chance to explain. Well, if that's the way he wanted it. I picked up my bag and headed out the door.

Like our previous performances, Flame was on fire at the Tuskegee concert. In front of his student body, he was even more explosive. Everyone in our group was comfortable but me. The old building where we'd first met and once shared such warmth had now become cold.

I had phoned Wesli before the performance and told her about my situation. She volunteered to take me back to Auburn after the concert so I wouldn't have to deal with the drama. The thought of accompanying her to a football party wasn't terribly appealing. However, when compared to the option of being around Rory, I accepted her invitation.

When I got to the dressing room after our performance, Wesli was already waiting. It brought a smile to my face to see her, and I was glad I'd given her name to security so she could have access to backstage.

"Hey, lady," I said. "Let me change clothes and we can go."

"Go?" Toi yelled from behind me. I didn't know she was there, listening to my conversation.

She had a smirk on her face that I could not figure out, but before I could ask her to get out of my business, she said, "Bacall, I . . . I didn't mean to spread your—"

I cut her off. "Save it, Toi. Save your drama for someone who wants to be entertained."

"OK, fine . . . be that way. I just came in here to deliver a message from your precious Rory. He's around the corner and wanted me to tell you he needs to see you." Toi still had that smirk on her face, but I ignored it.

I was excited that Rory wanted to see me, but having my pride, I debated whether or not I should go to him.

"Go," Wesli said, as if reading my mind. "If he's ready to talk, you need to do it now. Even if it's just for your own peace of mind."

"Thanks, Wesli." I smiled, knowing she was right. "I'll be right back."

I rushed into the hall, then stopped when I turned the corner. I knew my eyes had to be out of focus. Rory was pinned up in a corner—with another woman. His arms were wrapped tightly around her. They were locked in a deep conversation that seemed so intimate I didn't have the key to enter.

"You know I'll always be here for you," I heard Rory say. "I care too much not to." He stroked her hair. Then he must have felt my presence because he turned toward me.

I was even more astonished when I recognized the girl. It was Ashley. Yep, the lady who caused the enormous scene at the beginning of the school term.

What's going on? I wondered. What business did she have to discuss with Rory? Somehow my eyes wandered down to her stomach. I was astonished to see that it was the size of a beach ball. Then my gaze met Rory's. This was too much for me to digest.

Finally, the words that were stuck in my throat released. "And you have the nerve to be mad at me?" I turned around and quickly walked away.

❦ ❦ ❦

I sat silently in the car as Wesli drove. She knew something was wrong, but she didn't pressure me to talk. Instead, she drove straight to the party. I didn't feel like being bothered with people or music, but I didn't want to spoil it for Wesli.

Less than five minutes after we were inside, I felt someone tap me on the shoulder.

"Bacall, is that you?"

I turned to face Jackson Reed, an old friend. We never dated, but he had always let me know he was interested. I didn't return his affection, though I was glad we remained friends.

"Jackson," I said, hugging him. "It's been ages."

For the next hour, we caught up with each other's lives. We chatted and reminisced, but most importantly, we laughed, which helped spice up my somber mood. Although I was still devastated by what I'd witnessed earlier, I was determined not to sulk all night.

When the DJ slowed down the music, Jackson stood and extended his hand. I took it and followed him to the center of the dance floor. There were no feelings on my part. But the beat had me groovin' and my old friend had my hips movin'. I was so relaxed, I never noticed how close we were dancing.

All of a sudden, someone touched my shoulder, and I moved away from Jackson. Before I could turn around fully, a fist flew over my shoulder and swirled toward my dance partner's jaw.

It took me some time to realize what was going on, and when I did, I screamed. "How dare you, Rory! And, for what? Because I'm dancing with a friend?" I reached toward Jackson. "I should be the one playing the fool. After all, you got someone pregnant. Just get out of here, Rory."

Jackson stood and lunged toward Rory.

"Jackson, please," I begged him. "He's not worth it."

I glared at Rory and he stared back at me. We were on two different wavelengths. I had had it. I was tired of his up-and-down moods. It was clear that we had reached a boiling point in our relationship. We desperately needed to cool off, but I didn't know how we would do it or if we could. We were both immensely hot.

8

Kindling

Before Rory and Jackson could go at it, several football players grabbed Rory. I turned around and started to walk away.

"Oh, so it's like that. You just gonna walk away. Walk out on all we've built," Rory yelled as he struggled against the men holding him. "You gonna let these tired football players throw me out of the party?

I had to admit, Jerome Rocker, our defensive lineman who weighed a whopping two-hundred-sixty-one pounds, and T-bone, Auburn's linebacker weighing close to two-hundred-fifty, were handling Rory quite roughly. However, part of me didn't think the guys were rough enough. I had given my whole heart to Rory. Yet his actions all day had stomped on my emotions. Why should I care if he got stomped? Heck, if I were big enough, I'd have thrown him out myself.

"Man, y'all get yo' hands off me," Rory demanded.

Somehow, Rory broke free from the football players'

grips and stepped in my face. Wesli jumped up to defend me.

"It's not a good time. Just get out of here, Rory," Wesli whispered, trying to put out the fire.

But Rory appeared to want to add fuel to it and tried to push her out of the way.

Wesli stood her ground and continued. "You both need to cool off. Rory, you don't want any trouble. I'm sure the tabloids are waiting for a juicy story. The last thing your career needs is bad press. Just go!"

"Bacall is my girl, and I'm not going anywhere till we talk!" Rory shouted.

Tears skated down my face. "I have nothing to say to you . . . nothing at all!" I yelled. "If you want to talk so bad, go back to 'Skegee and talk to Ashley. You two have a bundle to talk about."

"If you'd quit blabbering, I want to—" Rory tried to utter.

"Blabbering? Blabbering?" I screamed, cutting him off. "Oh, no, see, you have nothing else to say to me. Go tell the band we're no longer an item. That should make you happy, seein' as how you hated they all knew 'bout us anyway."

Before I knew what was happening, Rory wrapped his arms around me, pulling me close to his chest. I was shocked by the move, and for a moment I relaxed, wanting to stay in his embrace. His hug was warm and cozy, but it couldn't come close to fixing our problems. And I was too angry to forgive and forget.

I pushed away from him, my rage too much to contain. "You're standing here calling me your girl. But you didn't want anyone to know about us. I must have been crazy to agree to keeping our relationship a secret!" I screamed. "Why should I stay with someone who wants to keep me hidden? Get real, Rory. Get real."

All of a sudden, T-bone pulled out a knife and waved it

in Rory's face. I was terrified. Everyone at Auburn knew T-bone was loony enough to truly use the thing.

Rory, on the other hand, thought he was playing. "Bro, quit trippin'." Rory laughed.

"You think I'm playin', man?" T-bone waved the knife in the air.

When Rory shook his head and continued chuckling, T-bone lost it. He dived toward Rory and slit his leather jacket.

It took Rory only a moment to realize what had happened and he charged T-bone. Now it was a full-blown fight.

I wanted desperately to stop it, but Wesli held me back.

"You can't go over there," she said, pulling my arm. "T-bone has a knife."

"And Rory is going to get hurt because of me!" I screamed over the noise that filled the house. "Let go of me, Wesli."

My friend slowly released my arm, but as I tried to move forward, Jackson stood in my way.

He said, "What can you do to stop those big jokers from goin' at it, Bacall? You just gonna get yourself cut. Is that what you want?"

"Well, somebody has got to do something! If Rory gets hurt, I'll never forgive myself," I whimpered.

I tried to move past Jackson, but he continued blocking my path. As the fight went on, he tried to pull me out of the room.

"No!" I shouted over the other screams. "Leave me alone, Jackson. I can't leave Rory. Not until I know he's all right."

Rory and T-bone looked as ridiculous as the fake wrestlers on television as they tussled on the floor. Unlike those staged shows, this fight was real. I knew it would only be a matter of time before the knife found flesh.

I looked around at the crowd that had developed. I was appalled. No one was doing anything to stop the madness. These people wanted to see a show.

I could no longer just stand by. Though I was furious with Rory, I knew I loved him. There was no way I could watch him get hurt on my account.

When Jackson and Wesli were focused more on the brawl than on me, I dashed to the tangled bodies. As I leaned over T-bone, I tried desperately to swat the knife away from his wrist. But with one slap, he tossed me across the room.

Seeing me shaken up must have given Rory extra energy. My man mustered up his strength and turned the knife on T-bone. In self-defense, he slit the side of T-bone's face.

The crowd oohed and aahed at the sight of blood, but before T. Bone could retaliate, the police busted in.

"Break it up, break it up!" two uniformed officers yelled.

Without asking questions, the cops handcuffed both guys. I hated seeing my sweet, suave star treated like a cold, cruel criminal.

"Man, be glad they takin' us in," T-bone yelled as the policeman pushed him through the door. "'Cause for what you done to me, I woulda killed you," he threatened. "And, I still might . . . pretty boy. I don' care, you s'pose to be a singer."

"No one is killing anyone," the police officer said as he jerked both men to the patrol car.

While T-bone yelled defiantly, Rory was silent. It seemed that the thought of going to jail weighed him down.

"Officer, please," Rory said. "I was only protecting myself. He had the knife."

"Tell it to the judge," the other officer responded, not wanting to hear the story.

I followed Rory to the car. "I'll bail you out," I blurted to my guy with tears rolling down my face.

"No," Rory said angrily. "Get Blain! I don't want you near me."

* * *

I couldn't sleep the whole night. The events of the day played over in my mind—from the concert, to discovering Rory with Ashley, to Jackson, and to Rory being dragged away by the police. It was hard to believe all of that had happened in a few hours.

I did what Rory asked. I called Blain to put water on Flame's fire of trouble. And I stayed away, returning with Wesli to the apartment we had shared.

In my old bed, I tossed and turned until I couldn't take it anymore. I got up and went into the living room. Wesli still had a few of my things. Among them were my gospel CDs. It always seemed that when I was down, there was a Christian song that could lift my spirits. But no matter how many songs I listened to that night, it didn't work. So I returned to bed, accepting the fact that nothing would shake my sadness. Nothing—except talking to God.

I got on my knees and prayed. "Lord, please help my man. Well, he might not be my man anymore, but please help Rory. Regardless of what happens with us, I do care deeply for him. And I know You care even more. Please get him out of trouble. I want that more than I want us to be together."

I meditated on the words I'd just spoken, then climbed into bed. But I still had a restless sleep.

The next morning, I was awakened by a knock on my door.

"Callie, what do you want for breakfast?" Wesli asked.

I sighed. "All I want for breakfast is Rory at my side."

Wesli came into the room and sat on the edge of the bed. "I'm sorry you're still feeling so bad."

I shook my head. I couldn't believe all that had happened.

"He's probably still in jail. And even if he's out, he wants nothing to do with me."

"Callie, Rory's not totally innocent in this thing, you know."

I knew she was talking about Ashley and the baby. I had finally told her everything last night before we went to bed.

"You know, Wes . . . I never wanted to be one of those girls who marries a man with baggage. You know, a guy with kids or an ex-wife. But now that I'm in love with a guy who's gonna have a kid, all my logic seems to be gone. I just want to be with my man. Only now that I realize that, he wants nothing to do with me."

"Quit beating yourself up," Wesli scolded. "You know I like Rory, but if homeboy can't appreciate you, then move on without him. I don't know what he was trying to tell you last night, but his tactics were cruel and unnecessary. Grabbin' your arm . . . what was that? The last thing you want is some brother being physical with you. I mean, who wants an unfaithful, abusive, destructive man? Maybe your first instinct to get away from Flame was right. After all, how many times does a hot fire have to burn you before you move your hand?"

I let Wesli's words sink in. Sadly, I believed that she was right.

All through breakfast, I thought about Wesli's words. As I tried to give myself reasons why Rory and I should remain a couple, a part of me felt like the fire in our relationship was already out. In my mind, I kept trying to restart the flame—I didn't want our love to die. But I didn't know what Rory wanted.

I didn't even know where Rory was. Everyone on the tour was scheduled to leave that morning for L.A.—except for me. I was attending the listening party for Karrington's album and would be returning to Los Angeles tomorrow.

But I didn't know if Rory had made that flight back or was still being detained by the Auburn police.

After breakfast, I called Blain's cell phone, but there was no answer.

"Blain would have called you if there were any problems," Wesli tried to reassure me.

By the time I had to get dressed for the listening party, I still had not heard anything. I tried to focus my attention on the event at hand.

Wesli helped me dress in the red satin gown that Brooks and I had picked out when we went shopping in Los Angeles. At the time, I didn't know where I might wear this outfit, but now I was glad I had bought it.

"Girl, you look great," Wesli said as she stood back to admire me.

Although I smiled, my heart was in turmoil. I couldn't get Rory off my mind.

"You better stop thinking of that boy."

I shook my head. We had been friends so long it wasn't hard for us to know what the other was thinking.

"It's time for us to get out of here." Wesli dangled her car keys in front of me Not only had she been a gracious host, but she was going to be my chauffeur to the listening party. It was a big deal, but the Gomp was down the street.

Forty minutes later, Wesli dropped me off in front of the church. Karrington's party was being held in the church ballroom, and if I knew my father, the company had spared no expense. This was going to be a class-act event.

I looked at my watch and sighed. I was twenty minutes late. My folks were surely wondering where I was, being that I hadn't checked in with them or Brooks. But I had done that on purpose. The last thing I wanted was to answer tons of questions about Rory.

Walking up to the side entrance, I saw my father. I smiled but then frowned. It looked like he was in a heated discussion with someone. As I got closer, I saw that my dad was with the man of the hour—Karrington.

I wasn't trying to eavesdrop, but their voices grew louder with every comment. It appeared they didn't care who was listening.

"I can't believe you snuck this song onto the album," my father said angrily. "I specifically told you that 'Jump' wasn't right for God's Town Records."

"Well, sir, I didn't know I needed your permission. True enough, we disagreed. But I'm the creative director and it is *my* album."

"Need I remind you . . . this is *my* record company," Dad said through clenched teeth. They were silent for a moment. "Son, this stunt you've pulled jeopardizes our relationship. The trust is gone like yesterday's rain."

Karrington shook his head, but remained quiet.

My father said, "I should recall every album and drop that song. Shucks, with the attitude I'm sensing, I could drop you as an artist and be done with this project altogether. So don't get cocky and smart!"

"I'm sorry, Reverend Lee." Karrington humbly dropped his head. "I didn't mean any disrespect. Really . . . I just didn't think I needed your permission."

"It's not that you needed my permission," Dad retorted as his voice cooled down. "But after we spoke last time, I assumed you were going to leave that song off the album. I guess I was wrong."

"Sir, I'm sorry if I misled you and I'm sorry that you disapprove. But please, give this song a chance. I really believe in it. The kids today are listening to this kind of music."

"We're not trying to be like all the other music out there."

"I agree, but with all respect, sir, I don't want to be an artist who only appeals to saved folks. I have a heart to reach those who don't know our Lord and Savior. I believe that Jesus Christ has called me to step out of gospel music's comfort zone and do something daring and different."

My father looked at Karrington intently, as if carefully considering his words.

Karrington continued, "We need to spread His Word to those who need to hear. Those outside the church. Please give this a chance to work."

I was captivated by Karrington's plea. My father had always been a conservative southern preacher. Maybe this was his chance to get with the times. As long as the gospel was not compromised, no one—not even my father—should care if the music was hip-hop or R & B with a swinging beat. Dad's company needed to try to reach people other Christian companies wouldn't. After all, that's what Jesus did.

A few moments later, my father said, "Well, Son, I still have reservations about whether or not 'Jump' will fly. However, you've made a valid point. We'll give the song a try and see what happens."

"Will you guys hug already?" I walked up to the two men and smiled.

"Bacall!" My father was so ecstatic that he picked me up and spun me around.

I giggled like a little girl—the way I did when my father spun me around when I was a child. Boy, did I miss those times.

After my father put me down, I hugged Karrington.

"Come on, my children," Daddy said with a big smile as he wrapped his arms around both of us. "Let's go inside and make *our* company successful by promoting this album."

Karrington smiled and my father knew the question that was in his future son-in-law's mind.

"Yes, Son," my father said, "you heard right. *Our* company. You're engaged to my Brooks. In my eyes, that already makes you my son."

❦ ❦ ❦

I had been at the party for two hours, listening to Karrington's mini concert, which was excellent. The controversial song, however, had not yet been sung, and I wanted desperately to hear it. But as I waited, Karrington signaled to the band, indicating the end of the concert.

The crowd stood, giving him a standing ovation. I stood with the rest, knowing his album would be a huge success. Not because my dad worked on it. Not because the choir was awesome. Not because the song titles were powerful. But because the songs were truly anointed.

Karrington held up his hands and everyone returned to their seats. "You are too kind . . . but the applause should go to heaven, 'cause God made this project possible." Again, the group cheered. "And just like the album title, 'God Cares,' remember He does care for each of you here tonight . . . and so do I. There are some very special people I must thank." He turned to the singers who stood behind him. "Choir . . . without you, this album would not sound the same. Your voices carry out what God has placed in me to give to the world." Karrington had to wait for the applause to die down before he could continue. "To Reverend and Mrs. Lee . . . I appreciate and love you so much. I thank you for the leeway you've given me to spread God's Word musically . . . my way." Karrington paused as he tried to hold back his tears.

I glanced at my father. I could tell he was touched by Karrington's words, but he simply nodded his head in acceptance.

"Lastly . . . I'd like to say thanks to my fiancée . . . Miss Brooks Lee. Honey, will you please come up here?" As my sister walked toward him, Karrington said, "You are my friend. You make me love you the way Christ loved the church. Everything I do is by the help and strength of you and the Lord. Thanks for showing me every day that you care for me. I can't wait till God gives you to me completely and makes you my bride."

When my sister reached her guy's side, they embraced tightly. Everyone felt their love. As the crowd stood once again and applauded the beautiful sight, I dashed outside into the chilly air.

My sister was in love and happy. I, on the other hand, was in love and miserable. My heart was sinking lower than a submarine in the Atlantic Ocean. Here I was, at an event where I should have been happy for my sister and, once again, I was ashamed of my thoughts. Brooks needed my support, and I was too caught up in my own miserable feelings to take part in her moment. But there was no way I could sit there faking it. I hoped coming outside would refresh me.

As I looked to heaven for comfort, tears streamed from my sad eyes. I was in love with a man for the first time in my twenty-two years of life. It seemed, however, that love wasn't going to be enough to keep us together.

"Rory, why aren't things working out between us? Why are we falling apart? Why is what we have slipping away?" I shivered in the cold February air. "I love you, Rory," I cried.

Suddenly I felt two strong arms grip me. The touch warmed me like an electric blanket. I so badly wished they were Rory's arms around me. But I knew they probably belonged to my dad, coming outside to cheer up his little girl.

To my surprise, I heard a sweet voice. "I love you, too, my Lady Bacall. The lady I love with all my heart, with all my soul, and with all my mind." Rory turned me around to face him. "I'll give you everything I've got to give. We will make it. So don't ever question us again."

"I thought . . . I thought you hated me," I said with confusion. "Last night you said you didn't want me around."

His lips graced mine. The kiss was soft, sweet, and special. It wasn't a good-bye kiss. It was a sign of two people in love.

"Did that feel like I don't want you around?" Rory asked softly.

I shook my head.

"I never said that. I just didn't want you coming to the police station. I didn't want my lady involved in all that mess. You helped enough by trying to stop the fight. It was on me to get out of the trouble." He pulled me close to his chest. "I'm sorry I was so hotheaded when I came to that party. Can you forgive me? Can we move on?"

"I want to forget yesterday," I told him sincerely as I looked into his eyes. "I want to pretend all the things that happened . . . never happened. But what about Ashley . . . and the baby?"

"Bacall, honey, Ashley is pregnant, but it's not what you think."

How could it not be what I thought? He had another woman mixed up in our lives forever. He would never be able to cut things off completely with Ashley now.

But I wanted to hear Rory's explanation. I wanted desperately to believe there was hope for my guy and me.

"See . . . the night I met you, my roommate Jordan, thought when I left the apartment to set up for the party, I wouldn't be coming back. When I came back to change clothes, I caught him gettin' busy with Ashley. That's why she and I broke up that night. Remember when you saw Ashley and me in the hallway arguing?"

I nodded.

"She wanted to still be my girl. Get that! And she had the nerve to be mad at me for not wanting her. But the thing you need to know now is that the child is not mine. It's Jordan's. But when she told him, he said it was her problem."

"Oh, that's awful," I said.

He nodded. "Ashley was apologizing for doing me wrong. I told her she did me a favor, 'cause if she hadn't cheated on me, I wouldn't have found my true love."

I looked into his eyes. I felt horrible for judging him wrongly. I had assumed the worst. But I had to admit I was relieved.

People began to exit the church as the party came to a close.

I pulled away from Rory. "I've got to go inside and say good-bye to my family."

As I turned toward the church, Rory lifted me over his shoulder and walked toward the parking lot.

I was stunned. "What are you doing?"

"You can call your folks tomorrow. Tonight . . . this night is for you and me. I'm taking you someplace special."

I wanted to protest—I didn't want my parents to worry. But I just smiled. I was going to spend a special night with the man I loved.

❦ ❦ ❦

Three hours later, around midnight, Rory and I drove into *Hot-lanta* our nickname for "Hot Atlanta."

"Where are you taking me?" I asked him again for at least the hundredth time.

He smiled, as he had been doing all night. "I promise, we're almost there."

When we stopped in front of a house, I knew immediately where we were. He had described it to me so many times, so perfectly, that I knew—this was his home.

"Isn't it too late to be coming here?" I asked as he pulled me from the car.

"No. My mom stays up late. Besides, I want her to meet my special lady."

His mother was sweeter than my mom's peach cobbler.

"Oh, Bacall, it is so nice to finally meet you," she said.

"Rory has told me so much about you. I really appreciate you taking care of my baby."

I beamed. I was thrilled that Rory had told his mother about me.

We were in the house for less than ten minutes when Rory took my hand to leave.

"Where are you two going so late at night?" Mrs. Kerry asked.

"Someplace special, Mom. I'll call you tomorrow."

I kissed her good-bye, then we hopped back in the rental car. This time, I didn't even ask where we were going because I knew what Rory's answer would be. Less than twenty minutes later, I discovered that he really was taking me someplace special—a secluded cabin.

Rory never explained how he acquired the intimate spot or where he'd gotten this wonderful idea. My man simply opened the plain wooden door and whisked me inside.

I was amazed at such a romantic setting. It was quaint and cozy. Two things stood out—the fire burning in the fireplace and the queen-sized bed that took up a good portion of the room.

He placed one hand on my hip, the other around my neck, and slowly pulled me toward him. As we kissed, everything inside me felt sensual. We edged our way to the bed.

So many times we had been in this position, and somehow, I had always resisted the temptation. This time felt different. I was losing control. The last word I wanted to say was no, and no never crossed my lips.

"I love you," Rory said as he stared into my eyes. "I wanna show you how much. Please don't pull away this time. Don't stop what I know will be good. Let me give you all of me." My boyfriend kissed my skin and melted my resistance with his words.

I breathed deeply. "I'm scared, Rory."

"Don't be, honey. I promise I will take care of you."

"This is weird, Rory. I know it's wrong, but . . . it feels too right to stop. I'm confused. I don't know what to do."

Rory put his finger on my lips as if to hush my concern. Then, he stroked my hair gently. It felt wonderful to me.

He kissed me again. "I love you, my Lady Bacall."

The enticing kiss made my heart race as if I'd been on a treadmill for thirty minutes. Everywhere he touched me, I felt pleasure. With each caress, Rory wore down my resistance. The scary feelings faded.

Within minutes, all our clothes were off. Rory's gentleness eased my tension. We nestled ourselves into the cushy covers and moved slowly down the irreversible path.

I was so excited, wanting to show him my love, that I couldn't think of it as being bad. I couldn't believe this was out of God's will. I put my energy into enjoying the heated moment. When the two of us became one, I didn't want the moment to ever cease. Just as Rory had placed logs on the fire to keep it going, so too did I desperately want to keep our romantic union kindling.

Blaze

The next morning, before the sun rose, I woke up in a place where I didn't want to be. I was no longer innocent. I was no longer pure. I was no longer what I had been for twenty-two years.

Although I couldn't take back the previous night's actions, I wished with all my heart that I could. I wished I could recapture what was now lost forever.

Frantically, I whispered, "Oh, my gosh! What did we do?" As I thought about it more, my words became louder. "What did you do to me? Oh, no, what did I let you do?"

It took Rory a few moments to awaken from his peaceful slumber. "What's up?" he asked sleepily.

"What did we do?" I repeated. I covered my face with my hands.

Rory frowned. "Last night was great! Why are you acting weird about it?"

"I gotta get out of here, Rory. Where's my stuff? I . . . I gotta go!" Like a patient in a mental institution, I felt like I was losing it. The sinful act was done and I was sick with grief and shame.

"First of all, calm down," Rory instructed. "Neither of us has to be anywhere today. We can catch a flight to L.A. tomorrow. So relax. I'm sure we can talk through your problem."

"You don't get it," I yelled. "I gotta get out of here."

Rory took my hand. "Make me understand. Tell me what's wrong? I thought you enjoyed last night. I did." My boyfriend's eyes were filled with confusion.

I pulled away from him. "Please don't." I began to sob.

"What?" Rory asked with concern. "Did I hurt you, baby?"

I did feel sore. When I moved abruptly, parts of me felt torn, scratched, and raw. But that's not what hurt me the most. The part of me that felt the most pain was my heart. I had let the Lord down. The promise I'd made to Him when I became a Christian, to save myself for my husband, was broken.

"Did I hurt you, baby?" he repeated.

I shook my head. He smiled.

"See, it did feel good, didn't it?" he said, a bit cocky.

I had to admit, last night did feel good. But today, I felt terrible. Doubts rose within me. Rory had no obligation to me in the eyes of God. There was no ring on my finger. My guy, whom I loved very much, could leave me without a second thought. He'd hit the jackpot. So why should he stay?

My insecurities began to mix with my doubts. Rory was becoming a big star as quickly as a forest catches fire, from one dry tree to the next. And that would mean girls—women all over the place. "Flame" would be able to have his pick. If conquering was his objective, I'd just given him a reason to leave me.

I didn't want to talk to Rory. No way could I share my sad feelings. Yet he kept pushing.

"I'm not lettin' you clam up on me," he said holding my

hands. "You can't shut me out. I love ya, babe. Don't treat me as if I don't matter."

"You wanna know what's bugging me?" I screamed. "We shouldn't have done it!"

I couldn't even look at him. I ran into the bathroom and my reflection in the mirror stared straight at me. I dropped my eyes. It was bad enough that I couldn't look at Rory, but I couldn't look at myself, either. I felt used and dirty.

Questions were still popping into my mind. Could I be pregnant? Did I contract any diseases? Would our relationship ever be the same? Did I love Rory enough to give so much away?

I turned on the shower faucets. Crazily, I hoped the water would wash away my pain. As I let the water run to get hot, I sat on the toilet. I felt afraid, not knowing how the private parts of my body might be affected. I sighed with relief when I didn't experience any more discomfort.

When I finished however, I noticed red spots on the toilet paper. Seeing those precious drops made my tears start to flow.

My cycle had already come and gone for the month. The spotting was a sign of something else. I remembered stories in the Old Testament where a bride gave her husband the precious gift of blood after they consummated their marriage. This was the sign that the woman was pure.

I cried tears of disappointment. I'd never be able to give that gift to my husband. Even if I ended up marrying Rory, the gift was too sacred and special for just a boyfriend. Yet the present was opened and couldn't be returned.

As my sobbing grew louder, I heard the bathroom door open.

"Baby, what's wrong?" Rory asked. His voice was full of concern. I could tell he wanted to comfort me, but there wasn't anything he could do.

"Get out!" I rose and shouted at him. "I'm . . . not dressed."

Rory stood his ground. He threw me a towel, then tried to hold me. His gentle gesture made me really lose it.

I started beating my hands against his chest, hoping to push him away. I was shaking, screaming and stomping.

"What is wrong with you?" he asked. "Why do you think we shouldn't have been intimate? Do you think I'm gonna leave you? Why are you doing this to me?"

"Everything isn't about you, Mr. Rising Star Flame!" I screamed. "I'm not your groupie. I'm not a chick who would just be glad she spent the night with a singer. I'm your *girlfriend*, remember? I'm the lady whose feelings you should have taken into consideration. We . . . we just shouldn't have done it."

Rory looked puzzled. If I wasn't acting crazy, he probably would have wanted to go another round.

But I would no longer surrender to those heated feelings. I had to stand on God's Word. I hadn't done it last night, but I would do it now—I would stand. Even if it meant losing my love. If I had stood firm last night, I wouldn't be in this mess now.

"You know, Rory." My voice shook. "It says in First Corinthians that it is better to marry than to burn. We're not married. We didn't wait. We should have asked the Lord to melt away our lust, rather than try to extinguish it ourselves." I wanted to just sit down and cry, but I continued. "I don't know 'bout you, but I feel God's wrath on me. And I know . . . I know we should have waited."

With a shocked look, Rory turned around and left me alone.

❦ ❦ ❦

By the time I came out of the bathroom, I had calmed down. I couldn't blame Rory. I was just as responsible for what happened as he was.

When I walked into the living room, he had the fire

burning once again, but he was fully dressed.

"Bacall," he called my name softly. "I want you to stay here with me. I promise, we'll just talk."

I nodded and sat at the table. Rory joined me, but remained silent.

Finally, he said, "What do you think about the tour?"

His question surprised me, but I was glad he'd thought of something else to talk about. We spent the next few hours discussing the last two weeks—how things went, what went well. Although I could feel the friction in the air, I was glad to see that, no matter what, we would be able to remain friends. We carefully avoided any discussion of "us" and where we stood.

When Rory went outside to gather more wood, I comfortably nestled by the inviting fire. I watched Rory run in and out of the cabin. Even though my mind was racing with questions and my heart was still filled with pain, I wondered how I could live without this man?

Everything about Rory was large and strong. It hurt to face the fact that his faith was small and weak. I knew that, no matter what, I would now stand strong. What happened last night would not happen again. I also knew that we could still have a relationship without being intimate. But I didn't know how I could make Rory see that.

After placing a fresh log on the low, crackling fire, Rory knelt beside me. As he gently caressed my hair, I stared into the orange glow. It seemed as if the pit that held the burning logs was boldly staring back at me. It was like I was being pulled into the heat of the flames, and the fire mysteriously let me know it understood my pain.

Rory broke my trance. "Bacall," he whispered, "what are you expecting from me? Do you want to go down to the courthouse and tie the knot right now?"

I remained silent still staring into the flames.

"Well, if you're not saying that we should get married,

does that mean we won't have another wonderful moment together? 'Cause if that's the case, I gotta be honest. I don't know if I can do that."

My heart felt tight. Marriage wasn't the option I was proposing. We were too young, with too many other things going on. But I did want to abstain. I knew it wouldn't be easy for either of us, but we could do it.

"Honestly," he uttered slowly, "it's amazing that I went seven months without having all of you. Girl, you don't know how bad I struggled." He paused. "I thought last night was the start of a new closeness between us. But now, you're turning away from—"

"I'm not turning away from you," I said, cutting him off. I stroked his face, wanting desperately for him to not only accept, but agree with my decision.

All my life I'd waited to fall in love. Finally, I had something extraordinary. My feelings for this man were deeper, stronger, and sweeter than I'd ever imagined. I couldn't let him give up on us. He had to see things my way.

"OK, so it'll be a little tough," I admitted, trying to downplay the situation. "I'll admit that."

He pulled away. "Don't kid yourself, baby. It'll be very hard for me to stay your man and not love you in every way."

"But what about wanting to please God?"

He shook his head. "I'll be the first to admit that maybe I'm not where I need to be in my relationship with Christ."

"Well, I'm no saint, either, Rory. If my Christian walk was straight, then last night would never have happened. It's not about us being perfect. It's about striving to be."

"Baby, that's just it. I'm not ready to walk away from sex. I'm just not there. I knew this about myself before, but I decided to give you time. Now . . ."

He let the word hang in the air. I tried to swallow the huge lump in my throat. There was no way I could take anything negative.

"We want different things," Rory said softly. He didn't even look at me as he spoke. "I won't ask you to change. I know you can't do that. So I've got to do what I don't want to do, but what I know is right. I've gotta let you go."

Inside I screamed, *No!* Once again, my tears flowed, enough to fill a pond. But even seeing my pain, Rory didn't back down.

"I'm sorry, Bacall. I do love you. But I know we can't go on this way." Rory spoke through his own tears.

In despair, I wondered why it had come to this.

Rory ordered in dinner and we ate in silence. Every move he made I loved—the way he held his fork, the way he sipped his soda. Watching him, I didn't know how I would be able to move on. And because I didn't want to, I made another attempt to keep my man.

"I know you love me. Just look at us . . . we're both in pain." I picked at the Chinese food on my plate. "Our hearts are being ripped to shreds. It doesn't have to be this way, Rory." I paused, trying to hold back my tears. "Don't give up on us without trying to do it my way. Please, baby. I believe you love me more than . . . sex," I pleaded with puppy-dog eyes.

"Yes, I love you more than I love that. I . . . I just can't be with you and not want to give you all of me. Sex allows me to express what I feel for you. And, I deeply long to receive your love back."

"I could give you my love in other ways," I challenged. "We can enjoy each other, and love each other without intimacy. Please, Rory . . . say you'll try."

He shook his head. "I'm sorry." He dropped his eyes.

I got up from my seat and walked over to the fire. I bent down and stirred the flames. What I felt for this guy was hotter than the heat rising before me. Not all of my feelings were lust or passion. Most were feelings of intense devotion. I was totally committed. But now it appeared that I'd have to let those feelings rise away like the smoke from the flames.

Rory knelt beside me. "I know this is hard for you to hear," he said, "but you've gotta understand. If I'm not gonna be with you intimately, it's gonna be because you aren't my lady. I's gonna be hard to leave what we have. But, baby, it'd be unbearable for me to look at those luscious lips of yours and not be able to shower them with kisses. Kisses that will tell you much more than words ever could. It'd be excruciating if I couldn't breathe all over your beautiful dark body and let you feel what holding hands just can't explain. I couldn't take it if I held you in my arms . . . felt your soft body against mine . . . and then couldn't let you experience just how magical our love really is."

Hearing those words made me slip back into last night's mind-set. I was sweating, and it wasn't from the heat of the coals. I was hot for my man. He stared at me and our eyes locked. I knew we both felt the burning desire. I thought I had shaken all of those feelings away. But Rory was right. Being together would be harder than being apart.

By the grace of God, we made it through the rest of the evening without falling into sin. We talked into the night until Rory made a pallet on the floor and I climbed into the bed. But I couldn't sleep. It was hard to believe this was really happening. Rory not mine? Yeah, I knew that if I had to choose between my guy and my God, the Lord would win hands down. What I hadn't expected was to love a man so much and have it hurt so badly to lose him.

Rory's reasons for not wanting to stay a couple showed me that he loved me enough to allow me to stand on my beliefs. I just wanted him to stand with me.

Seeing his silhouette in the night made my heart yearn for him. How would I make it without him in my life? When I thought harder on that question, I knew Christ would see me through all this. Truthfully, I didn't want to get over Rory.

But as the night continued to pass, I came to realize that Rory and I were finally coming to the end. This was different from the other times when we thought we wouldn't make it. In those times, even in deep confusion, our love didn't fold. But like a bad hand in poker, I knew it was time to throw it all in.

It seemed like an eternity since I had been in Kelly Evans's office, but it had only been three weeks. Many things had happened since I'd been here before the mini tour.

For the last week, I'd remained secluded in my apartment. When I returned from Atlanta, I could not face anyone. Rory Kerry's absence from my life had left my world feeling like a terrorist group had attacked it. It was blown into pieces

Although I was in a bad place, I was happy sulking and probably would have stayed that way for weeks. Especially since I was certain that word had traveled through the company about our breakup. Two days after he'd come back to Los Angeles, Flame had done a television interview. And, in front of that audience, he admitted something that deeply hurt me. He told the world that he'd lost the love of his life.

His exact words were, "The girl who had my heart is no longer my girl. Yep . . . I'm a free man. Really, this time!"

Hearing him confess those words so soon after we'd called it quits devastated me. But what could I do? I'd made a choice. A choice to be strong, even though my flesh was weak. Weak for a guy I'd probably always love. He had a part of me that I could never get back.

But even though I was hurt and wanted to continue to sulk, I had to return to work when Kelly summoned me in for this meeting. I had no clue what was so important.

I held my breath when I stepped inside the office, then

exhaled when I saw that Rory wasn't there. Still, I knew it was only a matter of time before he walked in. I had been briefed that this meeting had something to do with Yo Town's soaring artist. Who else could that be?

I was nowhere near ready to see Rory. Actually, I was a tad annoyed with my former guy. We'd been home a week and he'd never even called. Not one single call to see if I was OK. I hadn't dialed his digits, either, although it wasn't because I didn't want to. I just knew that if I did, I'd sink back into the deep waters I'd just swum out of.

"So, what's going on?" I asked Raven and Kelly as I sat at the small conference table.

"Frankly, hon, everyone knows you've been dumped," Raven coldly replied. "Get over it. Men come and go. Besides . . . Flame's hotter than we all envisioned. How long did you think your little fling was going to last?"

The one thing I was trying desperately to do was walk in the Spirit. Letting "Miss Know-It-All" get to me wasn't helping me accomplish my goal. I wanted to smack her.

However, the stern look I gave her said what my mouth wouldn't.

I was pleased when Kelly interceded for me. "You know Raven, everyone doesn't handle breakups the way you do." The way he spoke, I could tell he was disgusted with her. "Please excuse yourself and let me talk with Bacall alone."

Raven rolled her eyes, then stood and walked out the door. It didn't take a genius to see that I wasn't the only one with love woes.

Although I didn't really respect Raven, I wished I had her tough skin. It would be nice to be able to move on without letting the pain get me down.

Kelly cut off my thoughts. "Ignore her, Bacall. I'm sorry she's so rude. Anyway, let me get to the point of this meeting. I want you to hear what the world is saying about Flame's intro tour."

"I already know . . . it was a success," I responded. "Gotta go." I didn't want to be obnoxious, but the last thing I wanted to do was talk about Flame.

"No, wait . . . hold up. Please sit down," Kelly instructed. I returned to my seat and he continued. "One thing I've always admired about your father is his professionalism. From what I've seen from you, you share his work ethic too. You've always done your job well. Now, just because things are rocky with you and Flame, don't let that affect your professionalism." Though Kelly's tone was firm, I knew he was only trying to pass on his wisdom.

"I appreciate that, Kelly. I'm sorry."

Before he could continue, there was a knock at the door, and Raven peeked into the office.

"May I come back in?" she asked, politeness dripping from her voice. I knew being nice to Kelly took everything she had. If she wanted to keep her job, though, she wouldn't trip with her boss.

"Come on in." He motioned with his hands.

When Raven walked in, Toi and Camille followed her. I rolled my eyes. Though I hated not singing with Rory, being away from these girls was going to be a joy. Seeing them made me glad the tour was over. My season for singing had come and gone. Now it was time for me to resume my managerial position at Yo Town Records.

"Hey, Bacall. Aren't you glad to see me?" Toi asked sarcastically.

I'd never been fake and I wasn't going to start now. But Kelly had just talked to me about being professional.

"Let's just say . . . it's good to see you well." I smiled and stood. "Kelly, it's been great talking to you. I'll let you get on with your meeting. I've got tons of work on my desk. Just e-mail me with whatever you and I needed to discuss."

Once again, I tried to exit the office. Only this time, Rory blocked the doorway. Even though I'd known he was coming, seeing him stunned me. Just looking at him made me melt like an M & M candy. He looked splendid, striking, and wonderful. Disturbing chills went up my spine as I remembered that the vision I adored was no longer mine.

Holding back my tears, I whimpered, "Hi."

"Hey," he said slowly as he leaned forward to give me a hug.

I felt the stares from everyone in Kelly's office, and I knew they were wondering how I would react—how we would treat each other.

Actually, I didn't know how to respond. Should I let him hug me or should I kindly decline?

Somehow, my body automatically slid into his arms. The magnetic charge he sent off was definitely positive. Lost in his tight embrace, I forgot about our spectators. At that moment, I wanted to stay in his arms forever.

"I miss you," my former man gently whispered. "I miss this. Having you close like this . . . makes me crazy."

I was crazy for him as well. My legs were weak and my heart was racing. Just as firemen were needed to put out bursting flames, I needed help putting out my feelings for Rory. Unfortunately, even though I thought I had buried my feelings deep inside and had worked over the last week to make sure they didn't resurface, my emotions once again started to blaze.

10

Inferno

Before I got too caught up in Rory's embrace, Kelly Evans rescued me. The strong voice of Yo Town Records' vice president broke the romantic mood.

"Rory, Bacall, could you join us?" He motioned for us to sit down.

Just a moment before, I'd been eager to leave. Now, I wasn't so sure. Being in the same room with Raven, Toi, Camille, and Rory was definitely awkward. Yet I didn't want to leave.

I also didn't want to make more waves. I complied with Kelly's request.

"I know you all are wondering why you're here," Kelly started. "As you are aware, Flame gained several fans on the tour." I couldn't hold back my smile as Kelly continued. "After reading the reviews, we found that he wasn't the only one who acquired a following. People want to see his background in the foreground!"

Wow! I knew the stage act was dynamite, but I never

imagined people thought the three of us were that good. Our focus and purpose was to accent the artist. Guess we'd accomplished that and much more.

Kelly continued. "The chemistry between the four of you is explosive. In order to keep the heat rising, we want to make you ladies a group. We aren't certain how this will turn out, but, of course, we have high hopes. What we're proposing is a two-song deal. If, after the trial period, we all want to continue with this venture, we'll give you gals an album deal."

Was I hearing him right? My main goal was to get away from these girls and Rory. Now the company wanted me to be in a group with these chicks who didn't like me, and to tour with my ex? There was no way this crazy idea could work.

Anyway, I had more important things to do than get on stage and shake my tail. On top of that, I couldn't let my parents down. They'd never respect this as my career choice.

Even with all the reasons I had to decline right then and there, I didn't. I remembered my childhood fantasy—my dream of becoming a huge star. I guess part of me didn't want to let go of this chance to make that wish come true.

Maybe this was my chance! I shook my head. With these girls, alongside this guy, under these stressful conditions—what was I thinking? Let's just say none of them were ever a part of my childhood vision.

There was no way I could agree to this deal. But I listened as Kelly tried to persuade me.

"Bacall, I want you to not only be a member of this group, but to oversee the process. You can have creative control, and I'd like to cowrite the songs with you. We need a fast tune and a ballad that will fit the three of you."

Now I was intrigued. I had to admit, this project could work. Most of the legwork was already done. We had an image. We had a following. And we had a slammin' name, Matches.

"Each of you ladies will receive a nice signing bonus," Raven interjected.

"Because of your expertise and extra duties, Bacall," Kelly added, "you'll be compensated additionally. We're all set to go. We've arranged studio time for you to get started. We want to promote Matches right away. All you ladies have to do is agree and sign."

I was blown away. There were many things about this that still didn't appeal to me. But some of it was too good to pass up. Having creative control would be a great experience. Plus, I already had some sad tunes swimming around in my head that were dying to come out and swim to shore.

But how could I go forward? Did the good outweigh the bad? Did I even want the responsibility? Those were questions I didn't have answers to.

I looked at Kelly. "I need some time."

"OK," he replied. "Think it over. However, I would like an answer today."

I got up and left. While I walked to my office, Kelly's offer consumed my thoughts.

Any girl who ever wanted to sing professionally would jump at this chance. The offer was a dream! We would be on the company's A-list—our group would be a top priority. Not many new artists can say that. Sure, some had record deals, but most companies didn't push new artists.

The decision was still not easy for me. Call me dumb, or maybe I'm just not like any other girl who has ever dreamed of singing in the big league.

I took the long way to my office, hoping the stroll would clear my head. When I arrived at my door, Rory was sitting in my chair waiting for me. How presumptuous of him. I wanted to throw him right out. Yet his familiar smile stifled my anger and made my guard come down.

"Why do you have to think about this?" he asked. "This is a great opportunity for you. Is it me? If so, I believe you can handle it," Rory offered without my asking for his opinion.

"Oh, you think?" I blurted out sarcastically.

"Yeah," he responded without a doubt. "Look . . . I'm sorry I didn't call you."

Excuses. Explanations. He owed me none. Yet conflicting emotions still filled me, and I realized that I desperately needed to get over him. This back-and-forth thing, this moping around, this frustration was going to tear me apart.

I knew the feelings I had for Rory wouldn't evaporate overnight. I'd just have to divert my time, attention, and energy elsewhere. Maybe Matches was the medicine I needed.

"Rory, could you excuse me?" I asked, "I need to be alone."

He looked at me for a long moment before he finally left my office.

I sat in my chair and sighed. This was a lot to handle. I needed to run it by my dad. Picking up the phone, I dialed Alabama. It wasn't that I needed his permission, but his support would be nice. After all, I knew God spoke to him concerning me.

The phone rang only once.

When I heard him breathing, I said, "Hey, Daddy!"

"Hello, baby doll," he exclaimed, letting me know how happy he was to hear from me. "I was hoping you'd call soon. It's been over a week since we talked. You cut out on Karri's release party and then called hours later to say you were OK. Since that time we've heard nothing. Your Mom and I were worried. Then today I finally heard about what's going on."

That made me angry. Folks were always blabbing to my father about my personal business. Yo Town Records was huge, so anyone could have been the informant. I knew I should have told my family right away.

"So, who told you Rory broke up with me?" I asked.

My father was silent for a moment, then said, "Oh, I get it. That's why you haven't called. So, you and your Mr. Fire, Flesh, Fear—"

"Flame," I cut in.

"Whatever. So, you two are no longer an item, huh?"

I could have hit myself upside the head. Obviously, my father hadn't been talking about Rory.

"Uh, no, Daddy, we're not together anymore."

Now I was in trouble. I wasn't ready to discuss the reasons. But my father knew me well and he didn't press.

He simply said, "Well, sweetheart, whenever you want to talk about it, I'm here to listen. But that's not why I called. I've heard someone wants to make my baby girl a star, and I have a feeling you want to take the offer." He paused. When I remained silent, he continued. "I know you've always wanted to sing R & B."

I'd had a hunch he knew about my desire, but it was weird hearing him say it. Of course, he was right on. I had a burning desire to sing ballads and hip-hop tunes.

"You know how I know?" Dad interrupted my thoughts. "It's in your eyes. I can see it, Bacall. I have for a long time. You're my baby girl, remember?"

"Yes, Daddy," I replied, feeling secure in his words.

"You're grown now and I can't tell you what to do. But I will tell you this—God takes us through things for reasons. If you feel you need to jump off the branch to see if you can fly, go ahead. Remember, when you're out there trying to soar, God's eye is on the sparrow. So He's watching you, too."

I smiled. "OK, Daddy. I hear you."

"I'm in the studio singing for Jesus. You hear the music?"

"Yep. It sounds great as always."

"Call me later. I'll tell your mom that you're OK. Love ya."

I hung up the phone and smiled. My dad was awesome, and I loved him so much. He didn't tell me I shouldn't do it. Nor did he say I should. He simply reminded me to remember Jesus whichever way I went.

I knew what I wanted to do. I leaned back in my chair and sputtered out loud, "OK, Matches . . . I'm ready! Let's set the world on fire."

❦ ❦ ❦

The spring season brought with it my new mission. My goal was to become one of the greatest singers of the era. Yet as I stood in the crowded studio trying to record our first song, "Never Get Over the Feeling," I had trouble making it all come together.

Kelly was frustrated with me, and I could tell the others in the studio were anxious as well. We had done take after take, and not one was good enough to keep. My mind was there. I had written the song. But I wasn't feeling the vibe. It just was not excellent. And who'd want to record mediocre music?

Maybe I was too angry to sing, but I couldn't figure out what was bothering me. I wasn't angry with Toi or Camille. They were hitting their notes just right. Couldn't even say I was angry with Kelly for pushing me so hard. No, my anger wasn't coming from the outside; it was all inside. I was mad at myself. Remembering the initial resistance I had toward this project made me doubt whether I should be singing this song at all. The confusion was making me crazy.

Just as I was about to give up, Rory walked in.

"OK, let's try this again," Kelly said with frustration in his voice.

As the music played for the seventy-first time, I looked at the guy who was no longer mine, and I knew the song would be easy to sing. It was as if I'd never heard the chords before but knew it would sound perfect now.

"Seems just like yesterday . . . when we fell in love this way. I've got to stop lovin' you. Time for me to start anew . . . and let go of your love."

The words flowed beautifully from my mouth as I looked at the man I loved. I could not imagine getting over my feelings for him . . . ever!

My eyes stayed on Rory, and it bothered me that he didn't seem to notice me at all. He was on the other side of the glass, playing with the volume buttons. Never looking at me or inside my soul to see that I was singing only to him.

Knowing he could care less, it was easy for me to utter the next words.

"You want to be left alone . . . branch out on your own. So I'll let you go, but I'll never let go of the feeling!"

With those last words, Rory's head raised and his eyes met mine. The intensity was still there—for both of us. As he watched me, a tear flowed when I sang the chorus.

"The feeling runs deep in my heart so deep, deep down inside my soul. I'll never, ever let go of your love."

I sang the words with sincere sorrow.

"The memories linger on and on, and will last with me forever and always."

The last chord played, and there was silence before Kelly yelled, "That's it! That was awesome, Bacall."

Kelly sounded as relieved as he was excited.

But I wasn't relieved at all. I was too full of emotion to enjoy a successful recording. So I did the only thing I could—I dashed out of the room. I didn't want to look at anyone, especially not Rory. I couldn't handle the feelings this recording session had brought on.

On the day we performed the video of our first release, the same thing happened. I couldn't sing with feeling.

I didn't know what it was. We had an awesome set: a girl

walking along Malibu Beach in the moonlight, depressed about her recent breakup. The crew was sensitive to it being our first time performing in front of the camera.

Yet I couldn't work magic when the director said, "Action!" I couldn't do the moves. I couldn't sing the song. I couldn't act the part.

As if sensing my need for a rescue, Rory casually strolled onto the set and sat in the chair next to the director. He crossed his legs and relaxed. His eyes focused on me, and I aimed the second verse of the song at my former beau.

"Baby, I miss you so much. Ooh, I loved your gentle touch. Maybe I smothered you? Wish I knew what to do to hold on to your love." The words that left my lips sounded sweet.

As I sang, Rory looked directly at me. Yet I knew he wasn't seeing me. He didn't understand my words. He was more into his celebrity, as people on the video crew kept walking over to him, giving him his props. I was just another piece to help create his puzzle of fame.

This made the rest of the song easy.

"You're so blind, you can't see you're the only one for me. So I'll pray for your sight but till then I'll hold tight . . . to the feeling!"

A week later, when I saw the finished video, I knew it was perfect. When I viewed the final cut, I was amazed at how the film had captured my emotions. Watching it in the editor's booth made me feel the sadness and loss all over again.

This was getting to me. It wasn't fair. Rory had no problems going on with life. But I was stuck in a holding pattern, like an airplane unable to land. At times, I felt as if I was being tortured and I couldn't stop the pain.

I knew I had to do something about my misery. I had to take control over the way I was reacting. I was starting a new career. I had to focus. This was my shot at my dream.

Even though Flame and Matches were connected, I needed to light a spark that was all my own. And I was determined to do it.

❦ ❦ ❦

"Seems like you think things are all about a match . . . and not the book of matches," Toi remarked sarcastically as we posed for a group photo.

She is jealous, I thought. *Jealous that I'm receiving all the attention.*

I continued posing, ignoring her. I'd been sensing resentment from Toi and Camille for the past few weeks. Now, Toi's rude words confirmed my suspicion.

"Why are you always in front?" Toi complained. "We've taken about—what?—forty pictures? You're dead center in *all* of them. Dang!"

"It's not like I agree with Toi on hardly anything, but she's right," Camille interjected. "Bacall, you have been hogging the spotlight. It's a group thing here . . . not Bacall and Matches."

"What's the big deal? This is *my* song climbing the charts. It's my concept that makes our image. And lest you forget, my voice that the people love." I paused for a moment. "Besides, the photographer told me where to sit. Deal with it . . . or leave. Either way, the show will go on."

They stared at me, like I was crazy. I hated to be blunt, but they needed to understand that they were not in any position to make demands. I thought their silence was a way of letting me know they were going to accept the situation.

Arrogantly, I teased, "So nobody's walking away? Guess you realize that background is better than standing on the outside looking in."

"Just 'cause I'm here," Toi exclaimed, still clearly fired up, "that doesn't mean this is over. We'll play it your way for now. But just for now."

I rolled my eyes. I knew she was just talking junk. Toi wasn't going anywhere.

"To be honest, Bacall," Camille began as she pulled me to the side, "I'm shocked at this change in you. Although we've never been close, you've always seemed so positive. What you were . . . seemed to be of God. Now, I believe you're coming from the opposite direction." She stopped when I raised my eyebrows. "You're a preacher's daughter, Bacall and you know God for yourself. Don't forget that. Don't let the devil guide you. Don't get so caught up in the heat of your little moment of success that you place yourself in an inferno!"

11

Explosion

"Dang, they play the music loud here," I said to Camille as she and I stood backstage at the Summer Musicfest. "It sounds like the speakers are about to blow,"

It was late June. We had two songs tearing up the airwaves as quickly as a child opens birthday presents, and we were invited to be on the hottest summer tour. Eight top R & B artists filled the ticket. We were to do shows in fifty cities over a three-month period.

Things had changed between Camille and me. Ever since she made her comment at the photo session, we had become friends. I hadn't realized it at the time, but I had changed. I had stopped focusing my energy, time, and desire on Jesus Christ. Doing interviews for TV, radio, teen magazines, and black magazines, showcase to spotlight, I had become a tad too big for my britches.

That day in the studio, Camille's words of truth pierced my heart. I needed that dagger to relieve some of the pressure I was feeling. Although I was still enjoying the ride, I was no longer letting it drive me crazy.

"Where's Toi?" I asked, trying not to be angry. Toi was supposed to be standing with us, ready to go on stage. But recently, whenever she was supposed to be with us, she always managed to be someplace else. "Why does she keep doing this?" I continued to question Camille. "We've had nine shows on this tour and Toi hasn't warmed up with us yet. I'm sick of this! Have you seen her?"

The look in Camille's eyes told me there was something she was hesitant to say. I couldn't understand what was holding her tongue.

"What's the big deal? You know something. What is it?"

Camille took a deep breath. "She's with Rory. They've been together all month. I don't know what's going on, but they seem very close. I'm sorta surprised you haven't noticed."

"Contrary to what everyone thinks, Rory is not the center of my life anymore," I responded forcefully, trying mostly to convince myself.

I had certainly not been standing around thinking about him or whom he was dating. I did notice him one day in the office acting chummy with Raven. If what Camille was saying was true, Rory was a very busy boy. But did I care? Not one bit.

Finally, I asked, "Do you want to go to his dressing room and get her or do you want me to?"

"If you go, fireworks might start popping," Camille joked, but I knew she was serious.

"It's OK. I'm over Rory. And anyway, I'd never stoop to Toi's level. Don't worry. I'll get her without a scene."

The journey to Rory's dressing room wasn't a pleasant one. Who was I kidding? Yeah, five months had passed, but I wasn't totally over him. I'd just placed my energy in another direction, hoping to fool myself into believing the love was gone.

As I walked, I knew I had to gain strength because there

were many people who didn't want me to act refined when I saw Rory with someone else. Folks like a mess. But I wasn't going to give them a scene. I was going to behave like the woman who raised me—my mother. She'd always been a strong woman, pioneering into places no one wanted her to be. I'd tear a page from her. I would do the unexpected.

My thoughts were interrupted when I bumped into Bum, the biggest star and headliner of this tour. I'd never seen him alone. He was always escorted by his twelve-man entourage.

Bum and his crew formed a semicircle around me.

"Hey, pretty lady, why ya always struttin' so fast? Don't never give a brother a chance to rap. Since I finally got you still, can ya give a brother a second of yo' precious time?"

"I'm about to go on, so I can't talk right now," I answered with a slight grin.

"Yeah, I've checked you ladies out. Sexy!"

"You've seen us perform?" I was surprised. Bum was a big star. I never thought he'd pay attention to a starter group like us.

He nodded. "Heard your fast tune, 'Changes' on the radio. Thought it was dope! Wanted to see you perform, so I peeped out a show. You were . . . " Bum moved closer to me.

Even though I'd never met this dude before, I had heard quite a bit about him. Most of the rumors weren't friendly, but the worst I'd heard was that he was a member of a Detroit gang. Now, I was never prone to believe gossip, but all the fellas surrounding him were the image of trouble, with their beepers, chains, picks, bandanas, gang colors, and guns.

"I was . . . what?" I asked as I moved away from him.

"Let's discuss the rest of what I was gonna say over dinner. We can hook up after the show."

"I'll get back to you," I said, looking at my watch. "I have to be on stage in five minutes." Lost in his weird charm, I'd almost forgotten I had a show to do.

I quickly walked away from Bum and his men and headed to Rory's dressing room.

As I got to the door, I spent a second talking with the One I hadn't taken much time for lately. "Heavenly Father, go with me into this room," I prayed.

When I opened the door, the sight I witnessed disturbed me. They weren't kissing or fondling, yet their chemistry was obvious. I guess I did care.

A mischievous smirk crossed Toi's face when she saw me, and I remembered the time she threatened to get even with me. Seemed as if she was successfully doing that. She might as well have placed a dagger in my heart and turned it.

Rory's reaction, on the other hand, was the opposite. He acted as if he didn't want me to see him with Toi. He moved quickly from Toi's side to mine.

"To what do I owe the pleasure?" Rory's tone was polite, though I could tell he was nervous.

"Actually, this isn't a visit. I came to borrow your little toy," I rudely replied. "We're on next, and we can't warm up without your friend here."

Rory turned to Toi. "I thought you told me you had thirty minutes."

"Since you're on after us, I'd say Flame is the one who's on in thirty minutes. We're up now," I answered for her.

Toi didn't appear eager to leave. So I grabbed her arm and tugged her out the door.

"Are you trying to ruin things for me?" she asked angrily. "I was coming. Rory is my man now. To use your words, deal with it!" She jerked her arm from my grip. "I plan to give him what he never got from you."

"And if he's not careful, he'll have to get treated for it." I laughed.

Toi lunged at me. We fell to the floor and started scuffling, pulling each other's hair. I'd never fought in my life, and this sorry performance couldn't count as a fight either. Neither of us landed a punch.

Screams filled the hall and Rory flew out of his dressing room. He helped Toi get up from the floor, and I felt hands behind me helping me to my feet. I looked up and saw Blain.

"Y'all look like fools!" Blain yelled. "Save the energy for the stage. You're holding up the show for this junk. Let's go, ladies. We'll talk about this stupid stunt later."

Toi and I glared at each other, took less than thirty seconds to straighten our hair and clothes, then gracefully walked onto the stage.

I knew my little fight with Toi was about much more than her being late for the show. I had to find a way to move on from my life with Rory.

Bum asked me to go out with him every night after we met in the hall. One night, I decided to accept his invitation.

Four weeks later, Bum and I were still going out together. I knew being with him was a tad dangerous, but I felt I could handle the challenge. Bum showed me a wild and crazy world. Different from the confined one I'd lived in all my life. At twenty-two, I figured I should experience new things.

In Charlotte, North Carolina, Bum and I were in one of the local clubs when Rory came marching over to me. I was glad Bum was not at the table, though he had left a few of his boys to watch over me.

"What are you doing here, and what's this?" Rory demanded as he lifted the glass of wine from my hand.

I rolled my eyes. "What's the big deal? I'm out on a date. Not that it's any of your business." I tried to snatch my glass from him, but he held it back.

"Don't you know what kind of guy this dude is?" Rory asked angrily.

"If I were you, I'd keep those negative implications to myself. Look around. These guys don't take kindly to anyone downing their boy."

"You're taking this too lightly, Bacall. You've never been in a club."

I could tell Rory was genuinely concerned, but his words still angered me. "I've been in clubs before. I performed in them with you, remember? Or have you forgotten everything we did together?"

"As soon as we finished singing, you jetted," he retorted. "Now look at you."

I sighed. Why was I explaining anything? I couldn't believe Rory was trying to control me. I once again reached for my glass, and this time, when I snatched it from him, I drank the contents in one gulp.

Rory shook his head. "So you're bad now, huh? Doing things you've never done before."

"Oh, *now* you want me not to do things I've never done? You didn't have much of a problem with that when I was with you. All of a sudden, you're playing Saint Flame. Now you want to preserve my innocence. It's a little late for that, Rory. Get out of my face."

"You heard the lady, Mr. Fireman," Bum teased from behind Rory. "You best get to steppin'. There's nothin' to put out here. We like the flames of passion we're ignitin'. An' we gonna keep on fannin' 'em, right, baby?"

"Yeah . . . uh-huh!" My words came from the combination of wanting to hurt Rory and having more to drink than I was used to.

Rory took one look at me, then turned and walked away. I was glad he left without a scene. We didn't need another brawl. But there was a part of me that wished he'd fight for me.

I ordered another drink, and just as I finished it, I heard my song, "Changes," over the intercom.

The DJ raved, "Let's give it up, people, for Bacall Lee. She's the lead singer of Matches. And we're thrilled to have her partying with us tonight."

Hearing the applause, I got up on top of the table. I tried to lip-sync my song, though I mumbled and missed many of the words.

"My life has been an up-and-down roller-coaster ride, since I've been with you . . . and I never know which way you're gonna act. You catch me by surprise. Lately, when we're together, you never act the same. We argue, fuss, and fight. I don't know who's to blame! Can't you see I can't take these changes anymore? If this keeps up, I'll let you go."

Bum and his crew enjoyed my inebriated act. They cheered, encouraging me to go on. From the corner of my eye, I saw Rory. The look of disapproval on his face motivated me to continue.

"I can't take these changes. One day, we're together, the next day you're gone. No . . . no more changes. If this keeps up, I'd rather be alone."

I stumbled and almost fell. Bum reached up and finally helped me down.

"Come on, baby. Come with me," he said. Taking my arm, he led me through the crowd, past people still cheering me. In a drunken haze, I followed Bum to a secluded room in the back of the club. The door was barely closed before Bum was all over me.

Even if I hadn't been drunk, even if I'd had all my strength, there was no way I would've been able to push him off of me. Bum was more than double my size; there was no way I could move him.

"No," I whimpered softly. My voice sounded small. "No," I whimpered over and over again. Inside, those noes were loud screams.

Bum ignored my cries and slid his rough hands up my bare thighs. *How did I get here?* I pondered, knowing I was in big trouble. Yes, I had dated Bum. Yes, I was in his company alone. But never did I lead him on. Why was he trying to take me?

"Please . . . please," I mustered up the strength to say. "Please, no . . . no . . . no!"

It was as if Bum couldn't hear me. This guy on a date-rape mission cared nothing about my demands. He ripped the bottom buttons from my shirt.

"Girl, don't trip! You know you want this," he said huskily. "You been teasin' a brother for weeks. Only way that was cool was 'cause appetizers have been keeping me full. Well, now I got an empty stomach and I'm ready for a full-course meal . . . that's you, baby!" His words, along with the alcohol that filled me, made me sick to my stomach. "Tonight you're ready . . . all primed and wined up for the pickin'. I put a little somethin' in yo' last drink to relax you, but I guess I didn't put in enough. Dang! Relax. Don't fight Bum, baby. You gonna love this."

With everything in me, I tried to get away, but it was no use. I felt my clothes sliding off me, and I closed my eyes as tears rushed down my face. At that moment, I felt Bum move away from me, and my eyes snapped open. The first thing I saw was Rory. He had come to save what Bum was about to steal.

Rory threw Bum across the room. It only took Bum a moment to realize what had happened and he lunged at Rory. They beat each other, tossing chairs and overturning tables. I stood motionless and held back a scream when Bum cocked a gun to Rory's head.

"Bum! Bum, listen," I pleaded. "He didn't mean it. Put the gun down, Bum. Please!"

Fists beat against the door. "Open up," voices yelled.

I sighed with relief, knowing it was club security. But why, I wondered, didn't they just walk in? Why were they knocking? Then I realized the door must be locked. Rory locked it when he came in—probably thinking that would keep out Bum's boys. Now, the locked door was keeping out the men who could save us from this madman.

Hearing a key turn in the knob, Bum quickly tucked away his gun. "This ain't over," he threatened.

Rory stood, unshaken. "Oh . . . and I'm scared."

"You oughta be," Bum said before he stomped to the door and opened it. "What's up?" he spoke to the guards as if nothing had happened. Then he marched out of the room—but not before he gave Rory one final, long stare.

❧ ❧ ❧

"How long have I been asleep?" I asked groggily as I looked up at Rory, Camille, and Blain.

We were in Flame's tour bus, where Rory had brought me after the fiasco with Bum. Though I had fallen asleep almost immediately, I knew Rory hadn't left my side and, along with Blain and Camille, was keeping a close watch over me. The fact that he was so caring touched my heart, even though I felt dejected after replaying the unsettling events that led to my being here.

It was all my fault. Tough consequences of sinful actions. It all started with my sexual relationship with Rory. Our intimacy made my emotional tie to him so strong that our breakup took more from me than I was willing to admit. I didn't truly face my feelings. Instead, I tried to channel my sense of loss in another direction.

I was trying to find love in fame and fortune, trying to make success my lifeline. That was the reason I got so big-headed. That was the reason I found myself dating an even bigger-headed star, who took me down a desolate path I would have never traveled otherwise. All this bondage because I took my eyes off Christ. I could only hope this was the end of my downward spiral.

But those thoughts made me think of Bum and his threat.

In a panic, I sat up in the bed. "Where's Bum?"

Blain gently put his hand on my shoulder. "Don't worry, Bacall," he said in a soothing, protective voice. "I've got men following him and his crew. You guys are safe."

He must have seen the doubt in my eyes.

"Don't give me that look, Bacall. You're safe. Flame might not believe Bum will try anything stupid, but I know "Stupid" is Bum's middle name. I'm aware of that joker's track record. He's been in the pen several times. Gotten out and gotten right back into trouble. Why he's out now is beyond me. I know he's gonna get himself killed or kill somebody. But I promise you guys won't be his victims." He took my hand and clutched it. The sweet bond we shared long ago was present once again.

I sighed. Although I was still uneasy, Blain's words comforted me.

Camille held my other hand, and I weakly smiled at her. She had tried to warn me about Bum and what being around him would bring. More than once, she told me he would bring me nothing but harm.

"I know," I said, nodding at my friend's sad face. "You told me not to get involved with him."

"Yeah, I did. But I won't go there. Just listen to me this time and get some rest." She squeezed my hand.

Blain's cell phone rang, and he stepped away while Rory and Camille continued to hover. Blain spoke into his phone, then his voice grew louder.

"What? Are you sure?" he yelled.

Rory, Camille, and I exchanged glances, and my heart began to beat faster. I had the feeling that we were about to experience more negative results to my not following Christ.

He hung up the phone and turned to us. "Get off the bus!" he hollered. "There might be a bomb. Go!"

"Man, be real," Rory said, not believing Blain's words.

"Please, Flame, don't argue!" Blain screamed. "Pick up Bacall and head out. The longer we stand here, the more we put ourselves at risk. This could be real."

Rory swooped me into his arms, and Camille rushed in front of us, opening the bus door. Blain followed right behind us, grabbing his briefcase and folders he had spread across one of the tables.

We ran away from the bus, but were barely four feet away when an enormous blast boomed behind us. The noise was as frightful as the bursts of fire and debris that swarmed in the air. I was shaking as much from the eruption as I was from the realization that Bum's threat was real. Crouching in the midst of the blare, I felt like a soldier witnessing the horrors of war. It was that awful of an explosion.

12

Ashes

I slowly opened my eyes and looked around the room. I had been recuperating in the hospital for three days, though it seemed a lot longer. My mother sat in a chair in the corner. Her eyes were closed. She had to be tired. She hadn't left my side since she arrived. The record company had notified my parents immediately after the accident, and together with Brooks, they rushed to Charlotte.

My head ached and I raised my hand to the bandages covering my head. I had sustained a severe head injury when one of the bus's tires hit me in the back of my head. It knocked me unconscious and put me in a coma for seventeen hours. Fortunately, after a CT scan, the doctors said I would be fine. God's grace brought me back to this side of heaven. I knew it was because He had something for me to do. However, I was so out of His will I didn't know what His plan was for my life.

The debris from the explosion did varying damage to the four of us. The doctors said mine were the second worst.

Rory was the luckiest, though normally, I wouldn't have called a broken arm and numerous scratches lucky. Rory was treated and released the same night.

Camille had burns of multiple degrees on both her legs. She was heavily medicated to relieve her intense pain.

Blain was in the worst shape. In addition to suffering from severe smoke inhalation, he had burns over 85 percent of his body. He was thrown into the air, and the fumes and flames followed him. His body landed on the ground with a sickening impact. His prognosis was grave.

The first day, I wanted to see Blain, but the doctors wouldn't allow me to move. Although that pained me, I decided it'd be smart to do something I hadn't done in a while—I listened to those in authority.

Actually, not being able to see him was a good thing because when I thought about it, I realized I did not know what to say to him. Seeing my strong, healthy friend lying there helpless and in pain would hurt too much. So I didn't rush the visit.

Now, three days later, I still hadn't seen my friend.

I tried to sit up in bed, and the movement caused my mother to awaken. She rushed to the side of the bed. I knew my mother loved me, but we had never enjoyed a close friendship. We were forming a unique bond in the midst of this tragedy.

"How are you feeling, sweetie?" she asked with concern filling her voice.

I nodded. "Fine," I responded, though I was still feeling weak. "Have you heard anything about the others?"

"Camille is doing about the same. Still in serious condition. We just praise God that she's no worse." My mom paused for a long moment. She took my hand and gripped it tightly. Her voice shook with emotion. "The doctors still aren't optimistic about Blain. Your father spent time praying and sitting with him last evening."

I tried to blink back my tears.

"There is one piece of good news. Since you're doing so much better, your doctor has cleared you for visitation. Whenever you're ready, an orderly will wheel you down to see Blain."

I sat up higher in the bed.

"I . . . I just want to prepare you," my mother continued. "I don't think he's gonna make it, and he might not look like the person you know."

I had been praying for Blain's miracle. There was no way I was going to believe God wouldn't answer my prayer. Even though Blain wasn't a Christian, and even though I'd been out of God's will, I still expected Blain to be healed.

"I don't know what to say to him, Mom. Is he even conscious?" I asked in tears.

She gently wiped my face. "I'm told he's in and out."

"If I go to see him, what should I say?"

"Well, from what I understand, you need to tell this man about Jesus. You need to share the gospel. He needs to confess Jesus Christ as his personal Lord and Savior. I know that might sound like a scary task, Bacall, but who knows . . . maybe you were called for such a time as this."

Her words were challenging, but I began to feel up to the call. A sweet peace came over my spirit. God wants us all to know Him and make Him known. Even though I wasn't sure what I would say, I believed He'd enable me to talk to Blain.

"Do you remember our study?" Mom probed.

I grinned through my tears. "Esther 4:14 . . . how could I forget?"

Last summer, my mother led my sister and I through a study of the book of Esther. We used a fulfilling study guide by a lady named Dee Brestin. I needed that at the time because I was a soon-to-be college graduate, and I had to have faith that God would show me His vision for my life.

Even though I was searching for direction, going through a Bible study with my mother wasn't very appealing. But by the time it was over, I was a much richer Christian—all because of my mother.

How ironic that I might be able to use that study now. Esther had gone through many things that I was experiencing—she had lost her virginity to please an earthly king, yet even out of her sin, her heavenly King used her to save the Jews. Maybe that was how God was going to use me. Even though I felt unworthy, wretched, and filthy, the Lord still deemed me useful.

But it was still a scary thought, even knowing God would be with me.

"Mom, do you think I can do it?"

She nodded. "Definitely. And if you don't, who will? If you don't, what's going to happen to Blain?"

A predicament was before me. My lost friend might die. I had the privilege of helping him find Jesus Christ. I prayed that the Lord's divine providence would prevail. As Romans 11:33 says, "Oh, the depths of the riches of the wisdom and knowledge of God! How unsearchable his judgments, and His paths beyond tracing out!"

Maybe Mom was right. God could use this valley experience to send me mountain climbing for Him. Who knows?

Later that day, I sat in my hospital room alone. "Lord, You know I've never fasted before," I prayed as I held the open Bible close to my chest. "I think now is the time for me to start. I remember when You were with me in high school, and I shared the gospel with my friends. Twelve of them accepted Christ as their Lord and Savior. You were with me in college when I lifted You up before my seven girlfriends, and You drew them to Yourself."

I reflected on past times when I had helped bring someone to Jesus but didn't actually see the fruit. Sometimes people had heard the gospel, and I reinforced the information. Other times someone else reinforced the information I gave. Many times I had watered the plant that grew into someone's salvation.

I continued in silence, *Lord, every time I've witnessed to anyone, that person had a willing heart to hear the truth. All those people longed for understanding. I had no pressure. But Blain doesn't want to hear. His ears have been closed ever since his parents were killed. He still blames You and hates You for it.*

But I want to reach him, Lord, and I know I can if I can hear from You. That's why I want to fast—so I can clearly hear You. I want a sensitive spirit, and I want Blain to have an open mind. Only You can change his heart, Father. I paused and squeezed my eyes shut. *Thank You for hearing my prayer. Amen.*

Just as I finished, my doctor came into the room.

"I'm glad to see you're awake," Dr. Jefferson said as she walked to my bed. "I want to make sure you're getting better."

I waited for the doctor to complete her checkup before I spoke. "Dr. Jefferson, I want to go on a fast."

She frowned. "Are you talking about a total fast—no food or drink?"

I nodded.

She shook her head. "You're not strong enough for that. My job is to get you completely healed, and you need the nutrients."

"What about a food fast? I could drink water."

The doctor sat on the edge of my bed. "Why do you want to do this?"

I lowered my eyes. "There's a friend who needs help and I have to hear from God," I said softly. "I need to fast and pray to do that."

Dr. Jefferson nodded as if she understood. "Would you agree to a partial fast? I think I can go along with fruits, vegetables, and water."

I smiled, pleased with the compromise.

When Dr. Jefferson left the room, I leaned back against the bed. I'd made a commitment to God not to move regarding this area until a complete day passed. But did Blain have twenty-four hours? I had to trust God to keep my longtime pal alive that long. Truthfully, I still believed in his recovery.

There was a quick knock on my door, and Dr. Jefferson peeked into the room again. "Your father is waiting out here," she said. "He's been trying to catch you awake, but he knows your rest is important. Shall I let him in or are you tired?"

"It feels like I've been resting for a month. Please send my daddy in," I said.

My father entered, carrying a red teddy bear in one hand and a gorgeous assortment of lilies in the other.

"There's a lily in the valley and that lily's my baby girl, Bacall," my dad sang. He leaned over and kissed me on the cheek. "Pumpkin, you've had your dad worried. And you know I try not to worry about you too much. But it's been difficult. When you started dating seriously last year, I was worried. The thought of you managing out in big ole California, even though I sent you there, worried me."

My father sat on the edge of the bed. I could tell I'd put a tremendous burden on his heart. Seeing the concern cross his face made me sorry that I hadn't been his li'l treasure. In fact, I'd been a lot of trouble.

He continued. "When you sang backup on an R & B album, I was worried. Then when you decided to sing in an R & B group, I was worried. When you went on a big tour, I was worried. As word got to me that you were really enjoying yourself, I was worried. Then I got that phone call about thie explosion and once more, I was worried beyond belief. But when I walked into this room just now and saw you with this Bible in your hands, my heart felt good. All that needless worry flew away like a robin flies south for the winter. My prayers have been answered. My baby girl has come home."

He didn't have to say it—I knew he meant that I had come home to Jesus. That's what I was trying to do. I wasn't there yet. I was far from it. I had been far from it for a while, straying too far. Yet, at that very moment, my desire was to please Christ alone. I truly wanted to live victoriously on this side of heaven.

"Knock, knock," my sister announced at the door.

"Come on in!"

We embraced tightly.

"I've been so worried about you," Brooks cried.

I brushed the water tears her cheeks. My father wiped his away before he thought I saw them.

"I'm OK, you guys," I told them. "I'm back on God's side."

Their smiles made me feel better. "Thanks for not giving up on me. Your prayers probably got me over."

"Daddy," Brooks nudged our dad, "we better let Bacall get some rest. Sis, I won't see you back in Alabama. Karrington and I have to meet with our homebuilder in Atlanta. But you take it easy. I love you." She hugged me again.

My father put his arms around me. "Get some rest, Pumpkin. And remember that your daddy loves you."

As Brooks and my father turned to leave, Kelly, Raven, and Toi walked in. I was genuinely glad to see them all. This disaster had erased any ill feelings I had harbored.

"Hey, it's good to see you guys," I said. "I'm honored you all came."

Kelly set two dozen yellow roses in the last empty space on the dresser. "We're the ones who are glad to be here," She said. "We're glad you're OK and up to seeing us."

Raven and Toi nodded. I smiled again to let them know I was glad they came.

Brooks and my father remained in the room. I figured Brooks wanted to know more about the people I worked with, and my father probably wanted to talk to Kelly.

We chatted for a few minutes, but as time passed, the smiles on their faces turned grim. I knew Blain and Camille were weighing heavily on their minds. As Raven and Toi continued to talk, Kelly pulled my father to the side.

I stopped listening to Raven. Instead, I focused on my father and Kelly. I couldn't hear their words, but their expressions sent me into a panic.

"Dad . . . what's going on?" My voice shook. "It's not Blain, is it?"

My father rushed to my side and held my hand. "No, honey. But you do need to brace yourself. This isn't good news."

"Rory's missing," Kelly explained. "After he was released the other night, no one picked him up. To our knowledge he left on his own. He hasn't come back to L.A. and we don't know where he is."

"Has anyone called his mother?" I asked. "He would have definitely checked in with her."

My dad gripped my hand tighter and Toi began to cry softly. My eyes moved to Raven, who turned toward the window.

"His mother," Kelly began slowly, as if that would soften the impact of what he had to say, "was involved in an accident the night of the explosion. Her house was set on fire and . . . she was trapped inside. The police couldn't even identify her body. That's how bad it was."

I buried my face in my dad's chest and sobbed uncontrollably. How could this happen? But I knew the answer. It was all my fault. If only I could go back and change everything with Bum.

"We heard that there's a hit out on Rory." Kelly said. "I don't want to believe it, but the fact is . . . Rory is missing.

We have to prepare ourselves that that might be the case."

"He's dead," Toi blurted out. "I know Bum had him killed. He told me the night of the bomb that Rory was as good as dead. He said it when I came to the club looking for Rory. Now . . . I may never see him again."

Brooks went over to comfort Toi. She responded graciously to Brooks's kindness and placed her head in an understanding bosom.

My body trembled. Rory gone? That couldn't be. The emptiness I felt at the thought of his loss confirmed how much I still loved him.

I closed my eyes and silently prayed that God would not make Rory pay for all of my mistakes.

❦ ❦ ❦

I tried to stay in the Spirit all night. My hope was in a miracle-working God. I couldn't look at the circumstances because I was in a hopeless situation. I wasn't going to lose focus again.

The next morning, Dr. Jefferson told me I could visit both Camille and Blain. I was eager to see my friends. I had been told that while Blain was in the same condition, Camille was faring a bit better.

As I was wheeled to Camille's room, a revelation came to me from above. I had spent so much of my time thinking about Blain, that I never thought about Camille. She too needed to be saved.

All the times we had been together, I had never shared my faith with her. Yes, Camille was supposed to survive this thing. She was getting better each day. But what if her future was as dark as Blain's? Even if Camille wouldn't accept Christ, I knew I had to at least present my friend with the option.

I thought about the silly things we'd discussed, like our rising popularity and new lipstick colors. Obviously, those things paled in comparison to God's truth. I was thankful I had another opportunity to witness to her.

When I rolled my wheelchair into her room, the vision before me was refreshing. I don't know what I expected. Maybe I assumed she'd be tired and wretched-looking like me. But Camille looked just as beautiful as ever. I was elated to see her up and eating.

"Wow," I remarked in an astonished tone. "You look great!"

Camille smiled widely. "Girlfriend, come look under these covers and see my ugly, bandaged legs. The nurses change the dressing every five minutes, it seems." Her smile disappeared. Even though she was joking, I could tell she was serious, too.

"Oh, don't worry about that," I said as I wheeled my chair closer to her bed. You'll be up and walking soon."

We chatted awhile about the horrible hospital food and the nice nurses. Then, our talk turned to the serious issues that were heavy on our hearts.

Camille thanked me for my loving friendship, sincere concern, and encouraging words. I told her she meant a lot to me as well. We couldn't physically hug because she was strapped to her bed and I was confined to my wheelchair. But the moment felt like an embrace of love.

I took a deep breath before I said the words that I had come to say. "Do you remember telling me there was something special about me . . . something you wished you had?"

Camille nodded but frowned.

"Well, that was the Holy Spirit living inside of me shining through. I want you to have that same light . . . that same hope . . . that same God."

"Bacall," Camille began, "I'm a Christian."

I opened my mouth wide with surprise.

"Guess you couldn't tell, huh? I haven't shown it a lot recently, but I know and love Jesus Christ. My walk needs to grow, though. Maybe you can help me." She smiled. "I sense you're back on track."

"I hope I am," I said. "I'm just baffled that I didn't know you'd accepted Christ into your heart. I was concerned about you."

"Relax," she said, then giggled. "I'll see you in heaven."

I spent a few more minutes with my newfound sister in Christ. Sharing my favorite healing Scripture, Luke 8:48, "Your faith has healed you," filled us both with hope. On that spiritual high, we prayed for my upcoming talk with Blain.

Leaving Camille's room was easy. God had done a marvelous thing. In contrast, going to Blain's room was hard. I had no clue what God was going to do in there. Yet I trusted, obeyed, and proceeded.

I took a deep breath before I entered. When I pushed open the door and saw him, I knew he was not well. It didn't take a doctor to tell me that Blain was barely holding on.

He seemed to be having trouble breathing, and from the look in his eyes, I could see the pain was intense. However, a smile was plastered on his mummylike face.

I stood near the door watching Kidz No Mo, as they stood around his bed singing, "Amazing Grace." I'd never heard the spiritual sung so beautifully. Not only was the melody special, but the passion was intense and real.

Even though I tried to enter the room quietly, one of the members noticed me and motioned for me to move closer. Apparently, they wanted me to sing with them. The moment I opened my mouth, I felt all the tension inside me leave. God's presence was with me. I felt like it was a miracle.

When we finished the song, the members of the group hugged me.

"We'll let you have some time with him," one of them said before they said good-bye to Blain and walked toward the door. "He hasn't been able to comprehend too much. So

I don't know if he'll hear you."

When they were all gone, I pulled my wheelchair close to Blain's side. Then I sat and waited for God to give him enough energy to realize I was there.

Faith worked, and I watched God perform the second miracle. After about fifteen minutes, Blain was fully awake.

"Bacall," he softly called.

I leaned as close to him as I could.

"Don't try to talk," I said. I wanted to get the right words together in my mind. I didn't know if I'd have another chance with Blain. But before I could say a word, Blain spoke.

"Bacall, I'm ready to know Jesus. I'm not angry or bitter anymore. I do believe. What do I need to do?"

This third miracle blew me away. I had fasted and prayed for Blain. I had asked for my friend to be willing to hear about God. My heart was thankful to the Lord.

I gently placed my hand in his and wondered if Blain had been told his prognosis. Surely, he knew he might die. But he didn't seem upset by this.

"What makes you want to be a Christian . . . now?" I asked.

"I can't remember ever praying as an adult." Blain sighed. "But I did the other night. I remember saying, before the bomb went off, that if there is a God, I wanted Him to allow me to protect you guys. He heard me. He answered my prayer. Now He needs to hear me say I love Him. He needs to hear me answer His call."

Blain continued sharing his awesome thoughts of Christ. Then I shared with him the great things I knew about God. He was like a sponge, eagerly soaking up all my knowledge of the One he wanted as the head of his life.

After Blain prayed the sinner's prayer and confessed Jesus as his Savior, he also surrendered his life. Blain vowed that, however long or short his days on earth might be, he'd serve

God with each minute.

It was a powerful time. Blain was as physically weak as Samson when he lost his hair, yet he had the spiritual strength of Paul in his last days.

Tears ran down my face, "You saved my life," I sobbed. "How will I ever repay you?"

"Hush," Blain interjected. "We're even. You just saved mine."

❦ ❦ ❦

Seven days came and went as I recuperated at my parents' home. There was still no word about Rory. So I placed the matter before God and prayed for the best. The good things were that Camille continued to get better and Blain had hung on for another week, surpassing the doctor's expectations.

Blain was strong enough to talk on the phone. In our last phone conversation, he told me that he called his wife. He asked Valerie to come to his side.

"I apologized for the way I've treated her," he told me.

"That's great. I'm sure she forgave you."

"She did, especially after I told her I was born again."

After that conversation, I was sure Blain would recover. But as I began my second week in my parents' home, I received the dreaded phone call.

Blain had passed away. Though I cried uncontrollably when my father told me the news, there was joy in my heart. God had a new servant with Him.

But it wasn't going to be easy. I knew as long as I stayed on earth I'd miss Blain. We had a connection unlike any other relationship I'd had. I would never forget him. I praised God for allowing me to know Blain.

Although I was disappointed that God didn't spare my friend, I couldn't be angry. Blain was ready when his chariot came.

I kept my focus on the positive things. It was clear God was always on the move. He had a divine plan that was carried out. It was hard to see Him moving, and I couldn't say I truly understood all that He was doing. But I knew that He wanted me to trust Him. His providence would prevail.

God could have allowed Blain to die without being born again. But He spared him until Blain knew Him. Although I felt like a worthless lump of clay, God used me to help in that wonderful process. Just like in a fairy tale where the frog turns into a prince, God took my mess and made beauty out of ashes.

13

Dim

There were more flowers at Blain's memorial service than the dozens that had filled my hospital room. Seeing so many at one time is usually a precious sight. However, this occasion was sad.

Although it was far better for Blain to be where he was, he left loved ones behind who would miss him terribly. His mother, Miss Edythe, his wife, Valerie, and their two young daughters.

Blake was eight years old and Bryce was merely six. They reminded me of my sister and me in our younger days. I couldn't imagine what my world would have been like without my dad. All my life I had leaned on him.

However, my soul was comforted as I realized God would fill the void in those little girls' lives. I only prayed they let Him.

My parents accompanied me to L.A. for Blain's funeral, which made it much easier. As I leaned on them, I was able to help others deal with this loss.

For me, losing Blain wasn't the saddest part. The worst of it was knowing that most of the people at the memorial service didn't know the Almighty. They were so into their money, possessions, power, status, and fame, they did not believe God could give them anything. I was filled with sadness knowing these people might gain the whole world but lose their souls.

My parents and I sat in a pew close to the front. I turned around, occasionally scanned the crowd hoping to catch a glimpse of Rory. The bond Blain and Rory had developed over the last six months was strong. I knew if Rory was all right, nothing would stop him from coming here. Not even the serious threats from Bum would deter him from saying good-bye to his friend.

But as I looked at the hundreds of faces, Rory was nowhere among the crowd. I sighed and turned around as the service began and the minister prayed, then others shared their thoughts and feelings about Blain.

Finally, it was my father's turn. When he told me he would be speaking, he didn't mention what he planned to say. But I knew what these folks needed to hear. They needed to be told how to change their ways and get right with God.

"I had a chance to speak with Brother Price over the phone before his passing," my dad began. "We had a blessed time in the Lord. I've been the pastor for Kidz No Mo, the group he'd managed since their inception. And yet, Brother Price was never comfortable in my presence. Whenever he saw me, he'd run the other way. Y'all knew him . . . just picture it."

Dad had a knack for lightening a dismal mood. Small bursts of laughter filled the room. One of Blain's best traits had been his ability to brighten people's day. What a joy to see that my friend could do the same in death.

Then Rev changed his tone. "But he did a one-hundred-

and eighty-degree turn. On the phone, he asked me to be his pastor. I considered it an honor and I agreed to his request. I always knew Blain was a good man. But in his last days, he turned into a great man. You see, at the end of his earthly life . . . the Holy Spirit dwelt in him."

I could tell from the squirming in the seats and the low murmurs that folks were uncomfortable. No one wanted the preacher to preach.

But that didn't stop my father. He didn't let up. My dad always loved being salt—salt that would sting in the wounds of sinners.

"I didn't have to ask Brother Price what he wanted me to share with his family and friends in the event he turned for the worse. He brought it up on his own. Knowing we all have to travel out of this life eventually, he wanted this message told whether he lived to be ninety-nine or he passed the next day. The words I speak now are not my own. They come from your friend, Blain Price. Listen now . . . hear Blain's last words to you. Understand his last wish for you. Accept his last prayer for you. The only way you'll see him again is if you accept Jesus Christ as your Savior."

My dad's strong voice boomed through the room. "Blain asked me to be passionate when I shared this with you. He didn't know a bomb was coming for him. You never know when a bomb could go off in your life. I'm ready if my bomb blows up today. Are you? You've got to be ready, and the only way to be prepared is through Christ." My father kept challenging the congregation.

"The only way you'll ever see Blain Price again is to have your name written in the Lamb's Book of Life. You need to find the One he found. You need to love the Lord he loved. You need to have the God who was living inside him, living inside you. Yes, it's dark right now. We've lost a loved one. It hurts, for we no longer have Blain with us. Feel free to mourn his passing, but get over it, folks. This brother has the victory. And what a joy for those of us here who serve the same God! We know one day we will rejoice with Brother Price in heaven. If you're not already signed up to go . . . don't you want to sign up now?"

My father gave an altar call. The sermon would have been worth it, even if no one came to Christ because just then Reverend Lee had planted many seeds.

The crowd was moved by my dad's challenging words, but there was a hovering silence. Finally one stood and walked to the front of the church and many followed. My father prayed with those who wanted to know God. Twenty-two people went forward to give their lives to the Lord. One of them was Blain's widow, Valerie.

"I hate having to spring this on you," Kelly said.

I sat in his office with my mouth wide open. "How could they let Bum walk?"

"I can't believe it myself," Kelly continued. "But I told you I'd pass along every piece of information I get about this case. I don't want you in the dark."

I shook my head in disgust. Bum had been arrested for setting off the bomb—one count of murder in the first degree and three counts of attempted murder. It had taken the cops three weeks to gather enough evidence to charge him. When the CT3 explosives were found in Bum's possession everyone was sure that Bum would be put away for life. Toi's testimony of Bum threatening Rory's life should have sealed the case.

However, due to a technicality, the jerk was getting off. The police hadn't had a proper search warrant when they obtained the evidence, so the judge wouldn't allow the material into evidence.

Knowing Bum was free while Camille was still confined to a hospital bed gave me no pleasure. I believed it was only a matter of time before Bum would come my way and try to finish me off.

The judicial system irritated me. There was a vast difference between knowing someone did a crime and proving it beyond a shadow of a doubt. Sometimes, justice didn't get served. I hoped this wasn't going to be one of those times.

But, as Kelly continued to talk, I refused to live in fear. Inside, I claimed and quoted the Scripture, "No weapon formed against you shall prosper." Though it didn't look like it, God was going to bring justice for Blain and anyone else Bum had hurt. I wished I could help bring him down. Yet, even though I wanted in, I stepped out and turned the issue over to God.

"There are a couple of other issues we need to discuss," Kelly said, bringing me back to the present. "Flame is losing his popularity. His latest release, 'Hot Date,' is going nowhere on the charts. A lot of his fans are angry because the tour was canceled."

"How could people be angry?" I lashed out. "We don't even know if Rory's all right. You're telling me his so-called fans care more about whether he sings in front of them than if he is even alive to sing at all?"

I shook my head. To think that both Rory and I had always dreamed of stardom. For what? To please people who only cared about what we could give them?

"Fans aren't the only ones uneasy over Rory's disappearance," Kelly continued. "Flame has missed four television performances. Those network executives lost ratings when he didn't appear as they'd advertised."

As I folded my arms in front of me, Kelly held up his hands as if trying to stop me from being angry.

"Our public relations department is doing everything to keep Flame in the best light. I just wanted you to hear it from me, not from someone else. Flame's not the hot artist he was a month ago. But don't be discouraged. When we find him, we'll get him back on top again."

I heard Kelly's promise, but for some reason, I didn't think it was genuine. I was beginning to detest the record industry. It seemed all Kelly cared about was how much money Rory could make. Didn't he care if Rory was dead or alive?

Kelly didn't say they were going to toss Rory out, but if things continued going south for Flame, Yo Town Records would probably put out the heat by extinguishing Flame from their label.

"The other thing we need to discuss is God's Town Records," Kelly continued, sipping a cup of coffee.

What else? I thought.

Kelly said, "My understanding is that you are being groomed to advance in your father's company. Being vice president is tough. You won't be able to please everyone. You might even bump heads with the big guy . . . in your case, that's your father."

"What are you trying to tell me?"

"When a president, owner, or founder of a company cares too much about to his own desires, as opposed to what is best for the company, someone in an influential position needs to step in and help sway the change."

"Are you talking about God's Town and my father?" I asked.

"God's Town needs some fresh and innovative talent. Even Karrington Ford's releases are the traditional tunes. Now, I have heard some cuts on that album that are slammin'. Like that tune, 'Jump.' Even though it's gospel, it could blow up on the R & B charts."

I remembered the controversial tune that had almost caused a rift between Karri and my father. But with everything going on, I hadn't heard the song to render my opinion.

Kelly was right, however. Most of Dad's other artists

were traditional.

"Now, I'm not suggesting there's anything wrong with traditional . . ."

"But when that's all you've got—"

"Exactly," Kelly said before I could finish my sentence. "Then the company isn't diverse enough to successfully compete in the marketplace. I think you're going to be a great asset to God's Town and Yo Town . . . after all, we are a family."

For the next two hours, Kelly and I discussed that issue and tossed around other ideas. Our talk provided a light in the darkness of all the gloomy news. I didn't know if Kelly planned it that way, but it helped me not to be so upset. Sitting with him for that time taught me quite a bit.

As I drove to my apartment at the end of the day, I prayed, "Father, help me as I try to untangle this web of situations. I'm still concerned about Rory. Please protect him and cover him with Your blood. I know that in Your time, You'll allow me to know where he is. I don't want to get anxious, but it would be nice to get a word soon. I still care deeply for him and I've just got to believe he's OK. Thank You for hearing my plea. In Jesus' name, amen."

As I got to my apartment door, I heard the phone ringing. I fumbled with my keys as I tried to rush to get inside to answer the phone. I was certain the call was from my parents, letting me know that they'd arrived home safely from their trip. Just as I managed to open the door, my answering machine picked up. Grabbing the phone, I tried to catch the caller before they hung up.

"I'm here, I'm here, I'm here!" I yelled into the receiver.

"Where's ole dude?" a rough male voice asked.

"Bum?" I mumbled, trembling inside and out.

"You know my name, but that ain't the answer. I'm gonna ask ya one mo' time. Where's ole dude? I know ya know. Tell me now, or I'm gonna find him later. Either way, he's mine. And when I find him . . . he's dead."

"Can we talk about this?" I pleaded.

"Talk?" he yelled as if I was crazy. "You didn't wanna talk that night. You wanted a brother up off ya. Now we get too comf'table talkin' here, and I might just have to come and finish what we started. 'Cause I still dream 'bout bein' witcha. Mebbe that's what I need to get yo' boy to face me again. Yeah. Don't you get too relaxed over there, sweet thang. Boom! Ya never know when I'm coming."

I heard the dial tone. I stared at the phone for several minutes, then hung up and fell onto the couch.

I sat bawling my eyes out for several minutes. When I finally calmed down from the shock of the call, I reflected on Bum's words. As harsh as they were, one thing was clear. Bum didn't know where Rory was. If that was true, then he couldn't have hurt Rory. Since Bum was the only one who wanted Flame put out, there was a chance he was alive. But why was he missing? And why hadn't I heard from him? Where was he?

Even with all the unanswered questions, a glimmer of hope started burning inside me. I had to find Rory before Bum did.

The next morning, I purchased a plane ticket under a false name and headed to Atlanta. The flight took so long it was like flying to Spain.

I was such an unhappy flyer. No attendant could please me. No movie could entertain me. No passenger could talk to me. I was in a zone—only thinking of Rory. I desperately tryied to put the pieces of this puzzle together. But all I had was a hunch to go on.

I didn't inform anyone of my trip—not my parents, not the company, not even my friends. With Bum still on Rory's trail, I couldn't take any chances. Plus, I did not want to be swayed from my mission. I did, however, take my cell phone and pager to keep in touch if I needed to.

When I arrived in Atlanta, the sun was already setting. I hopped into a rental car and began my search for Rory.

I'd only ventured to the isolated cabin once but, it was a moment I'd never forget. Rory told me then that the cabin was the place he'd go to think. It was his space that no one knew about.

He had to be there. I needed him to be there. I prayed he would be there.

I drove down some dirt roads and got lost four times. It was pitch black, but I continued my search and my prayers at the same time.

Suddenly, the road I'd been desperately searching for appeared. It was as if the goodness and mercy David spoke of in the twenty-third Psalm moved the road and miraculously placed it in front of me. I followed the winding path, and minutes later stopped in front of the small log building.

But the sight in front of me wasn't comforting. There wasn't a light on anywhere. I sat for a moment and prayed for protection. Then I got out of the car and cautiously approached the cabin. I peeked into the window, but saw no one.

"I came all this way for nothing," I mumbled in despair as I sank back into the car. I was so sure Rory would be there, and now I had no clue how to find the main road.

As I sat in the car, wondering how I was going to get out, my pager beeped. An Atlanta number flashed on my screen. All kinds of thoughts passed through my mind. First, I thought it was Rory. Then, I shivered with the fear that Bum had followed me. It didn't do any good to speculate, so with my heart pounding, I picked up my cell phone and dialed the number.

"Brooks," I cackled when my sister answered the phone.

She laughed. "Karri and I are in Atlanta working with

the builder Mom said she didn't hear from you today so I figured I'd try and catch up with you. Where are you?"

A flood of tears fell down my face. I broke down and told her everything. In times like these, it was great having a loving Christian sister. God always managed to put her near when I needed her most.

"Don't worry," Brooks said, immediately stepping into her rescue mode. "We'll be right there."

Less than an hour later, Karri's limousine driver found me.

* * *

"I'm so glad to see you." I sighed with relief as Brooks and Karrington stepped out of the limo.

"Girl, I can't believe you did this," my sister said, hugging me while Karrington added his own scolding glance. "Let's get out of here."

Karri opened the car door for Brooks and me to get in. Just as the driver was about to pull out, I noticed a flicker of light from the cabin.

"Wait!" I hissed. "Did you see that?" I pointed toward the cabin window. A second later, another short beam of light came through.

"You guys stay here," Karrington whispered.

He slowly got out of the car.

"Be careful, honey," Brooks said.

My heart started beating faster. Now I had brought my sister and future brother-in-law into this mess.

"He'll be all right," I said to Brooks as I squeezed her hand. I wanted to reassure my sister, though I didn't believe my own words.

We sat in silence as we watched Karrington enter the cabin. Finally, after several long minutes, he returned to the car. His look was so grim that tears began to form in my eyes.

"Well, we've found Rory," he said softly.

"Oh," I gasped, covering my mouth.

"Don't worry, Bacall. He's fine . . . well, maybe not fine. But he's alive, and right now, that's what's most important."

I couldn't get out of the car fast enough. We all rushed into the cabin. It was dark, but I was able to see the zombie who sat in front of the dying fire, rocking back and forth, clutching both arms with opposite hands. His appearance matched his surroundings—everything was a mess.

I couldn't believe the sad vision in front of me. He was frail, fragile, and worn.

Slowly, I walked over to him and knelt down. "Rory?" I whispered.

He didn't even look at me. Karrington helped me from the floor, then reached for Rory. It took more than an hour, but we cleaned him up, got him changed into clean clothes, and fed him scrambled eggs and toast. Still, he was unresponsive.

"Man, I know it's tough," Karri said with concern. "But God loves you. Call to Him. Let Him in. He wants to help you through this pain."

Rory tried to speak, "I . . . I . . . I don't deserve help. It's all my fault." His voice was filled with disgust.

"It's not your fault," I said. "Bum did this, not you."

Rory didn't look up. A tear streamed slowly down his face, and he slipped back into a trance.

I couldn't handle seeing Rory like this, and I ran into the bathroom. Brooks followed me.

"I'm glad he's OK," I sobbed. "But he's not OK." I cried.

Brooks placed my head on her shoulder and I could tell she shared my pain.

"I know how you feel, honey," Brooks said as she stroked my hair. "But we've got to be thankful that we've found Rory and that at least he's alive. God will take care of everything else."

I nodded, knowing her words were true.

Without a word, Brooks took my hand and pulled me to the floor. I knew what she was going to do. We needed stronger assistance.

"Dear Heavenly Father," Brooks began.

I was grateful to have a sister who turned to God in order to help me. Because she knew what I knew—only God could turn things around. Only God could give hope to a man with no hope. Only God could make Rory understand his worth. Only God could be the light he needed to find so his world could cease from being just like the pitiful fire in the next room—dim.

14

Spark

By October many things were different, including the weather. I swiveled in my chair in my new office at God's Town Records headquarters, looked out the window, and thought back over the events of the previous few months. It was clear that God's plan had prevailed. It took time for Him to unravel our tangled weave, but having life back in order was the best gift.

Over two months had passed since we'd found Rory in the cabin. Ironically, it was just a week before my birthday and that would have been our one-year anniversary. Though things were going well for Rory, I hadn't seen him since we left the cabin. Karrington had been discipling Rory, and I was overjoyed to know he too was back in a right relationship with God.

In the midst of surrendering his worries and pain to God, another miracle happened. We discovered Rory's mother was alive! She'd been kidnapped the night of her house fire by Bum's goons. The body the police found in the burning rubble was that of a twenty-year-old druggie.

Mrs. Kerry had been found after two men were arrested for placing the bomb under the bus. When the district attorney announced he was going to seek the death penalty, the men plea-bargained, then confessed everything. Their testimonies led the cops to Rory's mother and provided the evidence the prosecutors needed to reopen the case against Bum.

A new judge was assigned to Bum's case, and he overturned the previous decision, now allowing the CT3 explosives found in Bum's possession to be entered as evidence. That, along with the recording from my answering machine, sealed Bum's fate.

It didn't take a jury long to find Bum guilty. He was sentenced to life without parole. It was a tragedy that such a great rap star proved to be a thug, gangster, and murderer.

With all that had happened, I was more than happy to give up on Matches. The group's album deal was dropped. All three of us had different agendas.

Toi and I never became bosom buddies, but we didn't walk away enemies. Since Flame wasn't a hot artist anymore, Toi lost interest in him. She began recording a solo album with another record company, and I sincerely wish her well.

Camille was still in recovery. She'd had a grafting operation to remove the burned skin from her legs. Her focus now was on letting her body heal. Although she was in good spirits, singing was far from her mind. And rightly so.

I turned away from the window and stared at the papers strewn across my desk. Serving as vice president of God's Town Records was my concern now. Trying to find my voice in the company was all I wanted to concentrate on.

I'd only been here for a few weeks, and so far, my father and I were working well together. I prayed that would last. Maybe, with God's involvement, our different ideas would mesh comfortably under one umbrella and create more success for the company.

The one thing that bothered me was that I missed Rory a great deal. My stupid pride kept me from contacting him. Though I tried to fight it, he stayed on my mind.

"What are you thinking about?" my father asked as he popped into my office.

"God's mercy."

My father nodded and took a seat in front of my desk. "I don't know if I've said it, but I'm proud of you, Bacall."

I waved my hand in the air.

"No, no, now, I'm serious," my father continued. "Don't look at me as if I have nothing to be proud of. Hear me out. Unfortunately, you did what I preach against every week. You fell. You strayed away from God. You didn't practice the spiritual disciplines. But I'm proud because you learned from this. You let the lessons work out for your good. You'll be stronger from these trials. You're now letting God lead. He won't steer you wrong." My daddy beamed with pride.

I lowered my eyes and smiled. Yes, indeed, I had come a long way.

Later that week, I was in my bedroom getting ready for a formal family dinner. When the phone rang, I thought about not answering it since I was running late, but I picked it up anyway.

"Hello?"

"Bacall?"

Rory's voice brought joy to my heart. I'd thought of him so often, and now I didn't have to imagine our interaction. This conversation was real.

"It's good to hear from you. How've you been?" My question started a conversation that was as comfortable as if we'd been talking all along.

"I'd love to see you," Rory confessed after we'd been on the phone for a while.

"Well," I replied, "since you called me, I guess you know I'm not in Los Angeles."

"That's not a problem. I'm in Alabama, too. Tuskegee's homecoming is this week, so I came out for the game. I'm leaving tomorrow night because I've got a studio session Sunday back in L.A. I'm recording a new song I've been working on with a friend. So, if it's possible, I'd like to get together tonight."

"I'd like to see you, too," I said, though disappointment clouded my voice. "It's just that I'm going to my parents' home for this huge dinner we're about to have. My dad's two brothers and their wives are coming, and I know I can't get out of it," I uttered, wishing all the more that I could. "So I don't see how tonight will work for you and me."

He paused, then said, "Tonight will be great. Pop downstairs and see. It will do my heart good to lay eyes on you again."

No way, I thought. *No way!* My heart started racing with excitement, as I ran from my bedroom.

At the top of the staircase, I stopped and inhaled. Standing tall at the bottom of the winding steps was the young man who still owned a part of my soul. My entire family was surrounding him, their faces stretched wide with smiles. My father's grin led me to believe that the Reverend was pleased with Rory's unexpected visit. I was blown away.

Slowly, I walked down the stairs and took the bouquet of fall flowers from his hands.

"Look, Bacall." My mother beamed. "I got a beautiful bouquet, too."

I smiled and turned my attention back to Rory. He looked as sharp as ever. The same feeling I had the night I first met him was back, but because we'd been through so much, I suppressed my warm desire.

"Well," I said as everyone stared at me. "I guess you're staying for dinner."

Rory smiled. "I guess I am."

❦ ❦ ❦

My mother is an awesome cook. Even though she had hired help in the kitchen, she fixed the spread alone. My folks seemed to pick up on how excited I was to have Rory at our home. I was still in awe that they were in on his surprise visit.

"Let's go into the living room," my mother said as she led the way. "I want to make sure everything is set before we sit down to dinner."

Before I could get to Rory, Karrington cornered him and the two men went into a corner. I didn't mind, though. I knew Karri had helped Rory a lot, and they were great friends. And it had always pleased my sister and me that our guys got along so well. Although Rory wasn't my guy, it was still neat seeing my friend get along with her man.

I sat back and watched the activity in the living room. My uncles were already up to their tricks, and I hoped Rory would fit in all right. My father's brothers were known for their coarse joking. I'd put up with it all my life and had mastered the art of ignoring them. Rory, on the other hand, never had the weird pleasure of meeting them. I was worried they'd rub him the wrong way.

It didn't take long to find out if Rory would be able to handle it. The moment we sat down at the table and my father finished blessing the food, his older brother, Bill, started in.

"So, Firecracker . . ."

Everyone at the table laughed.

"What? What's funny?" He turned to Rory. "Uh, that is yo' name?"

"No, sir. My name is Rory Kerry." He chuckled along

with everyone else.

Uncle Bob cut in. "I ain't heard no song from ya in a while. You ain't gonna be no one-hit wonder, are ya?"

Uncle Bill laughed so hard that some of his food flew across the room. It was disgusting. Yet he didn't care.

"I've got a new release out now that's doing well." Rory said politely. "As a matter of fact, I'm performing on the Billboard Awards next week. Lord willing, it will be a success."

"Don't let yo' fans burst yo' bubble," Uncle Bob joked. "Or Flame will be fireless."

Rory laughed. "Yep . . . you're right."

Thankfully, Rory went with the flow. Even though I knew my uncles were harmless and just having a little fun, the whole scene bothered me.

I could feel my father's eyes on me, and I knew he felt my discomfort. He took the situation into his hands. Dad had a unique power to shut his older brothers down. He did so by gracefully changing the subject.

"Rory, my son-in-law-to-be, has told me about the great time the two of you have been having in God's Word. Care to share something about that? It's not that I don't care about your music, but I care much more about your soul," Dad said.

Rory replied, "Yes, sir, the time has been just what I needed. Karri knows the Word and has been challenging me to know it, too. He's shown me what it truly means to walk with God. I now know it's much more than being saved. After being a Christian for such a long time, I'm finally growing in my walk. And with everything I've learned about Christ's life, I'm now struggling to live the same lifestyle. I said struggling because I'm not there, but I'm pumped to be on the right road."

"Amen!" my father cheered.

My mother stood and smiled. "Would anyone care for dessert? I have sweet-potato pie."

"Ain't no need in askin' a bunch of black folks if they want 'tata pie. Just bring it on out here and watch us gobble it up," Uncle Bob said, slipping back into his joking mode.

My other uncle took the cue. "These boys talkin' 'bout the gospel. Shoot, I wanna hear 'em sang gospel. They probably don't know nothin' 'bout that. Neither one of 'em actually sing. This Kerry just moans on his records, and that Karri talks on his. Let's show 'em how to really praise the Lord."

In sync, the three Lee brothers headed to the living room and moved toward the baby grand piano. For more than thirty minutes, song after song rolled from their lips. The quality and content of the music was good enough to be recorded, but moments like these weren't meant to be sold. We all joined in and relished the fact that we were praising the Lord.

It didn't take long for my uncles to be ready to call it a night, but it was still pretty early.

"Hey, you guys," Karrington addressed Rory and me. "Why don't the four of us go out together?"

Karrington's plan sounded good to me. I didn't want the night to end.

"Sure, I'm game," I stated excitedly.

Rory said, "Let's hit a movie." As he spoke, he glanced my way and smiled.

Unable to resist his charm, I returned the gesture. It was clear we were both where we wanted to be.

Brooks said, "I'll grab the paper and we can decide what we want to see as we drive. This will be fun," she exclaimed.

I looked at Rory and smiled again. So far, it had all been good, and I was looking forward to the rest of the night.

Before we went into the theater, I excused myself and went to the ladies' room. I wasn't gone five minutes, but by the time I came outside, there was a crowd of women surrounding my date. Seemed his career wasn't doing too bad after all. He still had a bunch of fans. I didn't want to interrupt him. He was enjoying signing autographs.

When Rory noticed me standing off to the side, he paused, then cut through the crowd to come to me.

"Sorry, ladies," he said, turning back to the group. "I can't sign any more. I'm on a date tonight and I don't want to keep this beautiful lady waiting. Thanks for your support." He smiled and waved good-bye, then gently took my hand and we walked into the theater. We stood in the back, trying to find Brooks and Karrington, but before we could spot the two, we were stopped by another fan.

"Can I just say you are so lucky to be with—oh, my goodness . . . Bacall Lee?" the girl said with disbelief.

It was Benita Hanyes—an acquaintance from high school. Years had passed since I'd last seen her.

Benita continued. "It's been forever! I heard your sister is getting married to that cute gospel artist guy. Now I see you're datin' Flame. Girrrrl, what's the family secret?"

I laughed. "You're so silly. So how are you?"

"Obviously, I'm not doing as good as you," Benita stated as her eyes roamed up and down my companion's body.

I formally introduced Rory to Benita, then we excused ourselves to find Brooks and Karrington. We spotted them near the front, and as we walked down the aisle, I teased Rory.

"It seems like my friend really liked you," I said.

"It doesn't matter," he said, looking into my eyes. "Because I know there's no one for me—except you."

It was like the moment froze for us. It was special for me to know how much he still cared. The strong connection we felt toward one another was once again pushing its way to the surface.

By the time we got to our seats, the lights had already

dimmed. I sat next to my sister. The guys sat on the outer sides of us.

Brooks kept smiling at me. I knew what her smirk meant, but I tried to ignore her. She wasn't going to have that, though.

As I reached for some popcorn, Brooks taunted in my ear, "I know you still love him. It's written all over your face. Your body language can't deny my claim, even if your lips want to."

I rolled my eyes, but that didn't stop my sister.

"I think he feels the same way. But be careful, Sis. I hope the two of you aren't walking into trouble again."

I'd never told my sister that I was no longer as pure as she was. Yet it seemed she knew. I couldn't explain how I knew she knew; I just did, and that annoyed me.

She could sense my irritation. "Don't get mad. I said that out of love. So chill. I'll keep staying on ya till you're married."

Even though her words were unsettling, I knew I needed to listen. Reluctantly, I vowed to heed her words. Never again did I want to fall so hard for *a* guy that I forgot to please *the* Guy who counted most.

It was after eleven when we returned to my parents' house, but none of us wanted the evening to end. So Karrington and I partnered to tear Rory and Brooks apart in spades. We were laughing and having fun when Rory received a page.

He excused himself from the family room and took the call in the kitchen. When he returned, he was smiling. "I need a favor from you guys."

Rory sat down at the electric piano and started playing "The Star Spangled Banner."

We all looked at him and frowned.

"What are you doing?" I asked.

"You're never going to believe this, but that was the president of Tuskegee. He heard that I'll be attending the game tomorrow, and he wants me to sing the national anthem."

The three of us applauded.

"You'll be great." I grinned.

"No, I won't."

His words confused me.

"*We'll* be great." He paused. "Remember that favor? I want you guys to sing with me. We'll turn that stadium out."

I looked at my sister and Karrington, and we all smiled. I sat next to Rory, and the four of us began working on our arrangement. We worked for several hours. What we created was amazingly special.

I always loved singing with Rory, and the next day on the field reaffirmed that fact. Rory had a passion for singing that was contagious. Every time he took the stage, his heart and soul were in the sound.

Just like at the movie theater, crowds of women surrounded Rory on the field before we sang and then throughout every minute of the game. But no matter who was around him, Rory acknowledged my presence. Being a part of his world again felt great.

Immediately after the Tuskegee victory, a limo was waiting outside the stadium to drive Rory to the Atlanta airport. Sadness consumed me. Yet the gentle kiss he planted softly on my lips gave me something to remember.

"I'll call ya tonight," he said softly. "But I'll be thinking about you until I see your gorgeous face again."

I nodded because the words I wanted to say were stuck in my throat.

"Good-bye, Lady Bacall," Rory whispered in my ear before shutting the limousine door.

I watched the black car roll slowly down the street, and I felt like I was losing Rory all over again.

❦ ❦ ❦

Rory kept his word. Not only did he call me that night, but he called the next night, and the night after that, and the night after that. He phoned every night for three weeks.

It was awesome developing a relationship with him again. It felt comfortable and familiar, the way I always wanted us to be. It was what we had become. It was right.

How ironic, we were once again miles away from each other. Like the song he'd sung to me almost a year before. This time I was the one down South, longing to be with him in Los Angeles. Often, I thought of dropping everything and flying to L. A. to be with him. But being a lady, I couldn't do it. Fortunately, though, I didn't have long to wait before the invitation came from him.

"The Billboard Music Awards are this week," Rory said during one of our phone conversations. "I'd love to have you go with me. Don't know if I'll win an award, but I'm performing, so it should be worth the trip. What do you say? You down?"

"Yes," I agreed without hesitation, "I'm down . . . down South!"

We both laughed. I was joking but definitely telling the truth. Finally, we got serious and finalized plans for my trip.

❦ ❦ ❦

The days passed quickly, and before I knew it, I was in Los Angeles enjoying Rory's performance. As I watched him win the audience with his new song, "Out of the Furnace," I knew he had totally won my heart. Flame was smokin' up both the place and me.

I was as proud of him as the person sitting to my right—his mother. Knowing where he'd come from. Knowing the dream he had. Knowing how his style of singing had changed to honor God. Knowing all that, I couldn't help but be proud. He had turned from a sultry, sexy singer into a powerful, inspirational vocalist.

An added bonus to the night was that Flame received two awards: one for best male R & B artist and the other for best new artist of the year.

After the show, Rory's mother and I congratulated him, then waited to the side as others offered their well wishes. When he finally returned to us, he took my hand.

"I've been invited to lots of parties. Are you two up for it?" he asked.

His mother smiled but shook her head. "No, honey. You and Bacall go. Take me back to the hotel. This is a night for young people."

After dropping her off, we went by the party hosted by Yo Town Records.

Kelly and Raven were the first to greet us.

"Bacall, it's so good to see you," Raven gushed.

Even though we didn't have a great past, I had the feeling Raven meant what she said. We had chatted a few times since I'd returned to Alabama, and we'd been able to bury those negative feelings. She told me on more than one occasion that nothing ever happened between her and Rory, though she admitted that she did try. I was glad to know Rory had never conceded.

The way Kelly and Raven hung onto each other, I could tell they were back together. Their on-again, off-again romance was more confusing than my own.

"Well, you kids have a good time," Kelly said as he led Raven across the room to chat with some of their other artists.

Rory said, "Listen, there are some people I want to say hello to—"

I held up my hand, stopping him in midsentence. "Go

ahead. I'll be fine." I tried to reassure him.

He kissed my cheek. "I won't be long."

While Flame mingled with the others, I sat and watched. He knew my eye was on him because he kept turning toward me and winking. I took several deep breaths. Boy, did I want him in ways that I shouldn't.

"Lord, help me," I uttered desperately, trying to contain those lustful feelings.

"You want him, huh?"

I turned to the voice and was surprised to see Toi standing behind me. I didn't even know she was around.

"Why do you ask?" I said strongly. "Do you want him?"

"If you believe the gossip that has floated around about me, then I should want him, right? I dumped him when he wasn't hot, and now that he's rising again, I should want back in!" Her voice was filled with frustration. "Well, wrong! All of those rumors are lies. Rory dumped *me*."

I stared at her with my mouth wide open.

She continued, "I did want him, and I don't mean his money. I wanted something from him he wouldn't give me."

She glanced across the room at Rory, then turned back to me. She touched my shoulder and lowered her voice. "I now know that he couldn't get with me because he always loved you. It was more than obvious when he defended you against crazy Bum." She was quiet for a moment as we watched Rory move across the room. Finally, she said, "And as I watch you looking at him with that same intensity coming back from him, I'm glad you guys found your love for each other again. So let me answer your question. No, I don't want him. And even if I did, he's yours anyway." Without another word, she turned and walked away.

I watched her leave the room and then my eyes returned to Rory. I wondered if Toi's words were true.

※ ※ ※

Much later, after we visited several other parties, the stares of passion we had shared all night became more than stares. We couldn't even drive away from the last party. The two of us were touching, kissing, grooving, and about to do much more. Suddenly, I realized what I was doing. An awesome God intervened.

"I don't belong to you, Rory. Please take me to my hotel." I don't know where I mustered up enough strength and maturity to say those words. But I was glad I did.

"Oh, baby, I love you," Rory whispered. "We can stop. Let's go to my place and talk. You don't have to worry. It's not like we've got a fire going yet," he said, trying to convince me.

But I pushed away from his enticing clutch. "Yeah, you're right . . . things aren't as hot and heavy as they could be. But I've got to bow out gracefully right now because I'm reminded of what I learned as a Girl Scout. To get a fire going, it only takes a spark!"

15

Candle

The wedding day finally arrived. Anticipation had met its destiny. Everyone was in the best mood.

"You are more beautiful than I could ever have imagined," my mother said with pure joy and love.

Mother was busy with last-minute touch-ups, making her daughter beautiful. Fluffing out the gown, stroking the bride's hair, and draping on jewelry were only a few things that kept her moving faster than a high-speed train. Watching her made me long to be so blessed to give a child away in matrimony.

"Mom . . . you're gonna make me cry," Brooks uttered, her voice shaky with emotion.

Finally, when it was time, the gorgeous gown seemed to walk itself down the aisle to the happy groom. My father was bursting with pride as he held his daughter's arm. Love was in the air.

The atmosphere was more romantic than a Disney love story, yet equally adventurous and special. It was an outdoor wedding, even though it was Christmas Eve. The clouds and stars had been invited. Each showed up with the gift of a perfect setting.

The groom beamed with pride and love, obviously adoring the woman God was about to give him. The minister smiled, then glanced up as if he wanted to show heaven's approval.

"Who gives this woman away to be joined in marriage?" young Reverend Morgan inquired.

My father spoke proudly. "My wife and I are blessed and honored to give our youngest daughter to be joined in marriage to this godly man."

As my dad walked away, I snapped from my daze. I was the bride. I still couldn't believe it. Standing still, in front of God and next to my beloved Rory, I allowed my mind to race over the events of the last year.

When Rory took me to my hotel the night of the Billboard Awards, we agreed that we could never be together. It was right for us to part, but our decision tore me up inside.

Alone in my hotel room, I cried out to God. "I love this man, Lord, and I don't know how to channel that love in a way that is honoring to You. Help me deal with this strained situation. Help me be strong. Either help me move on or work this all out." Talking to God, I realized that I really didn't want things to end.

But I'd honestly given up on the thought of Rory and me working things out. He never called that night, nor did he try to contact me once I returned to Alabama.

To refocus my energy, I threw myself into accomplishing tasks. Between work and Brooks's wedding, my time was totally consumed. I had a company to restructure, and I took my job as Brooks's maid of honor seriously. My goal was to make both a success.

When day after day passed and I didn't hear from Rory, it seemed our flame was finally out for good. Even though I was busy with many things, it still hurt that I didn't have the relationship I wanted with Rory. But the Lord gave me something better. He gave me Himself. I was back in His Word. I was fasting. I was praying. I found I didn't need a romantic relationship with Rory because I had a right relationship with God.

OK, I still had deep feelings for my ex-boyfriend, feelings that I knew would probably always linger. However, those feelings didn't control me. I was following Jesus Christ remembering what the Bible said in 1 Corinthians: "He who is unmarried cares for the things of the Lord—how he may please the Lord."

I knew God was taking me through this to strengthen me. To make me more Christlike was His goal. To get me to keep Him first was His aim. Just when I thought I had all the strength I needed, God knew I could have more.

I allowed God to help me through the passing weeks, and as we got closer to Brooks's wedding, it seemed to get easier. The night before my sister's wedding, I attended the rehearsal. I knew most of the people in the wedding party. But I was shocked when a familiar figure casually strolled into the church.

"Why is he here?" I asked Brooks in a panic. "What's going on?"

Brooks sighed. "Rory's in the wedding, OK? Since he and my boo have this amazing bond, Karrington created a place for him in the wedding."

"Created a place? What does that mean?"

"Look, Bacall, what's the big deal? I need you to help keep me calm, not stress me out," my sister sputtered. "Rory is the 'best friend.' Like the maid of honor . . . Karrington created a position just like that for a guy. And . . . just so you get the full picture and have no more surprises, Rory will be escorting you."

I was so annoyed I didn't know what to do. But there was nothing I could do, and I didn't want to stress Brooks anymore. It seemed all the stress had been transferred to me. Now everything about her wedding irritated me. I started to think she had too many bridesmaids when there were only twelve. Their chitter-chatter bothered me. These grown women sounded like girls in a schoolyard. I wondered what made them so giddy, and then I finally figured it out. They were laughing about ways to get close to Rory.

I looked around for Brooks. I needed her to get these ladies under control. She needed to tell them that Rory was mine—even though he wasn't my guy. But I couldn't find Brooks anywhere, and I knew she was probably off with my mother making plans.

After I calmed down, I was glad Brooks was nowhere to be found. When it got down to it, I had no right to tell the girls to stop eyeing Rory.

Though it was tough, I made it through the rehearsal. After it was over, I watched Rory wander through the room, speaking in depth to everyone—except for me. He only briefly spoke to me in passing.

At the dinner, Rory's behavior continued. He went from table to table, mixing with the guests. I watched as he chatted with my parents, giggled with my uncles, rapped with the guys, and schmoozed the ladies. I tried to keep my emotions under control, but I was livid. Yet I was successful at keeping my outer appearance calm and collected. One would have thought my former beau's actions weren't phasing me a bit. Yeah, right!

I couldn't wait for the rehearsal to be over, and that night before I climbed into bed, I thanked God for His unfailing love for me. Through my anger, through my disappointment, and through my resentment, I knew He still loved me. I didn't have peace that night until I once again realized that Christ was all I needed.

The next morning, when I awakened, I vowed that I would get through the day just fine. I sat with Brooks as she watched her favorite musical, *Fiddler on the Roof.*

"Wasn't that wonderful?" She asked as the video came to an end.

I rolled my eyes. My sister had probably watched the movie a half-dozen times or more each year.

"You know what I think?" Brooks asked though she didn't wait for an answer. "I want you to sing 'Sunrise, Sunset' at the ceremony this afternoon."

Oh, brother, I thought. At first, I thought her request was crazy, but by the time we got to the church and I looked around the beautifully decorated room, I realized how appropriate the song was. Where had the time gone? I remembered the day Brooks and I were flower girls for our cousin Jenell. Now, my big sister was the bride. The song she had to have at the last minute was perfect. Time waits for no one.

Standing before the packed church, I sang the song as if it were the last song I would ever sing. As I sang the final stanza, I looked at Brooks and Karrington standing together at the altar, and I wondered if the time would ever come for me to stand with my groom.

Against my will, my eyes met Rory's. The warmth of the moment was heavenly. As Brooks and Karrington exchanged vows, Rory continued to stare at me with a look I couldn't figure out. It was as if he were staring straight through me and seeing my heart.

Finally, I could no longer take his bold stare and I had to look away. There was no need to fool myself into believing Rory was thinking more than he was.

I cried at the end of the ceremony and made my way down the aisle. I stood in the receiving line as if I didn't have any cares. But once we were at the reception, I again stepped into a world all my own. I was enjoying the moment for Brooks, but not for me.

All kind of music filled the room. First, the jazz band performed, then the guests were entertained by various gospel artists who had been friends of my family for years. Christmas songs, love ballads, and gospel tunes blended in an interesting mix that made the occasion even more marvelous. Hearing melodies and lyrics about the Truth put a beat back in my soul.

About an hour into the reception, Karrington and Rory took the stage.

"God has blessed me so much this year," Karrington said, placing his arm around Rory. "Not only has He given me a virtuous woman and a soaring career, He has given me a dear friend. Through our experiences and time together, a song was born. We've titled it, 'Carry the Flame.' My name is Karrington Ford and his name is Rory Kerry, also known as Flame. Please enjoy what God gave us to share with you."

Tears of joy covered my face. This was the secret song that Rory had been working on with a friend. How neat it was to find out that the friend was Karri. Even though Rory and I weren't going to walk together through life, I was glad to see he would be walking with God. His passion was where it should be, for a Heavenly God who is Creator, Lord, and King.

Together they sang, "Carry the flame for Him in your heart. Carry the flame that won't ever burn out. Carry the flame that never dies. Carry the flame all of your life. Carry the flame, carry the flame, carry the flame for Jesus Christ."

That nailed it for me. The song let me see why I went astray. I was carrying a torch for things other than Christ. Only when I sought Him was the light guiding my way clearly and brightly. Carrying a passion for God brings no darkness.

On the second chorus, the song gave me more things to

think about. Karri and Kerry were joined by all the top gospel artists. The sound was awesome. Even my dad joined in. One would have thought it was planned, but there was no rehearsal involved. They just felt the Spirit and stood up to sing.

The crowd cheered at the end of the song, and it took a while for everyone to come down from that beautiful moment.

Brooks came over to me and gave me a hug. "Wasn't that special?"

I nodded.

"After my sorors serenade me, it'll be time to throw the bouquet," Brooks said.

I smiled at my sister. "And . . ."

"Well, you've served me so well over these last few days that I feel bad asking you for one more thing. But I have to ask anyway." Brooks paused. "I need to have you standing there when I throw the flowers." It must have been my frown that made her continue. "Please, don't ask questions. Just be there."

Ten minutes later, I did what my sister asked. I stood with sixty other women waiting for a myth to land in my hands so I could be the next to marry. Yeah, right. Even if I caught the dumb roses, I wouldn't have anyone to get hitched to.

I waited for my sister with my arms folded in front of me.

Brooks counted. "One, two, three." Then she tossed her bouquet in the air.

Women jumped up like wild beasts. I had to get away from them, but before I could move, they all moved away. No one was left to catch the flowing, beribboned arrangement but me. Instinct made me raise my hands and catch the flying bouquet.

Folks started screaming. My parents moved closer to

me. So did Brooks and her new husband. What was the big deal? So I caught it? And?

Suddenly, the bright lights that illuminated the room were turned down. Voices from the crowd were yelling, but I couldn't make out what was being said.

In the next moment, I heard Rory's voice behind me. "They're telling you to look at the flowers," he said softly.

I couldn't imagine why he was telling me to do that. It was kind of silly since the lights were off. What would I see? But, I did it anyway.

I blinked several times. A sparkle flashed in my eyes. A two-karat, princess-cut diamond ring in a white gold setting lay in the flowers. Screams came from all sides of the room. It was only the noise that kept me from fainting.

My entire body was trembling at the thought of what this ring meant. It didn't make sense. What could Rory say to close the gap between where we had left to where we now stood?

It seemed I was about to get the answer to my question. Rory took my hand and moved close to me so only I would hear his words.

"Bacall, I knew I loved you the night we met on your birthday almost two years ago. From that moment, I've wanted you in my life. But God knew I wasn't ready to have someone like you . . . one of His own . . . with me. I was full of pride, thinking I had it all . . . or could have it all. Well, as the Bible says, 'Pride comes before a fall.' And I fell. Yet I fell into the truth as God let me see just how far off I was. I now know that many of the things I engaged myself in before I met you were wrong. They didn't make me a big man. You tried to get me to see that, but I was blinded with arrogance. What's worse is that I misused your love by asking you to make compromises."

Was I hearing him right? Did he finally get it? I thought about the times I'd wanted to hear those words from his lips, and I thanked God that I was finally hearing them. Although he was whispering to me, I wished every person who struggled with sex, and who struggled with thinking that promiscuity was OK, could hear his confession.

The man I loved knelt before me as those around us continued to cheer.

"I've asked the Lord to forgive me, Bacall, and now I want to ask you that . . . and more. God took me through things that almost cost me everything to let me see that all I needed was Him. When we stopped talking again a few weeks ago, I had no peace. You told me you weren't mine and that bothered me. In my quest to find answers, I learned you were wrong about that. God told me you are mine. It is His covenant. I haven't always obeyed Him, but that's changed. I'm on my knees right now to follow His command for my life. Lady Bacall . . . will you marry me?"

It had been a whirlwind year from the moment I had said yes, and now, here I stood next to the man God wanted me to be with.

"Dearly beloved, we are gathered here today . . ."

Like my sister, I was being married on Christmas Eve, but this ceremony was far less traditional than Brooks's. Rory and I were being married on a beach in Malibu—the same beach where I'd made the video when I was with Matches.

"Marriage is a sacred covenant, ordained by God . . ."

As the minister spoke, I casually glanced around. Rows of bonfires glowed around us. To my left, my two bridesmaids, Wesli and Camille, stood in different-styled tea-length dresses. The smiles they wore reflected what was in their hearts. Behind Wesli and Camille stood Blake and Bryce Price—Blain's little daughters, who were the flower girls. Rory and I had agreed to do this, wishing Blain was still with us. We took comfort in knowing that the one who'd saved our lives was resting in the peaceful arms of the One who'd saved our souls.

Behind us were rows of chairs, and I didn't have to turn around to know that while my father was probably beaming with pride, my mother and Brooks (who was eight months pregnant) were probably holding tissues to their eyes.

While Brooks couldn't stand up for me, Karrington was Rory's best man. Next to Karrington was Kelly, as the "best friend". I knew Raven was nestled somewhere in the audience behind us, hoping to soon change his marital status.

"And so, Bacall and Rory, you stand together today in the eyes of God to become one."

It was time for us to say our vows—but instead of just speaking, we had decided to sing our words of commitment. While I knew the melody, I didn't know what Rory was going to say. His song was filled with words like, *everlasting* and *love of my life,* and that brought tears to my eyes. His voice was sweet and sexy.

I, in turn, told him how much I loved him with my vows. I could tell by the way his eyes watered that I had gotten to him.

As we were pronounced husband and wife, I knew Rory and I would be together forever.

"Where are you taking me?" I asked as Rory led me down the beach.

It was dark, so Rory held my hand, although I was sure he'd be holding me even if the sun was shining brightly.

"You'll see soon," he said simply.

Finally, in the distance, I saw a shape on the sand. As we got closer, a tent came into clear view. It seemed my husband had found a secluded place where we would spend our first night as husband and wife before we left for Hawaii the next morning.

It was a simple setting—everything we needed was there: my husband and me. And God supplied the music: the roaring waves that lapped beside us.

We sat on the blankets and sipped the sparkling cider Rory had brought along. As he became more amorous, I became more hesitant, even though this wouldn't be our first time together.

My desire for him wasn't diminished. I just wanted the intimate part of our union to be greater than great.

"Don't worry, baby, God is in every part of our marriage," he said softly. "He longs for us to enjoy our bed. Even if our bed is the sand."

We laughed and embraced. For at least the thousandth time that day, I thanked God for this blessing. When I finally sought heaven first, God granted me the desire of my heart. He gave me Rory Kerry. A man who loved God more than he loved me. A man who, with every breath, would love me as Christ loved His church.

What a blessing and honor it is to know Jesus Christ, I thought. Before I met Rory, I thought I knew God. But I learned through the rough experiences of the last two years that I never truly did. If I really knew Him, I would never have turned away from His guidance. I pleaded for God to give me a man. I wanted to make my own mate. Would a person after God's heart try to rule her own life? No!

I had learned many great lessons in the past two years. I learned to always walk by faith. This is the only way to please our heavenly Father. And I learned to trust Him to supply my needs.

I also learned to pray, "Lord, may my desire match Your will for my life." I knew now that if I continually operated from that prayer, my steps would be ordered by God and I would enjoy this journey. Now, when I think of God's goodness, how can I not give Him my all?

One day, He will come back for us. I know now that on

that day, I'll be ready. He has given me a husband to love with every inch of my being. So I will do just that.

I left my thoughts and let my husband's kisses consume me. It was easy to enjoy our bed. Every sensual move aroused me.

"I'm blessed . . . because I have Jesus . . . and because I have you," I uttered tenderly to my man.

The passion we had for our heavenly Father, as well as the passion we felt for one another, was like an embedded wick deep in our souls that burned intensely. That luminous light reminded me of the only other object in the tent. Our love that filled the air was as precious as that pure, glowing candle.

Holy Ghost Re

The Chosen Vessels

Holy Ghost Revival on Azusa Street:

THE COMPLETE AZUSA STREET LIBRARY

Volume 4

Compiled and edited by

Larry E. Martin

ISBN 1-931393-26-5

CHRISTIAN LIFE BOOKS
P.O. BOX 36355
PENSACOLA, FLORIDA 32516
WWW.RRMI.ORG
WWW.AZUSASTREET.ORG
WWW.JESUS-IS-THE-ANSWER.COM

email: info@azusastreet.org

Dedication

Dedicated to the true evangelists,

God's gift to the church.

May they always labor that the fires of revival will never stop burning.

The Apostolic Faith Gospel Mission (Ca. 1906)

312 Azusa Street

Los Angeles, California

One of the earliest photos of the mission

Photo used by permission

United Pentecostal Church Archives

Contents

William J. Seymour at the Mission

Photo Used by Permission
Flower Pentecostal Heritage Center

List of Illustrations

Some of Azusa's Chosen Vessels

Larry Martin Collection

Foreword

As a fourth Generation Pentecostal, I cherish and value our history. I hold the men and women who blazed the trail of Pentecost here and abroad in high esteem. As Spirit-filled people we must know and understand our past and the foundation of Pentecost that was laid by our forefathers. Without a proper understanding of our heritage, and where we came from, we can't truly appreciate who we are, and what we stand for.

As a people, we must never lose our knowledge of William Seymour, F. F. Bosworth, John B. Lake, Smith Wigglesworth, G.B. Cashwell, D.C.O. Opperman, Frank Bartleman, Thomas B. Barratt, and countless others. They blazed the trail before us, and their stories and testimonies are invaluable to us.

Dr. Larry Martin is called of God to be a "Keeper of the Flame of Pentecost." I commend him for keeping our history alive, and I recommend his book *The Chosen Vessels* to any and all Spirit-filled believers. Read it and cherish our history, and never forget that "the sound of Pentecost" can still be heard, the wind of Pentecost is still blowing, and the fire of Pentecost is still falling.

In Christ,

Donnie Swaggart
Baton Rouge, LA
March 9, 2010

Preface to the Series

The twentieth century Pentecostal/Charismatic movement was born on the first day of the last century, January 1, 1901, in Topeka, Kansas. For several months, the fledgling faith slept like a babe in a crib. Then for a couple of years she crawled around in Kansas, Missouri and Texas. In April 1906, Pentecostalism stood to her feet in a dilapidated old mission at 312 Azusa Street in Los Angeles, California. Once standing, the movement swiftly ran around the world. More than one hundred years later she is still running strong as revival fires fall fresh on a hungry church.

This series of books is about the Azusa Street Revival that started it all. These books are not conjecture or hearsay. These are primarily eye witness accounts and material from original sources. Although these witnesses may lie silent in the grave, their testimonies live to speak to a new generation hungry for a move of God.

There are two primary reasons why I have collected and published this material. First, before any of these testimonies are scattered and forgotten, I want to establish a record for the future. A record that is available not only in libraries and archives, but accessible to all Spirit-filled believers, clergy and layman, who want to relive their heritage. The Pentecostal/Charismatic church must never forget what happened at 312 Azusa Street.

Secondly, I pray that the reading of these dramatic stories will create a hunger in the hearts of the people of God. Although the United States has experienced some revival in recent years, we have seen nothing that equals the Azusa meeting and the impact it had on the world. If the church is going to survive around the world, we must pray for a fresh outpouring for a new millennium.

This project was started with the assumption that I would publish one book, erroneously believing that only a little material would be available. Now, I have collected the material for at least ten books. Future editions will be published as the Lord wills and He provides the resources.

I have attempted to leave the record intact as much as was possible. In some cases, I have had to condense and to a very limited extent I have corrected misspelling (especially proper names) and punctuation. I have also changed the grammatical style (quotation marks, etc.) of some writers for the sake of consistency. In no instance did I add or subtract anything that changed the accuracy of the witness' account. If I have added editorial comments within the text, they are placed in brackets "[ ]" to distinguish them from the author's or editor's original comments that may be in parenthesis "( )."

I pray that my desire to present the original accounts as they were written will not cause any to be offended. Blacks are generally referred to as "colored" and some other language might not be considered appropriate by today's standards. Please remember that what is not acceptable today was the norm one hundred years ago. As you read, you will find that in most cases, the same language was used by both blacks and whites. In no case, is it my desire to offend. In fact, my prayer is that once again the children of God might worship together as one, regardless of race, ethnicity or affiliation. The "color line" is still washed away by Jesus' precious blood.

I am especially grateful to the guardians of our history for their diligence, without which this series would be impossible. I have studied at libraries, museums and archives from one end of this country to another. I could never thank every one who has contributed. Nevertheless, I must mention Assemblies of God archivist Glenn Gohr. His valuable assistance has greatly enhanced all of my projects. Also, this entire collection owes a great debt to Douglas J. Nelson the first Azusa Street scholar and Cecil M. Roebeck the most persistent.

A special thanks also goes to the many who provided me with materials and photographs with permission to reprint. Credit is given in the appropriate places. The entire series is better because of their generosity. I am also grateful to David Coleman for his excellent illustration for the cover.

This book is volume four in the series. Volume one, *The Life and Ministry of William J. Seymour* is the foundation for the series. To fully understand the revival, it is a "must" read. The next three volumes, including this one, contain testimonies of believers. Volumes five through seven are primary source materials that support the revival position. Volumes eight and nine capture the voices of the skeptics–religious and secular. Other volumes will come as the Lord provides. Our intention is to include a volume on William H. Durham and at least some of Frank Bartleman's more obscure works.

Like volumes two and three, this volume, *The Chosen Vessels* contains testimonies of the men and women who experienced the revival. Some of these exciting stories have never been published. Some have not been seen in fifty years or more. All are significant. Not every chosen vessel was famous or notable among men, but all have a notable story to tell–the story of a powerful God that visited an humble mission at 312 Azusa Street.

Finally, let us all pray that the love, humility, tears, hunger and Pentecostal power that were the spirit of Azusa will visit us again. Skeptics and scoffers did not stop the faithful, they must not stop us. Our world, our nation, our churches need Holy Ghost revival.

Larry Martin
Pensacola, Florida

Prologue

William Joseph Seymour (Ca. 1915),
pastor of
the Apostolic Faith Gospel Mission
312 Azusa Street, Los Angeles, CA

Photo used by permission

Apostolic Faith International Headquarters

Portland, Oregon

We pray God will mightily use you, for you are a chosen vessel to carry this Gospel.

Letter from Clara Lum to T. B. Barratt
November 22, 1906
from Azusa Street Lectures, Letters and Bible Lessons

A message that was given in tongues for God's people was this, "Humble yourselves under the mighty hand of God." He is now about to move on the world in a mighty wave of Pentecostal power and salvation. A sister had a vision of God's people as vessels that were full, and the Lord said, "The vessels must be emptied and I will fill them."

The Apostolic Faith
September 1906

THE APOSTOLIC FAITH

Pentecost Has Come

Los Angeles Being Visited by a Revival of Bible Salvation and Pentecost as Recorded in the Book of Acts

The first issue of *The Apostolic Faith* Newspaper

September, 1906

A Night at the Azusa Street Mission

Author Unknown

After some hearty singing and earnest prayer, a converted Jewish brother testified. Then a little boy mounted the altar and said plainly, "I thank the Lord for saving me, and now I am seeking the baptism. I want you to pray for me that I may get it. Tonight I had a toothache and I prayed for the Lord to take it away, and He took it away."

A sister said, "Rejoice in the Lord. Rejoice always; and again I say rejoice. I am rejoicing in the Lord; I am rejoicing in His salvation, I am rejoicing in His life, I am rejoicing in His presence with me, I am resting on His promises, and looking and expecting Him moment by moment. Hallelujah! Hallelujah! Praise our God for ever."

A colored brother arose and sang the verses of a hymn, the people joining in the chorus, "The Blood, the Blood, is all my plea; Hallelujah, it cleanseth me."

He then said, "Hallelujah! I am so glad I can testify that the Blood cleanseth me. Oh, the sweetness! My heart is full of love for Jesus. I am so glad I can take up the cross and work with Him now and follow Him. Oh, I know I am leaning on the Almighty's arms."

An old gentleman who has recently received the baptism said, "Just take the blessings that God sends down to us. Oh I thank God that He has found an old man, a sinner like me. I was not worthy of anything but He gave Himself to me. O glory, O glory! Then he spoke in another language, the interpretation being, "Glory to Thee my great Redeemer for Thy great love towards me . . . O how I praise Thee." He continued in English, "Oh glory to God for the gift He has given me. Now if there is any sinner here tonight seek Him. Now we all may have it without money."

Another testified as follows, "I praise God tonight that I am under the Blood; Jesus' Blood covers me and cleanses me from all sin. . ."

Someone else said, "I know that the Blood of Jesus saves me and sanctifies me and keeps me from day to day. He is my Healer, I praise Him and thank Him for the way He is increasing my faith and instructing me today. The Lord gave me a verse since I have been standing here, 'Wait on the Lord, be of good courage, and He shall strengthen thine heart.' I am just standing on His promises. With His stripes I am healed. I praise Him and thank Him with all my heart. He saves me and sanctifies me and baptizes me with the Holy Ghost"

A new song of much power was then sung through in the Spirit by all:

"Jesus Christ is made to me
All I need, All I need;
He alone is all my plea,
He is all I need
Chorus–
Wisdom, Righteousness and Power
Holiness forever more,
My Redemption full and sure, He is all I need."

A brother testified, "There is power in my soul tonight because God put it in there; it is the power of the Spirit that came down from the throne of God, from the Everlasting Father, before whom we must one day stand and give an account of the deeds done in the body. Oh how careful we as professing Christians ought to walk before this ungodly generation. The Lord showed me a few years ago that out of California would come a movement that would startle the world, and here is the prophecy fulfilled. Praise God for this personal Pentecost." He then said in another tongue, "Jesus died that you might be saved. Oh be saved tonight and seek Him with all the heart, and let Him have His way."

A young colored sister then said, "I want to praise God tonight. He is all in all to me. Glory to Jesus. Dear ones, you do not know how sweet it is to trust in Jesus. Do not sit back laughing and scoffing–oh you are laughing at Jesus, not at us." In tongues she said, "He that sitteth in the heavens shall laugh, the Lord shall have them in derision. Oh why will ye not come unto Me that ye might have life? Oh why do you resist My pleading with you at this time? Oh why do you not come to Me and turn to Me with thy heart?"

Speaking again in English she continued, "Dear ones, accept this blessed salvation. I do praise my blessed Redeemer for saving me from sin, and giving me a clean heart. When I was a sinner I would go to church and look around laughing, but oh I did not know I was laughing at Jesus, but, praise God, He is all in all to me now. He has taken all the laugh out of me, all criticism. He has given me a perfectly clean heart and filled me with love. Dear ones, oh it is precious to have a clean heart. He saved my soul and He has baptized me with the Holy Ghost." Again in tongues, "O why do you resist the strivings of the Spirit? Why do you not turn to Him in repentance?"

Returning to English she said, "Dear ones, it is so sweet to walk with Jesus. I take Him as my Healer. He heals all my diseases. O glory to God." She then finished her testimony in tongues, saying, "Why do you not look to Him and live at this time?"

Brother W.J. Seymour then started the congregation singing:

"Jesus, Jesus, how I trust Thee,
How I've proved Thee o'er and o'er;
Jesus, Jesus, blessed Jesus,
Oh for grace to trust Thee more."

He then said, "Glory! Beloved, I want to say 'Good night' to you all for a short while. It has now been over a year ago since I left Texas and come up in this portion of the country to labor and work for the Lord, and I am going back there through that old state where the Lord called me from a year ago. I am going to pass through there and see those precious children that prayed with me for Pentecost, and while I am gone I want you all to pray that God may use me to His own honor and glory.

"I want to read some of God's own precious Word in the first chapter of Isaiah." He read the first nine verses and said, "I am so glad the Lord God has raised up a people right in Los Angeles, and San Francisco, they seem like Sodom and Gomorrah, but out of these cities the Lord God has raised up a people for His holy name. He has cleansed them from sin, He has sanctified them, and has baptized them with the Holy Ghost and sealed them unto the day of Redemption. Glory to His holy name! I can go and rejoice with the people in Texas, telling them of the wonderful things that God has done in Los Angeles. They said I should be back in a month's time, and now this is the first chance I have had to get back."

He then read to the end of verse twenty, saying, "'But if ye refuse and rebel ye shall be devoured with the sword; for the mouth of the Lord hath spoken it.' Every man, every church, every home, that rejects the full gospel of the Lord and Savior, Jesus Christ shall be devoured. We are living in a time when the Holy Ghost is working–bless God–convincing men and women of sin and righteousness and judgment, and every man and every women that hardens their heart against the Word of God shall fall. If the men and women of this city will repent and turn from their sin and accept our Lord and Saviour, Jesus Christ, 'ye shall eat the good of the land.'

"Glory to His holy name! God has fat things to feed all His hungry people. Oh, He will fill you tonight. Oh, the music will be singing in your soul and, oh, the love of Christ that passes all understanding will be dwelling in you heart. Just read what He says, 'If ye be willing and obedient ye shall eat the good of the land.'

"Jesus says, 'Abide in me, as the branch cannot bear fruit of itself except it abide in the vine, no more can ye except ye abide in me.'

"Oh, beloved, if we abide in the words of the Lord Jesus Christ and feed off Christ, I'll tell you, we shall live off the good of the land–bless His holy name. We will have the fat–bless God–we will have everything to cheer our heart, we shall have healing and health and salvation in our souls. Oh, glory to His holy name. Oh, do not refuse the Word of God; oh, accept it, accept all the doctrine of our Lord and Saviour, Jesus Christ, and oh, beloved, it will fill you hearts with good things.

"But just listen to what He says, 'If ye refuse and rebel, ye shall be devoured with the sword: for the mouth of the Lord hath spoken it.' Beloved, if you reject Christ, if you reject His precious Blood, if you reject the Holy Ghost, ye shall be devoured with the sword; but if you accept Jesus Christ He will prepare a table before you, and the Lord God Himself will spread it and He will feed you Himself. When Jesus had gotten through feeding His disciples He told His disciples to feed His lambs and sheep. What are we going to feed them? We are going to feed them with the precious Word of God; we are going to teach them to accept Jesus Christ as their Savior and as their Sanctifier to destroy the root of sin, and then we are going to teach them to accept the Holy Ghost. He shall baptize them with the Holy Ghost and fire, and when He comes in He is going to speak through them, and he says, 'In the last days I will pour out My Spirit on all flesh.' Glory to His holy name.

"I want to say 'Good night' to you."

"God Be with You till We Meet Again" was then sung as Brother Seymour shook hands with as many as possible and left for the train. Brother Anderson spoke a few words of encouragement to the saints on the necessity of our continuing faithfulness in the pastor's absence.

This is a transcription of the service on May 1, 1907. It was recorded in shorthand by a Spirit filled lady who had the gift of interpretation of tongues. It was printed in the May, 1907 edition of The Apostolic Faith.

Front: William J. Seymour and John G. Lake

Back: John A. D. Adams, F. F. Bosworth

and Tom Hezmalhalch

Photo Used by Permission
Flower Pentecostal Heritage Center

Origin of the Apostolic Faith Movement

John G. Lake

Many have enquired as to what was the origin of the Apostolic Faith Movement that has now spread through the whole world in a few years, and produced this glorious world-wide revival that is now in progress.

In the year 1900 a brother by the name of Chas. F. Parham, of Bagster [Baxter Springs], Kansas, U.S.A., who then conducted a Bible school, was led by God to study the Word concerning the Baptism of the Holy Ghost, and was then led to visit various people and holiness bodies who claimed to possess the Baptism of the Holy Ghost.

After much consideration and prayer, the school was led to the conclusion that none of these demonstrated in proper degree the power of God, or real existence of Holy Ghost Baptism, as recorded in the Book of Acts. The school concluded that the Book of

Acts clearly demonstrated that those who received the Baptism of the Holy Ghost spoke in tongues.

After much seeking and waiting on God, finally the baptism fell, and a considerable number were baptized in the Holy Ghost and spoke in tongues. But being yet babes, and having yet to learn by the Spirit the necessity of a deeper walk with God than they had ever before known there was much stumbling, many errors, and manifestations of the flesh. Some even fell away, but blessed revivals took place and many were saved.

After a number of years, while preaching in the State of Texas, a brother by the name of Seymour attended Parham's meetings, and received the teaching. After due observation, it was revealed to him by the Holy Ghost, that this was indeed the true baptism of the Spirit, but that if a deeper and holier consecration unto God was apparent that a mightier power from on high would rest on the lives of the baptized.

He went to Los Angeles where he joined with a number of friends in praying for the baptism. In telling of his experience some years ago, as nearly as I can recall, his words were as follows: "Prior to my meeting Parham, the Lord had sanctified me from sin, and had led me into a deep life of prayer, assigning five hours out of the twenty-four every day for prayer. This prayer life I continued for three and a half years, when one day as I prayed the Holy Ghost said to me, 'There are better things to be had in the Spiritual life, but they must be sought out with faith and prayer.' This so quickened my soul that I increased my hours of prayer to seven out of twenty-four and continued to pray on for two years longer, until the baptism fell on us."

Speaking of the night in which the baptism in power fell on the little company of brethren at Los Angeles, he said: "We had prayed all night, when at four o'clock in the morning, God came through the window."

What he meant was that the Glory of God came through the window.

The power of God prostrated all the company on the floor. When he came out from under the power of the Spirit it was ten o'clock in the forenoon, and his friend, Brother Lee (known to ourselves), was speaking in tongues, magnifying God.

Soon the fire began to fall at the Asuza Street Mission, Los Angeles, which became known world-wide as a great centre of Holy Ghost power. After considerable time the work spread through out the whole country and world, until every land has its representatives of the Apostolic Faith Mission, and Pentecost is a household word.

Many have enquired: "How is it that you connect the Pentecostal movement with the Welsh revival?" We do so because of the fact that in many instances during the Welsh revival people were baptized in the Holy Ghost and spoke in tongues. In our assembly at Johannesburg there is a young Welsh missionary who testifies that he was personally acquainted with a number of these, and heard them speak in tongues during the Welsh revival.

The same wave of spirituality that touched Wales crossed the seas to America and a deeper manifestation of God took place. The fire spread to India, where a mighty manifestation of the power of God was felt, especially in the work of Pundita Ramabi and great numbers were baptized in the Holy Ghost.

The work in Africa took a still deeper phase of spiritual power, especially along the line of miraculous healing of the sick. From careful investigation we are free to state that in no land had such a demonstration of healing of the sick occurred in South Africa. We rejoice in this continuity of development and evident deepening of spiritual power over the whole world, as the fire has spread from place to place, and country to country, indicating a still deeper life in God the Holy Ghost, revealing more and more marvelous possibilities through the power of God and the precious Blood of Jesus Christ.

At present to us it is clear that the Spirit is now leading many in this movement, not to depend on the prayers of others and themselves for the healing of their bodies, but appropriating the glorious Resurrection life of Jesus Christ, and realizing His triumph over all the powers of the enemy and their own translation into the overcoming and triumphant life of the Son of God, knowing that by the indwelling Christ life they should be kept and are kept free from sin and its dominion, free from sickness and its power, through the Holy Ghost in them.

May God lead us all into the deeper and truer ascended life of our Lord, "For if when we were enemies we were reconciled to God by the death of his son much more being reconciled, we shall be saved by his life and not only so, but we also joy in God, through our Lord

Jesus Christ, by whom we have now received the atonement" (Romans 5:10, 11).

This article was published in September 1932 in The Pentecostal Outlook. *The editor added this note, "The above article was written twenty-one years ago, in June, 1911." Although Lake's account is not identical to some who were there at the beginning, it is nevertheless significant. John G. Lake was an early Pentecostal missionary and a prominent leader in the movement.*

Seeley D. Kinne

Larry Martin Collection
Courtesy of Jay Hearn
(Digitally Enhanced)

From Whence Is It?

Seeley D. Kinne

In a personal letter one says; "I am in trouble about some things. The present Pentecostal movement, is it of God, or is it a delusion? Have the people that talk in tongues, all over the land, got the real baptism?" As there are those who are candidly perplexed we will consider some of these difficulties.

Let us first try to get a look at things from above the scenes. A great battle is being fought between two great powers. One side is headed by Jesus Christ the infinite One, infinite in every respect that He can be thought of that is consistent with perfect holiness and love and benevolence. The other side is headed by that arch-fiend, Satan, Diabolis, the Accuser, who is full of the most insolent, malignant hatred to all that is good. So far as we know the principal battle ground is in this world in men. One of Satan's strong efforts is to counterfeit genuine godliness. To so imitate, appear as an angel of light, and so obscure the real as to make one feel there is no genuine work of God.

Man has been a constant failure and, looking from the apparent results, God's work and dispensations among men seem a failure. Moses was one of the best and greatest men God ever had, yet he angered the Lord several times. David and Solomon wrote some of the richest things in the Old Testament, yet there are serious sins recorded of them. So of the greatest men in the New Testament, Peter failed his Lord at the most serious moments. Paul assisted in the killing of the first martyr.

After man had failed and been swept away by the flood; again failed and God chose Israel a nation, and bestowed almost infinite pains to prepare them for the coming of the Messiah, they rejected Him and put Him to death. When the Holy Spirit had been poured out so wondrously upon the early church, they backslid and went into gross darkness for a thousand years. To this day degenerate, idolatrous Rome claims to be the original apostolic succession. The various sects of Protestantism stand out as the crystallized, fossilized successors of various mighty revivals of the Holy Ghost in modern times. The holiness movement split into factions over different phases of doctrine. So every dispensation God has given to man he has abused and degenerated from the life into a form, a doctrine, an experience, instead of keeping vital, living connection with the personal Christ.

This much we have written for a background to look at and compare the movement called Apostolic Faith and Pentecostal movement. That there should appear in this movement much that is faulty, spurious or Satanic would not necessarily convince a candid observer that is not of God, for the reasons above given that man has failed in the past of the grace of God, and Satan has succeeded in mixing in his workings.

The writer has been among the holiness people over thirty-two years, and heard many of the best preachers in that movement and attended some of its great camp meetings. I was in Azusa Mission soon after it was opened. I knew God was there. I had felt the same power of the Spirit many times before. I believed I had the baptism of the Spirit then, and that it was more than sanctification. About nine months after this and nearly three years ago, the Spirit succeeded in getting me under arrest and conviction by the word "for" in Acts 10:46. I saw that those Jews discovered the Gentiles received the gift of the Holy Ghost exactly as at the first; that is, with the sign of speaking in tongues. I said I never received the baptism as they received it. Many times during the first year and a half I was told I was a fanatic, teaching false doctrine, and was esteemed a dangerous man. Time and again after being told these things I went away and prayed and cried to God. I did want to be right. I sought to be perfectly open to the Spirit. I always came back to the same conclusion that it was God. One day I said, "Now I have done this for the last time, I know this is God." With all the prayerfulness, earnestness, and observation and light I have been capable of and, in addition to this, the deep powerful inward witness of the Holy Spirit, I know it is God. I submit the following reasons and observations:

1. When Pentecostal meetings are kept in the Spirit there is ordinarily more power than we ever saw in holiness or other meetings, and often they rise into a state of worship, revelation of the Divine presence, waves of joy, victory, love and praise with which we never saw anything to compare in the past. Pages could be written of the sights and scenes, many of them surpassing description. God has indeed visited men once more in these last days. We

have never seen such melting and breaking of hearts of both saved and sinner as frequently occurs in Pentecostal meetings. The outward visible glory of God is at times revealed.

2. Restoration of the gifts. While there has been considerable healing for some years and a little all along, there is much more in this movement than among other Christians combined, we believe, tongues, interpretation, prophecy, discernment and miracles heretofore very rare are found among us, and are increasing.

3. It has among its professors many of the deepest Christians who have been before the public for years. Their saintliness and grace has been much increased by this outpouring, and they have grown more in the months since being baptized than in the years of Christian life before. We have seen men and women who three or four years ago were drunkards, morphine fiends, fallen, changed into the sweetest, purest saints. Their growth has been wonderful indeed.

4. The power of the Spirit to expose sin and bring to repentance and restitution in this work is beyond all precedent in these days. The exposure of people who have been false and attempted to palm themselves off as Christians, and of those who have been deceived themselves, is often startling and most convincing.

5. More missionaries and a stronger missionary spirit is among its people than was ever known among any people in a much longer time. Saw near 50 missionary candidates at the Alliance, Ohio, camp last year. Through personal contact with and examination of everyone of them I can say I never came in contact with such a body of fervent, earnest, sensible, precious people in my life.

6. We are a persecuted people, a falsely accused people. But in many cases deep suffering has been borne in a saintly manner.

7. In its teachings under the openings of the Holy Spirit, the revelation of the personality, offices and character of the blessed Trinity, and especially of the Christ, are often very deep and wonderful. The character and workings of Satan are also uncovered. The nature, character and needs of men are more deeply discovered than ever before. There

is a character work going on in this movement that is a fulfillment of Luke 3:4-6.

8. If I might testify to my own experience, it would be to say that since receiving the baptism with signs accompanying has been the best part of my life. I am experiencing in a gracious measure what I have been under conviction for, for twenty-five years. Personal experience, communion, prayer, faith, everything multiplied. A deeper revelation of the personal Christ, and usefulness increased at least tenfold. A definiteness and certainty in dealing with souls. It is glorious. Hallelujah!

9. Such magnifying of Jesus as is seen in this work is beyond anything we have seen in the past. He is exalted and man is humbled.

10. This wave has only nicely begun. Wait a few years till some of those tutorage have time to develop under Divine training and you will see some men and women whom God can use to shake the strongholds of Satan.

11. Eros, perversions, self-exaltation, legalism, Phariseeism, fore-ordination, sectarianism, once-in-grace, free-love, forbidding to marry because the coming of the Lord is so near, Christian Science, Spiritualism, and other false doctrines Satan is trying to inject into the work. Some will get wrong. But these are not Pentecostal doctrines, and those who are trying to teach them in the name of Pentecost will soon fall out of the work or repent and get right. This is not a movement to formulate doctrines and theories, but to reveal the personal Christ. Those who stand and go through the sifting, continue faithful unto the end, will be gloriously saved and rewarded.

Seeley D. Kinne was a publisher and minster from St. Louis, Missouri. He attened the Azusa revival, but like many others, recieved his Holy Spirit baptism later. This testimony appeared in The Household of God *in March 1910.* The Household of God *was published by William Manley in Dayton, Ohio* *(see page 79).*

John G. Speicher

Larry Martin Collection

(Digitally Enhanced)

As Dr. Speicher Sees It

John G. Speicher

My dear Brother in Christ: Recognizing the value of your excellent paper as a means of communication, and in view of the many things that are transpiring in Zion City constantly, the many misunderstandings and the many prejudices, I beg of you the privilege of speaking through your paper to my many friends in this city and in many parts of this and other lands, hoping hereby to give a fair representation of facts as they appear to me.

In the first place, allow me to say that I am personally standing aloof from all the controversies as to the claims of either of the General Overseers. And I have taken no part in any way in any of the legal controversies entered into by any parties whatsoever. I have a deep conviction that there is another and better way for the solution of the difficult problems that are disturbing the peace of Zion. But I want also to declare that I have not given up my belief in the beautiful ideas of the Kingdom of God as set forth in the original plan of the Christian Catholic Apostolic Church in Zion. The only question is as to the feasibility of carrying into operation at this time these high ideals. There is no doubt in the world but that the real Kingdom of God upon the earth under the personal rule of Jesus Christ will be a highly organized government, but until then experience has proven that there is no man so strong, so pure, so full of divine love and unselfishness, as to make it desirable or wise to place all our earthly interests into his absolute control. Neither do I admit that the Christian Catholic Apostolic Church in Zion in either of it's branches represents the whole and only definite work of the Holy Spirit . . . [part of the article is missing here] . . . positions taken by many of my friends who are among the adherents of both or all the various divisions of Zion. I have no right to criticize them for their views, and I only claim the same privilege with them to hold to my views on these and all other matters; for, "are we not all brethren and have we not all one Father," and are we not all seeking the same "Heavenly City?" And have we not all trials and burdens enough that we can look upon each other with compassion and mercy, and seek to lighten each other's cares and sorrows, no mater how much we may differ theoretically?*

This is what I want to say to all the dear ones of Zion everywhere. It seems to me, in view of the apparent imminent coming of our Blessed Redeemer that, as we see the day approaching, we should be

*This article is from the Flower Pentecostal Heritage Center. When it was copied, a few sentences were cut off the page. A search of archives and historical societies in Illinois has failed to find an original.

exceedingly lenient in all our judging; casting away all prejudice, and with the spirit of forbearance seek to help those who differ from us by loving admonition and instruction. "Come, let us reason together." Let us reason concerning the things that pertain to our salvation and the salvation of the world and let us keep aloof from all controversies that will hinder us in the work of the Master.

It seems to me that what should concern us more than all other things is, first, our own growth and development in our Christian life and experience: and, second, the exercise of all our energies toward the conversion of sinners, beginning with those in our own households and neighborhoods.

This is one thing that especially attracted me to the people who worshipped in the Haven and the College on my return from California. I had been strongly set against this movement from it's very beginning in Zion City. I abominated it. I raised my hands in holy horror. The bugagoo of trance-evangelism, spiritualism, and other fearful isms rose up before me like a mighty nightmare. I opposed it with all my heart just as many of you dear people are doing today and just like you I refused to go near to investigate but took the exaggerated testimony of these who had been in attendance.

And I left Zion City for California in just this way, still bitter and opposing all these things which I did not understand.

But God was better to me than I was to His people. After several months of work and travel in the state of California I was thrown in contact with many of whom were known to me as former staunch supporters of Zion. I was especially impressed by the spirit of such people as dear Brother Overton of Santa Rosa, who has nearly $20,000.00 invested in Zion and who has no income whatever from his investments, but who has given his whole life to the work of the gospel. He entertained me in his home and spoke so kindly and considerately and had no harsh criticism for anyone. I attended the meeting and heard a dear sister speak, but I was not in a condition to receive or accept the things I heard and saw. Then in other places and finally at Azuza Street Mission in Los Angeles I saw and heard things that broke down my prejudice completely for I became convinced that it was no other than the wonderful power of the Holy Spirit that was working through his people. Not that all that I saw was to be accepted as such, for I saw much of the human element that entered in that caused me much distress at first, but this was so insignificant when compared with the wonderful results that I soon lost sight of the human in the more marvelous manifestations of the divine. And I also remembered that in the development of divine healing in Zion there were many things that were quite as objectionable. Hundreds of honest-hearted ministers came to Zion to investigate it's wonderful work but turned away disgusted and disappointed when they saw the leaders lay hold of the limbs of the lame and pull with all their might until sometimes serious injuries resulted. And they saw from 500 to 1000 sick present in one day in the healing room and only a score or two at the most were healed of all that great number. And they heard the extravagant utterances of the speakers and the harsh language and the peculiar testimonies of some of the healed.

But this in no way invalidated the claims that were made by the adherents of divine healing that it was scriptural and that it was applicable today, and that in the aggregate thousands were actually being healed of all sorts of disease.

But then, just as today, the great mass of humanity refused absolutely to investigate, but turned away because of the stories of gross inconsistencies which they had heard and because of divine healing differing from their preconceived ideas of things.

Now, let us soberly look at this "Tongues" matter and consider some of the facts, or all we can gather, and before we judge finally and refuse to believe, let us at least be fair enough to be intelligent critics if nothing more.

Let us consider the subject under several heads:

First—Is speaking in tongues scriptural? Second—What was the purpose of tongues? Third—Are the manifestations in Zion City genuine?

I want to take up these questions seperately. I want to deal fairly with them. I want to get at them just as I did with the doctrine of divine healing when I first heard of it.

First, as to the scripturalness of tongues, I need not try to convince any one of the fact that speaking in unknown tongues was a common thing in the early Church. We find it at pentecost. (Acts 2, 1 Cor. 12:10, 28 1 Cor. 14.) The fourteenth chapter of 1 Corinthians wonderfully reveals the condition of the church. Paul says in the 18th verse: "I thank God I speak with tongues more than you all." It was a source of thanksgiving to Paul that he spoke in tongues. Then we have Matt. 16:17, 18, which is so widely quoted in favor of divine healing: "These signs shall follow then that believe: In my nane shall they cast out devils; they shall speak with new tongues;"

etc. This undoubtedly had as much force for tongues as for healing. Then we have the incident of Cornelius and his household, (Acts 10:46) when they were baptized with the Holy Ghost they spake with tongues.

But I need go no further with this point. This is uncontroverted. The early disciples spake with tongues, cast out devils, healed the sick and preached the gospel generally.

Second–What is the purpose of tongues? I can do no better than to quote the Apostle Paul, (1 Cor. 14:32): "Wherefore tongues are for a sign, not to them that believe, but to the unbelieving." A sign to the unbelieving. God in His goodness willing to do so much to make it easy for us to believe. Faith is so weak today. Signs are as much needed as ever before. Praise God! He fulfills His word by sending latter-day signs.

So much criticism has been offered because of some irregularities, some apparent confusion; the confusion of the meetings; the lack of interpretation, and some other almost indefinable things. Paul says if there be no interpreter let them keep silent in the church (1 Cor. 14:28). But this simply proves that what has taken place in Zion City also took place in the Corinthian Church, that they spake without interpretation for a time. This is no longer done here, for now a number of persons have the gift of interpretation which did not pertain at the beginning of the speaking in tongues.

Third–Are the manifestations genuine, or from the Holy Ghost, or are they either spurious or demoniacal demonstrations?

So much has been said on this question, pro and con, that to express a mere opinion would have little weight. Let us have the "law and the testimony." First, what are the manifestations? What is it that is taking place in these revival meetings that are peculiar and subject to so much comment?

The things that impressed me particularly were the purported speaking in tongues, and the falling down prostrate of some of the people under the supposed power of God. The speaking in tongues was not confined to any one class, but old and young, men, women, youths, maidens and children would break forth in what at least appeared to be various kinds of languages and dialects. Some resembeled Chinese, some French, Latin, Spanish, Holland, and many others.

For a long time no one understood any of these tongues, not even the speaker themselves. Recently under the leadership of an evangelist, familiarly called Brother Tom, who comes from Los Angeles and who has been used mightily in many places in the conversion of sinners, there has come a greater freedom in speaking in tongues, and also a number of persons are claiming the power of interpretation. More wonderful even than the tongues is the way the Holy Spirit falls upon many of the people, even young children who put to shame the best preachers in the church in the way they stand before the people and preach the everlasting gospel. O, the power, the grandeur, the beauty of a child of six or ten years of age breaking forth in scriptural language and pleading with the people to turn to God with all their hearts for Jesus is coming soon! Then to go into tongues in such a beautiful way. And sometimes these tots speak for half an hour at a time, and it is all praise to God for the wonderful love of Jesus. This is the whole burden of their talk. Praise! Praise! Praise! The power of the blood! And pleading for their loved ones. O, how sublime! O, how pitiful! Truly the saying of Paul has come to pass, (1 Cor. 1:27-30): "God hath chosen the foolish things of the world to confound the wise; and God hath chosen the weak things of the world to confound the things which are mighty: and the base things of the world and the things which are despised, hath God chosen, yea and the things which are not, to bring to naught things that are: that no flesh should glory in His presence."

"He is taking little children and young people and simple hearted people and is speaking through them more powerfully than He has ever spoken through all the great Overseers and Elders and the hundreds of officers of Zion." (The ministry of Zion has been unfruitful for years. No one can deny it. We have been set aside and God is allowing us to pass . . . [missing text].

"But now," some one will ask, "are you sure these things are of God? May not the devil be deceiving the people?" All I can say in answer is this: "Beloved try the spirits." "Prove all things, hold fast that which is good." "No man can say that Jesus is Lord but by the Holy Spirit."

"No where do I find that the devil is in the business of preaching the gospel of Jesus or of praising God, or converting sinners. If he is in that business now, then he is converted and no such news has come to us yet. It is easier to say that it is of God. It presents less difficulty. "By their fruits shall ye know them." These people are themselves saved and are getting others saved. Some do foolish things and even wrong things, but they only claim to be human. They have the true missionary spirit. The vagaries, the fanatacism, the over zealousness of some will take care of itself as it does in all new movements. Give them a chance. Help to build up and do not tear down what is manifestly of God. Come and see. Lay aside prejudice and behold the wonderful work of God. Nearly all who have witnessed the recent scenes in the College and Tabernacle admit that at least some are genuine tongues and of God. If some, why not more? Decide for yourself and do not take the word of others.

I shall be glad to see any one and talk with them about what I have seen.

I am waiting on God for the enduement. When He is ready to send me forth again I am ready to go. Pray for me. Yours in the Gospel of Jesus.

John G. Speicher

This testimony was published in the Zion City News *on June 28, 1907. Mr. O. W. Davis, the editor of the* News *added this note:*

> *The recent rapid growth of the Apostolic Faith Movement in Zion City, which now claims the attention and sympathy of many of our best people, makes the following letter from Dr. J. G. Speicher of much interest at this time.*

Speicher was a medical doctor and a leader in the Austrailan faith healer John Alexander Dowie's Christian Catholic Church, serving as the "Overseer" of Zion City. He was one of the followers who deposed Dowie on charges of polygamy.

Charles Parham had first carried the Pentecostal message to Zion City, but no doubt Speicher's endorsement carried lots of weight with the movement. Some of early Pentecostalism's greatest leaders–John G. Lake, F. F. Bosworth, John Sinclair, William Piper and many more–came out of Dowie's church.

Is It the Latter Rain?

John G. Speicher

Editor Zion City News: May I again impose upon your good nature in order to inform my friends through the columns of your paper as to what is transpiring in our city, especially in the wonderful manifestations of which so many opinions have been given?

"There are many people in many parts of the world that are honestly desiring to know the exact and unvarnished truth concerning what is known as the manifestations of "Tongues," for no matter what decision we may come to as to the origin or source or cause of these manifestations, all who know anything about it most heartily admit that they are of a most unusual character, and that they are receiving greater attention than anything else that has ever occurred in Zion City."

"It is not my intention to review the work in general. Yet it is only fair to say that, as a constant attendant upon all the Tabernacle and other meetings, I have been thrown into close relationship with such men as Evangelist Thomas Hezmalhalch, John Lake, F. F. Bosworth, A. F. Lee, Elder Dietrich, Elder Brannen, Cyrus Fockler, and others, and they have proven themselves to be Christian gentlemen. Never have I heard one word spoken from the platform or in private that would bring the blush of shame to the face of the most modest woman or young girl. Their whole speech and conversation has been of heavenly things, and I am glad to say their ministry has brought great peace and joy into my home and into the hearts of the members of my family. And (no matter what their past lives have been) I am proud to be associated with these men in the ministry, and I would to God I had the experience and power that some of these men have in preaching the Word of God."

What I want to write of in particular are some of the experiences in my own immediate household. Just two weeks ago this evening there gathered in my home a company of young women for prayer and praise. My daughter Ruth, 16 years of age, was among the number. She had not been willing to admit that the manifestation of speaking in tongues was of God or that is was a desirable attainment. But during the course of the meeting several of the young women spake in tongues and seemed to address remarks to my daughter. When the interpretation was given it revealed that what was said was in admonition to my daughter telling that she was full of pride, that she was haughty, stubborn, disobedient to the voice of God, etc. That she must surrender to God and seek His face, and that then He would forgive her and baptize her with His Holy Spirit. At first she resented these personal remarks and felt inclined to leave the room, but as the girls pleaded with her, suddenly she fell upon her knees and implored the forgiveness of God, and sought for sanctification which she at once experienced. Then she also was baptized in the Holy Ghost and at once broke forth in praises to God in the Holland language. Since that time she has been overflowing with joy and she is constantly praising God in many different languages.

Yesterday dear sister Evangelist Johnson visited our home. Before she left we gathered the family together for prayer. While we were praying, my daughter and two sons burst forth in praise in foreign languages.

My eleven year old son has been speaking in tongues for more than a month and he is also able to interpret any tongue or language that is spoken by a person under the influence of the Holy Spirit.

We all ceased praying except my daughter who continued to pray most earnestly in tongues until she had spoken in more than twenty languages. Of these I could distinguish German, of which she knows very little; French of which she knows little or nothing; Holland, of which she knows absolutely nothing. She spoke for more than thirty minutes and was interpreted as she went along by my son, who told us what she was saying. That which she spoke in French was especially beautiful. The voice was ecstatic as she exclaimed, O, thank God for the deep, settled peace in my soul, O, I do not care for any of the things of this world. All I want is Jesus and He is coming soon.

In German she said among other things, "O, es ist so schone. O, Jesu Jesu, O, Unser Fader," etc. Then there was Chinese and many languages I have never heard but it was very easy to distinguish between them all. When she had finished in tongues she repeated in English what she had spoken and exactly corroborated my son's interpretation. Every word was either in prayer to God for His blessing upon some one, or else in praise to Him for what He had done for her and for us. She spoke with great boldness and power and the divine boldness continues in her daily life and she is a new creature. A great change has come into her Christian experience. She no longer cares what others may think or say or do. She has a deep longing to see sinners saved.

Now, this is the truth as best I can write it. I give it only that those which desire may get an idea just what some of these manifestations are like. Others have had greater experiences. These are not exceptional. I can only praise God, and ask Him to bestow the same precious gifts upon me in His own good time. I rejoice that I have been permitted to see this day. Who can desire to destroy a work that brings blessing to so many lives. Better were it that man should examine himself and see what he has done and is doing for God and humanity in bringing joy and peace into the hearts of the people, than to seek to take away from those whom God is blessing in this way the sweet peace that has come to them, and the new lives which they enjoy, which in no way injures any one, but is a boon and blessing to hundreds.

And the one great feature of this work is the wonderful missionary spirit that it inspires in the hearts of those who come under it's influence. About thirty of those who have been baptized in the Holy Spirit and speak in new tongues have gone out into other fields of labor and are being successful as soul winners.

May God prepare many more laborers for the harvest field, for the fields are now white unto the harvest. Do not hinder this work. Pray for it. Help it. Stand by it.

"Prove all things. Hold fast that which is good."

Jesus is coming again. Are you ready?

From Zion City News, *August 1, 1907.*

Apostolic Work

Addie M. Cook

"And it shall come to pass in the last days saith God, I will pour out my Spirit upon all flesh; and your sons and your daughters shall prophesy and your young men shall see visions and your old men shall dream dreams" (Acts 2:17).

"And these signs shall follow them that believe: in my name they shall speak with new tongues, they shall take up serpents, and if they drink any deadly thing it shall not hurt them, they shall lay hands on the sick and they shall recover" (Mark 16:17, 18).

We are glad to see that the Apostolic movement which began in Los Angeles, Cal., is spreading to many different parts of the continent, and some of the faithful ones in New England are praying "without ceasing" (Acts 12:5) that God will visit the barren portion of the country in mighty power. There is a great need everywhere and we rejoice greatly in all that God is doing in other places. Send your name and address written plainly to "The Apostolic Faith" Los Angeles, Cal., 312 Azusa Street, and ask for their paper. Subscription free.

This will give you a faint idea of the marvelous things God is doing. There are four or five different Apostolic papers printed in the country now and no price on any of them, no names mentioned as editors, all the work done without money or honor.

Don't pick up a few of the devil's counterfeits and hold them up before the world as a warning against this movement, and pass right by the hundreds of rich, beautiful, genuine nuggets of pure gold. Following are a few of the many testimonies we would like to present to our readers:

A leading Methodist layman of Los Angeles says, "Scenes transpiring here are what Los Angeles churches have been praying for for years. I have been a Methodist for twenty-five years. I was a leader of the praying band of First Methodist Church. We prayed that Pentecost might come to the city of Los Angeles. We wanted it to start at First Methodist Church, but God did not start it there. I bless God that it did not start at any church in this city, but in a barn, so that we might all come and take part in it. If it had started in a fine church, poor colored or Spanish people would not have got it."

Reports come from Denver that forty souls have received the Pentecost and are speaking in tongues.

"Cartoons in the newspaper were my first introduction to this meeting," said a brother, "and I said, this is what I have been praying for for years. I was warned by leaders that it was of the devil, but I came and got a touch of heaven in my soul."

There are three regular Pentecostal missions now in the city besides a number of cottage prayer meetings in which the Lord is working in power. In Monrovia, Pasadena, Sawtelle, Whittier and other points about here, as fast as workers are ready to go out, meetings are springing up.

Bro. A. C. Atherton, a Presbyterian evangelist from Greenfield, Iowa, hearing the glad tiding from Los Angeles, came 2500 miles, and the first night of the meeting he was slain under the power of God and said that one meeting paid for the trip. Afterward he received the baptism with the Holy Ghost and spoke in tongues. He then started home filled with a great cry to spread the good news.

News comes from Colorado Springs that souls are being saved, sanctified, and baptized with the Holy Ghost. Some are being healed also. A number are speaking in tongues. The Lord is calling some to be missionaries, and a number are expecting to go to different parts of the world. The gift of singing and playing instruments in the Spirit has been given. A child six years of age has the gift of tongues, also a person eighty years of age. A girl of twelve years preaches and sings in the Indian language.

A sister in Pasadena who was living a holy life before God and was honestly desiring all God had for her, arose in a Pentecostal meeting and said, "I do not ask for tongues but I want to love God with all my heart soul and my neighbor as myself," and immediately she began to speak with tongues.

Bro. J. C. Mackey, of San Diego, California, says, "I heard of the meetings in Los Angeles and it set me on fire. The Spirit said to me, 'You go.' I said 'I will.' I got my ticket and came and today I am saved, sanctified, and baptized with the Holy Ghost, and have the witness."

This article was printed in Word and Work *in April 1907 and tells many of the exciting things that were happening as the revival entered its second year.*

My Experience in the Baptism with the Holy Ghost

Saint Anonymous

My parents were charter members of the first Holiness Church organized in Southern California and the honor was conferred upon me of being named after its founder and first president. It was my happy lot to be taught principles of righteousness; and that salvation, when received, brought to the heart assurance of one's acceptance with God, and a life of holiness as confirming evidence. It was not, however, until I was almost twenty years of age that I became greatly concerned about my soul which resulted in deep repentance and a clear experience in salvation and holiness. That was in the fall of 1904.

During the year that followed a young friend and myself went to Colorado where we remained until September of 1906. Conscious of the presence and fellowship of the Lord whom I loved, I was yet conscious that there was something still lacking in my experience. But those among whom I worshipped seemed not to shed further light on my pathway than I was walking in.

During the spring of 1906 my mother began writing to me that a wonderful visitation of the Holy Spirit was falling in our home city, Los Angeles, Calif.; that a number of my old acquaintances were receiving the Holy Ghost with differing manifestations, chief among which was speaking with other tongues as the Church had done in the days following Pentecost. This was entirely outside my range of knowledge at that time either of the Bible or of spiritual things. Later she wrote that my father had received a beautiful anointing of the Spirit which had so mellowed his heart that even when he returned thanks at the table he would break down and weep. This was the first report coming to me which made a definite impression on my heart, for I felt this must be none other than a work of God if it bore such fruits of righteousness and tenderness.

Later on a copy of a little paper telling of God's work was received by me. My friend and I were then working on a large ranch in Southern Colorado. It would be hard to describe how the Spirit witnessed to my heart that God was working in a way such as I had never seen, but it felt in my heart something like the soft, warm, dripping of pleasant waters.

In September my friend and I returned to our native city. We attended on our first Sunday after arriving home, first the morning service among friends whom we had known, then went over to where the power of God was reported to us as falling. Never will I forget it. The altar service was on, people seemed everywhere seeking God. We were awe stricken, yet curious, and we just looked on. Much looked to us like the work of God, other things we did not understand. Soon a good woman, who had known me since I was a little boy, came over to me and as she approached and took my hand there was so much of love manifest by her and so much satisfaction expressed on her face that it did not take me long to begin seeking for myself.

With what reverence I attend the services, and as at first I knelt at the altar to pray a young man came to me and said if I would begin to praise the Lord He would fill me with the Holy Ghost. But I was not seeking the Holy Ghost just then. I had been separated from the fellowship of saints for some time and the first thought of my heart was "Search me O God, and know my heart: try me, and know my thoughts; and see if there be any wicked way in me."

Having assured my heart that it was all yielded to the will of God, and that I was fully accepted in the Beloved, I began seeking to be filled with the Holy Spirit and power. A remarkable experience came upon me one night a few days before I was satisfied that the fullness had been received. As I was praising and worshiping God, it seemed as though the Lord was dealing with my very physical flesh. After some time a lady came near me and quietly said, "Lord give this young brother rest," and immediately such rest came over my being as I had never expected to know this side of heaven. Quietly I waited before God marveling that one could live so near to Him as to be able to simply and quietly to speak to Him as this lady had and to have an immediate answer. I have never learned who this lady was.

After this experience I walked in rest and quietness, dwelling in the presence of God, with what seemed like a spiritual wall on either side of me. Yet I continued earnestly seeking in faith for the fullness which I believed was to be mine. It was on the night of October 2nd, that a young brother who had received the Spirit the night before, came and encouraged me to praise the Lord with my mind stayed on Christ Who had promised to baptize with the Holy Ghost and fire. That night, as I yielded, the Spirit came and I spoke with other tongues as the Spirit gave me utterance. The ecstasy I had expected did not, however, come that night. The next morning I ascended a hill near our home where was a grove of eucalyptus trees which I entered to pray. There the glory met me, as the Holy Spirit took my tongue and my whole being. How I was thrilled as language after language rolled from my lips as the Spirit gave me utterance.

More than twenty-four years have passed since then–years of blessed fellowship with the Father and with His Son Jesus Christ. Perhaps never a day since then has passed that I have not at some time in the quiet devotion of my own secret closet spoken in other tongues in sweet spiritual communion much to edifying of my own heart, and I believe to the glory of God.

There came also into my life with the baptism with the Spirit that happy consciousness that my salvation was in a Person more than in some certain experience. Before then I had worked hard trying to keep, my experience." If I were happy, I felt my experience was good; if trials oppressed, there was such a battle against doubts. But when He came, trying to hold on to my experience ceased and I found I had entered a life hid with Christ in God. Within I was so conscious of the living indwelling presence of the Spirit, while above all was the conscious presence and communion with my Father in heaven, and the Lord Jesus the precious Bridegroom of my heart. Yea, Christ seemed in heaven to be worshipped by me and in my heart to live through me at the same time. Rivers of living waters had come, and bursts of glorious sunlight from the world where blissful saints in glory dwell. The scripture was fulfilled, I had tasted the good word of God and the powers of the world to come. Not always since have I been permitted to live on top of the mountain. Many times have I been called upon to walk in the valley. But ever there has been the consciousness that I was not alone. The Spirit had come to abide forever.

Athough the author is anonymous, it is clear that this testimony was written by Ernest Swing Williams. First, parts of the testimony are identical to Williams' other written and oral accounts of the events. Secondly, he was named after James W. Swing, president of the Southern California and Arizona Holiness Association as stated on page 61.

Williams received his baptism at Azusa Street and later was promoted to General Superintendent, the chief executive position of the Assemblies of God.

This article appeared in The Pentecostal Evangel *on January 3, 1931. Used by permission* The Pentecosal Evangel.

Mr. and Mrs. M. L. Ryan

Larry Martin Collection

(Digitally Enhanced)

Brother Ryan Receives His Pentecost

Author Unknown

Rev. M. L. Ryan, a holiness evangelist and editor of *Light [Apostolic Light]*, Salem, Oregon, hearing the good news from Los Angeles, suddenly dropped in at the Azusa Street publishing office. After a few words of greeting, he went in to the upper room meeting and in about two hours after he arrived, he was baptized with the Holy Ghost and spoke and sang in tongues in the power of the Spirit. He has returned to Salem and a band of Spirit-filled workers have gone to Salem to help in a Pentecostal meeting there. Bro. Ryan says:

> "Little did I think that God had such a rich experience for so unworthy a person as myself. When I arrived in Los Angeles I had my mind made up I must seek for the Pentecostal Baptism at least one week before receiving it. To my unutterable surprise and joy, the power fell on me at once. The Holy Ghost prayed and spoke through me in tongues. One of the blessed privileges conferred

upon me was a place in that heavenly choir, the songs of which defy all power of human to imitate. Hallelujah for his unspeakable gift."

Ryan's testimony was printed in Word and Work *in April 1907. He became a leader in the early Pentecostal movement on the West Coast and an early Pentecostal missionary.*

Brother Andrew Johnson

Author Unknown

Andrew Johnson (or Jansen), of Sweden, then spoke. He passed on warm greetings from the Bible School at Oreboro, Sweden, also from brothers and sisters in Copenhagen, where they had had a glorious meeting recently.

Some years ago he was in Los Angeles, and had been much blessed in his soul. He was saved and experienced God's peace. In 1905 he became very hungry after God. He had a great desire to witness for the Lord. On May 13th he was baptized in water in the name of the Lord Jesus. He was consecrated by the laying on of hands, and witnessed for the Lord whenever he got any opportunity in stores and in the streets.

He was present at the very beginning of the glorious revival at Azusa Street Mission, but believes that he had received the Baptism of the Holy Ghost with signs before that revival commenced. This was the occasion he was at a meeting when Pastor Bramley was preaching. He listened attentively. His heart was filled, and he began to sing a new song. He sprang up from his chair and ran round the pulpit preaching. Then he sat up and clasped his hands and said, "I'm in Heaven."

He believed that he spoke in tongues at this time but after the revival broke out he became more hungry.

He went up a mountain side to pray. As he was alone with God he uplifted his hands and prayed for Los Angeles. Then he lost command of his tongue, and spoke in other tongues. But he began to fear that it might be himself. So he went to a revival meeting and asked them to pray that it might really be the divine gift. The power of God came upon him, and he sprang to his feet and began to speak in "tongues." Interpretation was given, and it was a warning to backsliders.

At Los Angeles he saw all kinds of people coming for the blessing. Many preachers came. A message came that he was to witness at Jerusalem. He soon saw that this meant Sweden, his homeland. On his way he stayed at New York, in the Rev. A. B. Simpson's Alliance Home. A sister was there trying "the Hunger Cure." She, however, got hungry for the Lord, and was soon filled with the Holy Ghost and healed immediately.

He took steamer to Gibraltar and witnessed there; then to Naples. "I had no friend, but I had God." As he sat in a public place he shut his eyes and prayed, and people passing by placed money beside him. Hallelujah! God is good to them that trust in Him. He had a wonderful journey to England, and left on November 19th, 1906, in a steamer for Gothenburg. One day after arrival he came to his home at Sherboro. He found himself dark in the spiritual world, and wondered if he was to go back to America. He soon found that God had work for him to perform. He began to attend meetings in a Baptist chapel. God bid him to lay hands on a brother, and the Spirit fell and he began to speak in tongues. A sister fell from the seat to the floor. Leaders of the church were angry, but the fire was now kindled. He was invited to Oerboro. Sometimes people would jump over the forms that he might pray with them. He went by request to the great Bible School at Oerboro, where more than 100 young people are sent out to many places in Sweden, from which requests come for Spirit-filled Evangelists.

"We must love our enemies. We lose much if we do not love. The witnesses of God have not much time left. Persecutions will only draw us nearer to Christ. I praise God for the gift of tongues."

Andrew Johnson was one of the first missionaries sent out by the mission. This report, from a German conference he attended, was printed in Confidence *in January 1909.*

Jessie Penn-Lewis

Larry Martin Collection

A Letter to Jessie Penn-Lewis

George Studd

Dear Sister in Christ,

Though a stranger to you, you may know my name and perhaps one or other of my brothers in England. But anyhow I feel constrained to write you a few lines in regard to your articles in the *Christian*–"An Hour of Peril."

For while I do see in your 4th article (Feb. 6th) that you admit that "large numbers in the U.S.A. have entered into an experience of the phenomena of the Spirit" (and this is most assuredly true), yet the whole tone of your articles is so much, so very much, of this movement is of the evil one; I am sure you are thereby preventing many from even seeking that fullness of the Spirit which has come through this movement to many of the best men and women, (sober and instructed in the Word) whom I know.

I have for the past 8 months come into close touch with this Apostolic Faith Movement, at first attending their meetings with some fear and suspicion–going by myself, and looking up to God to guide me in judgment and to keep me from evil. My unhesitating testimony is that while undoubtedly the Devil is working to imitate and counterfeit God's gracious work, as well as to openly oppose and ridicule it, yet I do not doubt–nay I am sure the work is of God.

I formed this judgment slowly and prayerfully–most certainly the outward manifestations of tongues and physical shakings etc. were not what drew me, nor made me form the convictions I have.

First and foremost, what moved me was the transformed lives, the beautifully transformed lives and manifest fullness of the Spirit of many whom I know well–some I have known for years before this movement began as earnest Godly men and women–to whom God came through this movement in His fullness–I have for five months now mingled with many of these, attending small prayer meetings in humble homes and elsewhere–and I can only say to the glory of God I never saw such a spirit of true intercession, such unity of the Spirit (in the prayer meetings) such spirit of worship and praise amongst a body of people–and it has been my privilege for the past 20 years to be associated with the saintly men and women in this country and in England as well as amongst the C. I. M. in China in 1887.

From the first I noticed that both in their literature and in their meetings and their personal testimonies:

1. They honor the Blood of Christ continually in its atoning and cleansing power.

2. They honor and give room to the Holy Spirit and expect Him to work.

3. They live in expectation and constantly testify to the near return of our blessed Lord.

4. They are missionary people in their prayers, their giving–and doubtless a good many have gone forth before God sent them and have made mistakes.

5. As to the money question (as far as I see them–and I have seen a good deal of them) they do indeed trust God for means–they neither beg, take collections nor even hint for money–and most of them that I know are walking of faith in this respect even as George Muller, Hudson Taylor and many others of blessed memory and some still living have done.

Of course I admit the Devil has sown tares with the wheat, and has mingled some spurious with the pure gold of God's own precious working–and he has thus succeeded only too well in scaring away many hungry, needy souls from ever beginning to seek God for the fullness they need.

Last September I left the Mission work with which I had been connected for more than 13 years because my colleagues would denounce, ridicule and oppose this Apostolic Faith Movement and this although living in Los Angeles, they had not attended one single meeting nor permitted themselves to come in contact with the Movement–hearsay evidence against it was readily welcomed and believed on almost any authority–things which I myself on investigation proved to be utterly untrue were not only believed but passed on to others–I don't say this bitterly, for I am still in love and personal fellowship with these same dear friends with whom I have lived and laboured for years–but just to show how much of prejudice and misrepresentation there is–I would add one other word of testimony viz. that it has been a great blessing to my own soul to mingle with and pray with these despised people–and I say it in the fear of God, before whom by His grace I am walking quietly and humbly, that He is responsible for the stand I have taken in favour of this Movement. Though, as I said before, I see and confess that the enemy has sown tares amongst the Lord's wheat–but where is not this true in any really spiritual work of God?–I have seen spurious Holiness work–as well as the genuine for years–as also in the work of conversion.

My old friend Cecil Polhill, (who went to China with my brother 23 years ago and is now on loan to the C. I. M.) has recently spent a month here in Los Angeles and has had opportunity to see the work and come in contact with many here–and I know he would endorse what I am writing–He is now on the Atlantic returning to England–and I wish you might have the opportunity of seeing and learning from him–He not only stayed in Los Angeles a month but he visited a number of other cities in the U.S.A. as well as Toronto, Canada–so that he really is able to speak from personal experience and close investigation.

Excuse me for writing to you at such length; but it has been on my mind for a week or more to write to you and to assure you I have not done so without much prayer and quietness of Spirit before God. I feel I ought to give you my testimony as you seem to get so much against this movement. Knowing the influence of your name and pen with earnest, godly people I felt grieved at the pessimistic and fearful way you have written of it. I think you will gather from this I am not averse to a word of warning being given (I believe it is needed) but, if I may speak out what is in my heart, I do feel that your articles are far too pessimistic and condemnatory of a movement in which God is surely doing wonderful things and bringing the fullness of blessing and the baptism of the Holy Spirit to many hearts not only in Los Angeles but all over the States.

Again I ask your pardon for writing you so long a letter; I would ask an interest in your prayers for myself that God's perfect will may be done in my heart and life.

I remain yours sincerely and humbly; in Christ,

George B Studd

This is a letter written from George B. Studd to Jessie Penn-Lewis. Penn-Lewis, well known in Great Britain and around the world, had taken it on herself to criticize the Azusa Street revival. Penn-Lewis had also been critical of the manifestations present in the Welsh revival. Some feel her influence led to the premature retirement of Welsh revivalist Evan Roberts.

Studd felt the criticism was unfair and takes her to task in this letter. To the best knowledge of this editor, this letter has never been published. Studd wrote from 227 South Main Street, Los Angeles, Cal. on March 4,1908.

Studd was a regular at the Azusa Mission. He occasionally taught in the day sessions. He is from a famous family in England. The family was very wealthy and Studd helped pay for the Azusa Street property. His brother, C. T. Studd, was famous, first as a cricket player and finally as a missionary to India, China, and Africa.

The original letter is in the Donald Gee Centre in Mattersey. The letter was given to the editor by Desmond Cartwright, with deep appreciation.

True Pentecostal Power with Signs Following

William Manley

The editor of this paper visited the meetings held in Los Angeles, not as a critic, but convinced before going that God was with His people there. The following notes were written by him while there.

The meeting last night was just what I expected. God had full control from first to last.

God's children here are filled with the Spirit. At times shaken and trembling under the power of the Spirit. They speak with the most intense earnestness I have ever seen and what they say is in the tenderest love. Not a harsh word spoken. No denunciation of any one, except in tender love. Some strong warning against the false teachers and blind guides in the churches.

The general appearance of the congregation indicate that they are poor, who hear about Christ, and hear Him gladly. I saw none whose garb indicated wealth.

About twenty-five colored people and about three hundred white people all one in the Spirit.

The singing had a deep spiritual power in it. No organ. No leader. From seven to ten the whole time was given to singing, prayer and testimony. Then a short fiery talk on some of the words of Isaiah by the preacher, W. J. Seymour, closing with an altar call for any who wanted anything from God. About ten bowed there, among them myself, for the fullness of the Spirit; for all God had for me on any line. I laid my whole soul, body and spirit open to Him to do as He pleased. I was very happy, and wholly surrendered to Him throughout the meeting.

Mrs. Evans, wife of a D. D., who speaks with tongues, said in her testimony that God had told her that she was to go to Oakland about the first of August to testify for Jesus, but that in four days she would see me face to face. That she had related this to Brother Smith, who replied that he had a letter saying that I was coming, And now she saw me, just as God had told her.

Two other women, both preachers and colored told that God tells them to go to Oakland. Both speak with tongues.

So you see God is going to bring a true Pentecost to Oakland. This is not my planning, but I am delighted.

A little boy about 12 years old, is sanctified and baptized with the Spirit, and speaks and sings with great power.

There was a most remarkable incident of the sweetest singing I ever heard by about half a dozen women, all in unknown tongues, in which at intervals one voice would die away in very plaintive strains, while the others carried on the song. Then the former would break out in rapid strong language filled with unction, and others would give tones as of singing in the distance. This was most enchanting, and filled with tender love.

This singing was led by Miss Moore who never could sing before, until she was baptized with the Spirit.

Several tramps and criminals have been converted and sanctified, and are speaking with tongues–all of them are very illiterate–showing the power of God in them.

The daily papers are throwing their influence against this work. But it is of God and they cannot overthrow it.

Part Second

Yesterday was the most wonderful Sabbath I ever knew. The Holy Spirit controlled during the entire day. Outbursts of Holy Spirit Pentecostal power came again and again in the meeting, both Saturday and Sabbath, thrilling every soul. Songs right from heaven, in foreign languages, in which sometimes ten to twenty voices mingled, all foreign; but the same languages, thrilling and finding or touching the same chord in the souls of all the children of God.

This is the most heavenly place I ever was in. My soul is charmed and filled, and is dancing for joy. This is God. Wonderful! Wonderful!! Wonderful!!!

Five persons who speak the language spoken in Palestine are commanded of God to prepare for that land, to carry apostolic power and tongues back to Jerusalem, as they had it on the day of Pentecost. God has shown them their tickets for the trip, and all supplies from Him. But no one knows where the money is to come from. I understand that God has shown them the vessel that they are to sail on, and fixed the time, first part of September. He tells them that Jesus will not come until this Holy Spirit Pentecostal preaching returns to the east again, and spreads throughout those lands.

Jesus has given by special revelation power to raise the dead to three Spirit-filled preachers–two women and one man. Two of these have already gone to India and the other, I understand, is going to Oakland soon.

A boy from India, about 22 years old, who could only speak a few words in English, has been converted, sanctified and baptized with the Holy Spirit and has been given the English language, and speaks the wonderful works of God in our own tongue, wherein we were born. Will this convince you that these people are given tongues by the power of God. This is God's work, and is marvelous in our eyes

A minister from England, who never could sing, is now baptized with the Holy Spirit, and sings with heavenly strains in some foreign tongue, and speaks several foreign languages. He had learned German, and told us yesterday that a colored woman here, who cannot read, is speaking as pure German as was ever spoken from the throne in Germany. Another man, a German, corroborated these statements.

Many persons were healed here yesterday. Oh, the power of God here is wonderful. Pentecost, true Pentecost, has come again. There is no use of denying it. God is here.

The public meetings which have continued for four months, closed last night for one week, that the workers may meet alone, daily, with the Father, Son and Holy Spirit for instruction.

Upwards of eighty are now speaking with other tongues.

The Nazarene minister, La Fountain, I am told, preached a sermon a week ago telling his people that this work was not of God, and warning his people against it. But the people are coming from there, and are seeking for the baptism of the Holy Spirit and some are speaking with tongues.

Part Three

Owen Lee, a young Irishman, a converted Roman Catholic, who has been sanctified and baptized with the Holy Spirit, and who speaks several tongues, was so overwhelmed for hours that he was speaking in tongues in a low tone, and with both hands making the deaf and dumb signs, as fast as his hands could move; at times with such rapidity that the eye could not trace or record the different signs given. In all this he did not seem to know that there was any person in the room but himself.

This young man arose several times, and in a very soft tone, with hands still making signs, and at times uttering some words in a foreign tongue, told us what the Holy Spirit had said to him.

He first arose and said he had been talking about Jesus and salvation to a large crowd of Catholic people and among them three priests. There were some Protestants in the crowd who listened, and were greatly moved. He asked all of us to pray for him, for God was sending him to his own people. He said God told him he would have more faith after this week.

The Lord told him we all lacked faith. That if we would only believe, great works would be done. That we must trust Him (God), and He will give us wonderful power this week.

A brother arose and gave us a description of a town in Africa with hills surrounding it, where he was to preach.

He is very happy in prospect of going to the dark continent.

Brother Anson [Ansel] Post, a former Baptist minister who is the most fluent and powerful speaker in foreign tongues, and who can interpret what he says, has been preaching in our tent in Pasadena, and several persons there have been filled with the Holy Spirit and speak with tongues.

A man, attending these meetings, in vision, saw two devils come in, one tall and stout, the other smaller. These two demons seized a man who was standing with a book in his uplifted hand and took him out.

The next night two policemen, one tall and stout, the other smaller, came into the tent and seized Bro. Post who was preaching with the New Testament in his uplifted hand.

At the trial Bro. Post made no defense and offered no witnesses but submitted to the powers that be. During this trial the man who saw the demons in a vision, saw an angel standing beside brother Post during the trial.

The Lord told Brother Post to fear not, that no man should set on him to harm him. That He had much people in this city.

The Court fined Brother Post $50 or fifty days in prison for disturbing the peace and for refusing to take down the tent.

This eye-witness account of the revival appeared in The Household of God *in September 1906. Manley was the editor of the periodical which was published from Dayton, Ohio.*

The Apostolic Faith Mission

Courtesy of the Apostolic Faith
Portland, Oregon

A Letter to E. J. Phillips

George H. Thomas

We went one morning to the Azusa Mission, where "Pentecost" is said to have first fallen in California. The first impression on nearing the mission was a wooden building that badly needed repairing and painting. On the outside were the words painted in large letters, "Apostolic Faith Mission." My guide tried the door which was unlocked so we entered and walked up a number of steps to a large room which is used as a meeting place, in which was a number of chairs, a reading desk and on the wall a chart. While we were looking round and speaking a coloured lady came out of another room and introduced herself. She was Mrs. Seymour the widow of the pastor who had been in the place for some years (I understand her to mean from those early days of 1906). She gave us the impression during the conversation, that the people who at that time worshipped there, and had now left and gone to other places of worship had gone back from the real thing and she and the small company who met there were still holding true to what they had at first. We went to the room beneath which was larger than the one above, but was now seldom used. The walls of this lower room were whitewashed and rough looking. Mrs. Seymour said that it had been a place of worship even before the falling of the Holy Spirit in 1906. The building was a striking contrast to the beautiful Angelus Temple which seats about 6,000 people and is filled with worshippers who believe in the Full Gospel. It shows too the wonderful workings of the Lord during the 20 years since the Holy Spirit came to Los Angeles. Besides the Angeles Temple there are two other large Pentecostal Assemblies in Los Angeles. Mrs. Seymour invited us to speak at their service the following Sunday, but we were obliged to return to San Diego, so had to decline.

This account of a visit to the Azusa Street Mission, Los Angeles is from a letter written from George H. Thomas to E. J. Phillips on June 4, 1926. This is a good description of the mission and it's ministry about four years after William J. Seymour's death. It is obvious that things are in a steep decline. The mission never recovered and was eventually forclosed on and torn down. Today the location is the plaza of the Japanese Cultural Center.

Thomas was an Elim minister from Britain who was working as a missionary out of San Diego, California and ministering to Mexicans. He was in Los Angeles attending a meeting of Pentecostal leaders when he visited the mission. Thomas later became secretary to the Elim Missionary Society in England.

The letter is in the Elim Archives and was given to the editor by Desmond Cartwright, with deep appreciation.

Kent White

Larry Martin Collection

A Letter to Alma White

Kent White

Dear Alma:

I am going to mail you some papers, and name some pieces that I want you to read. I am satisfied that you will read them now, for my next step will be to go into meetings separate from the Pillar of Fire Church, and this I do not want to do. Everything will be ended then. So this is the crisis. I know you will grant my request and read the articles I have marked in these papers. Then I want you to write and tell me what ones you have read, as I am going to keep a list and know what you have done. Of course I love you and want to be with you, but I am not without honor now only in my own home and Church.

In the first place I am going to convince you that the "Tongues" was not brought into existence by the colored man (Seymour) in Los Angeles, yet you and I must be just. We do not know what God worked out in Seymour's heart and life the few weeks after he went through Denver, before he broke out with the Spirit ("tongues") on him in Azusa Mission. I believe God chose him, one of the despised race, so that man might not glory, and then let him drop out. Anyhow it is the Holy Spirit's personal movement, not man's. I have been told that Seymour had the Holy Spirit at one time, and was very humble.

Now Alma, I am going to put the pieces down in the order that I want you to read them. Also Charles and others; and then you write me about what is being done.

When the Holy Spirit takes possession of the body and manipulates the vocal organs, a great faith comes for healing; and this gift of tongues fills the soul with the glory of God, for it is from this glory that the "tongues" arise.

You cannot throw God's word overboard. You do this and damnation will come sure.

Your scripture you got, Malachi 2:2-6, frightens me. It was surely of God. I had been feeling this; and then for you to refer to this it made me tremble. O my soul, it would kill me for things of this kind to come into your life, but I had had presentiments and fears, and have written them down. I even said this morning, that the way I felt I would not go out with a market basket on my arm, from Bound Brook to Zarephath, to get what I believe would be left of the Pillar of Fire organization after eighteen months, if they resisted and fought the Holy Spirit's gift of tongues.

Now Alma, God is going to sweep away some of the refuge of falsehoods in regard to the "tongues" that you are hiding behind. Then darling, you will have to look out. At three strokes God swept ancient Jerusalem out of existence, and sealed the captivity of seventy years. You think, dear sweetheart, of your blessings, papers, books, buildings, and our two boys, being turned to curses. I would now gladly die a dozen deaths to save you from such a thing if God would accept it.

Now Alma, you said you loved me still, even If I would not come home. I did not mean to say that I would not come home, but that God would not let me come.

After I left Brooklyn (on the 13th of August) the Lord showed me things that I did not see before. It was a painful ordeal through which I passed, when I was counting cost of boys and wife and the people I loved. But Alma, you cast your husband's testimony aside as unworthy, and God took me away from you. I can say with Job, "The Lord gave and the Lord taketh away; naked came I into the world, and naked I go hence." It is not that I do not want to come home, but He will not let me until there is a change. I wish the whole Church could know my heart as it is before God, but they will not unless you read them some of my letters and heart-utterances and experiences. Some day God will let them see. Some day indeed the mists will be cleared away, and you will see me right in the midst of the battle.

Now there are people in the Church who will accept the truth as soon as you get out of the way. You are standing in God's way. In mercy He is sparing you. You are standing out against His word and the Godhead. He may bless you in a measure on the ground you occupy, to encourage you and lead you on into this experience. Your past blessings may become a snare to you and let deceit and high-mindedness cause you to trample God's word down. You are now on the battlefield in line with God's shot. He may for a short time order His guns to one side. Then if you do not take warning He will shoot you down–three shots–three shots took Prince Scott off the field. The battle is on. The Bridegroom is waiting. God has no time to trifle. It would make angels weep for His batteries to be turned on you. I would gladly go and be shot to pieces myself in your place. I feel I cannot stand it. You are in the way of God's word.

The Pillar of Fire is not bringing the Latter Rain. The Latter Rain has got to come, and with it Satan will have his counterfeits. The Holy Spirit can work nowhere so mightily as He is now working in the ("tongues") movement on the earth. I am astonished at what I find out about it since I left home.

I would like for Arthur and Ray to read these tracts and papers that I mail to you. I want them to know that their father has some foundation for his course outside the Bible. Now Alma, if you love me you will write and tell me what pieces you have read as requested and who reads them.

In a far land,

Kent White

This is one of only a few chapters in this book that contain the story of a person who (as far as the editor now knows) was not present at Azusa Street. Yet, Azusa Street and William Seymour are both mentioned.

The letter is written by Kent White to his estranged wife, Alma. It was sent from Beverly, West Virginia on

September 1, 1909 and was published in Alma's 1926 book, My Heart and My Husband. *Kent and Alma White were co-founders of the Pillar of Fire (originally called The Pentecostal Union), a significant Holiness movement at the turn of the twentieth century. The Whites had a very unstable relationship based partly on Alma's unwillingness to submit to the authority of her husband. Kent believed that he, not Alma should lead the church. She forcefully disagreed.*

A final fracture came to their marriage when Kent endorsed the Apostolic Faith movement. He became acquainted with the "tongues movement" in Denver and received the Holy Spirit baptism evidenced by speaking in tonuges in England. The two separated and never reconciled.

Subsequently, Alma became one of the Holiness movement's greatest critics of Pentecostalism. No doubt, whether unfair or not, she blamed Pentecostalism for the loss of her husband.

In a chance meeting, William Seymour had stopped at their mission in Denver on his way to Los Angeles. Her book, Demons and Tongues, *contains this unflattering description of Seymour:*

> *He was very untidy in his appearance, wearing no collar, and had a greenish-looking brass button exposed in the band of his shirt. In my evangelistic and missionary tours I had met all kinds of religious fakirs and tramps, but I felt that he excelled them all. There was a cause for this. The Lord knew that Satan was going to use him the outbreaking of the so-called "Pentecostal" movement with the baptism of unknown tongues, on the Pacific coast; and permitted me to see the person that the devil was going to use, before the winds of perdition began to blow.*

White also said that when Seymour prayed at her table she felt, ". . .serpents and other slimy creatures were creeping all around me."

It should also be noted, however, that White's prejudiced view of Seymour was colored not only by her broken home, but also because she was an unrepentant racist and a very public proponent of the Ku Klux Klan. In 1925 she published a book, The Ku Klux Klan in Prophecy *where she said the Klan ". . . program must be carried out if the country is saved from moral, social, and political ruin."*

A Wonderful Ministry in Song

Sarah Haggard Payne

From babyhood I penetrated the regions of the unseen. I kept company with angels who guided me into safe paths as my feet wandered seeking, seeking that that would satisfy my not-understood desire; and but for their good offices, I would have drifted into destruction long years ago. I am writing this article at the age of fifty-four, and for the comfort of someone who perhaps walked and still walks in a similar path.

As far back as I can remember I loved music. I sang on any stage I was allowed to sing on at the age of six and have kept it up ever since, gladly accepting any opening until I have sung, an unknown singer, in jails, county poor farms, county hospitals, orphan homes, and countless places no one else would go to; in hundreds of schools all over the United States, all kinds of societies, Crittenton homes in many states, in houses of ill-fame and railroad shops, using all kinds of instruments, good, bad, and indifferent. I have sung on the streets time and time again, and more than otherwise have been received kindly, and hearts were comforted. But not until 1904, when I consecrated myself and my all to God, did I lift up a soul, to my knowledge, to God. If I did, I did not try to, and I did not know it. I always believed in God. I inherited faith from my parents. All children should. I believed, but so do the devils believe, and tremble. In the year of 1904 I gave up to God and answered a call that I had heard three times, and then and there on rising from the altar I saw and knew I was in the hands of the Holy Ghost who would be my teacher in all things.

I had never composed songs in the sacred line, only two, "The Magdalene," and "Come Unto Me," both showing the lack of holy inspiration, and fall flat even now when sung. At once I felt placed in a holy atmosphere of melody and began to hear voices, one or many, and musical instruments, but for years I was alone in my new discovery save my twin sister, Mrs. Mary Anderson (Walling, Tennessee) who heard heavenly singing, and several times she heard angel voices singing my songs, one of them being, "I Fell in Love with the Nazarene," she never having heard it, and she sang the chorus to me perfectly, just at the time I was having it published.

In 1904, a few weeks after my consecration, the Lord gave me a vision of a golden rainbow of seeming fire, out of which He spoke to me, promising to help me in my new work, sacred song composing. None scarcely believed this story, but God showed it to me too clearly to doubt it and through all the turbulent waters of tribulations at the hands of my friends, whose helping hand I needed, I stood alone, save God and the angel host who strengthened me, and comforted me with songs and music.

Then the Holy Ghost and fire came, and I feared no longer. I was in His school and learned all about composition in song, literature and execution on instruments, and when He comes upon me I can sing. So often I heard other voices sing with me, and many stringed instruments accompanying me, but when I told it people would shake their heads and look wise and troubled. They thought I was either a spiritualist trying to be a medium (and that is one thing I know nothing on earth about), or a crazy illusionist. But I knew where I was and where I had been from childhood. I had heard God's call and saw His leadings, so I spoke when I felt led and kept silent when led, and just let all say and think as they chose. I said like Esther, "I will go in unto the King, and if I perish, I perish!" Well, she did not perish, and neither have I. Praise God!

I received my baptism, immersion in the fire of the Holy Ghost in 1907 at the old Asuza Street Mission, and that same night heard the real message of His soon coming and a few nights later heard a legion of angel singers sing my song, "Behold, I Come Quickly," singing unbroken verses in the last chapter of Revelation with a line or two in other parts of the Bible, and as they vanished I arose and sang in pure joy the chorus, "Glory, Hallelujah, He is coming soon, Coming to the children of men!"

Then I, like others, saw wrong things among the members of the Pentecostal assemblies, even among those who spoke in tongues, and thoughts of doubt began to rise in my mind, not doubt of God's Word, nor in my own experience, but doubt concerning the people in this new movement, until I lost what I received at Azusa St., and grew dark in my soul and went into worldly things. While in this state I heard no more angel voices nor heavenly music. I investigated again and nearly made a fatal mistake by writing an article against the movement.

God spoke these words to me one afternoon as I stood on the pier at Ocean Park, Cal., "Ecce homo." I heard the words three times and seemed to see them written in the sky, and instantly I was transported from 1910 to the beginning of the world. All things were new, and God said, "It is good!" I went to an encyclopedia and found "Ecce homo" meant "Behold the Man!" referring to Jesus before Pilate. I did not speak a new language then but God did, and I was convinced, and sought a renewed connection with the third part of the triune God, the Holy Ghost.

In 1911 at a tarrying place, I received the desired touch of the King's sceptre and He said, "What is thy wish and what is thy desire?" I said, "That I may lift Thee up in this song work and that I may be freed from the flesh in song, that Thou mayest be able to lift the hearers up, up, up, high enough that they may be able to hear the heavenly music so that they can praise God as they never did in song before and rejoice as they should in Thee."

Sarah H. Payne lived in Ocean Park, California when she wrote this article. It was published in The Weekly Evangel *on January 13, 1917 as "The Fulfillment of a Life Dream: A Wonderful Ministry in Song." Although the testimony gives little details of Payne's experience at Azusa Street, it does tell the story of an early Pentecostal believer's struggle with doubt concerning the movement and demonstrates how common angelic and spiritual visions were to some early Pentecostals. Payne's article continued with several other conflicts that she faced after her Holy Ghost baptism.*

Used by permission The Pentecosal Evangel.

Barney Moore

Photo Used by Permission
Flower Pentecostal Heritage Center

Glorious Miracles in the Twentieth Century

Barney Moore

Under the preaching of a Methodist missionary from Utah I was converted in 1901. He was preaching nearly everything that is now preached in Pentecost, though he said he did not understand it, he just saw it in the Word. One Monday night, after much meditation and prayer, I went to the Methodist church and knelt at the end of one of the pews for quiet prayer. While praying, it was as though the heavens opened and a rushing mighty wind filled the church. When this power fell on me I went toward the rear of the building and then up the other aisle. By the time I had reached the front the power had fallen over the congregation and about a third of the people were slain under it. Some in the rear of the building fled to the street; the pastor ran behind the organ and his wife hid somewhere else. I saw the pastor when he put his head out and asked me to pray. When I started to pray something broke loose and I prayed right out in a language I had never heard. The pastor said, "What has happened?" I said, "What we read of in the second chapter of Acts has happened." The revival continued until eighty-five were converted and a high school teacher received the baptism in the Spirit. And such singing!

The pastor said, "I think, Brother Moore, you ought to go to school and prepare for the ministry." The way was opened for me to go to Taylor University, where there was a praying band, and the power would fall every time we prayed together. But we did not understand anything about Pentecost. When I would pray I would sometimes speak in tongues; and because this was all new to me I would sometimes get afraid that I was a little "off." I would frequently waken in the night singing in tongues and feeling as light as a feather. I knew this was extraordinary but did not understand it, but someone explained to me that it was what happened to those who had the call on them to preach, and I supposed that that was so.

My first pastorate was in Urbana, Ill. in 1904, and there the power fell. A lady spoke in classical Hebrew and Latin, and the people wondered what in the world had happened to her. The professors from the State University at Champlain came to listen, and they recognized and understood these languages. We asked the professors what she was saying, and they replied, "She is talking to us fellows who are too highly educated to take in the simplicity of the truth of the gospel."

The city officials became very angry at the demonstration of the power of God and incarcerated me for twenty-nine days in the city prison. Those were days of prayer and meditation. We were usually so busy we could not get as much time alone with the Lord as we would have liked, so the Lord took this way of saying, "Come ye a part and rest awhile." During the imprisonment I gained about a quarter of a pound a day; and when released I seemed to be fatter and fairer than my enemies. They could not understand this, for they had fed me on hard tack and bean soup, and an imitation coffee out of a peach can. They turned the heat off, and during freezing weather I lay on the concrete floor with a newspaper for my bed and a coat for a pillow. I would say Hallelujah on my right side, Praise the Lord on my back, and Glory to God on my left side, and sing when I sat up. This stirred the enemy in the hearts of the officers and they threatened to turn the hose on me, but I said, "You can never put out the fire that way, for this fire came from heaven."

But the city officials were called into question for this incident. The mayor, the police judge, the chief police, and all connected with it were dismissed, and I was exonerated. The prosecuting attorney told me to go ahead with a free hand and preach all I wanted to, that we were living in a country of free speech, with no ban on religion. I told him my lungs had been healed and that was the reason they could hear me preach a block or two away.

Later I was married, and while we were in a revival in Maryland we received the call to the foreign field; but money was so scarce in that section we did not know how the funds would be provided. About that time we heard of the power falling at Azusa Street in Los Angeles and a holy awe settled on both of us; we longed to go. We began to pray for funds and a letter came with $115 in it. Then more money followed, and we were able to go. While at those meetings we received light on what had been happening in our own lives–for my wife had also received the baptism in the Spirit, when a light like that of the noonday sun surrounded her and she spoke in many languages. She did not tell anyone about it for several days, but finally she ventured to mention it to one of the most spiritual women she knew, who replied, "I received the same thing several days ago in the kitchen." From Los Angeles we went to Oakland where for eighteen months we had a constant revival, preaching three times a day.

In the years that followed the Lord laid Japan very heavily on our hearts and in 1914 we set sail for that land. My first message in that country was given at Sister Bernaur's mission, her minister interpreting. Some students from the Imperial University happened to be present, one of whom was preparing to fill the place of ambassador. During the message the power of God fell, and this young would-be-ambassador went down on his back on the floor. This caused a great commotion and several hundred people gathered outside, it seemed as though the whole street was blocked with people. My interpreter, who was sitting on the floor in Japanese style, jumped clear over my head and made a rush for the door, and began preaching to the crowd outside, telling them that the prophecy of Joel was being fulfilled there that night. The Holiness church was close by and their meeting had just closed, so many of them were standing outside listening as this young man preached a most remarkable sermon on the power of God.

Afterward I questioned the young interpreter concerning how he received this great blessing. He said that he first went to the Salvation Army, where he found a little water and felt a little wet. Then he heard of Mrs. Bernaur's mission and went there, where he became very much wet and had waters to swim in. His face was beaming with light. He came with me to Kobe and it was not long before we had a good many of the Y. M. C. A. boys converted, thirty-five of them.

Our neighbor's son was converted through listening to wife and myself at family prayer. She would play on the folding organ and together we would sing songs. One evening he came in and knelt with us, saying, "I am saved." And we knew he was, we could feel it. Soon he brought in a dark-faced, evil looking young fellow, named Yamaguchi, a young man with dissipation written on his face. Our new convert got down beside Yamaguchi and said, "Repent in your heart of all your sins and they will be all taken away, and you will get the same thing I have." He worked with this fellow until he began to cry, then by and by he rose, saying, "It is in my heart."

Yamaguchi was the young man who brought groceries to Sister Atchinson. When she saw him coming the next morning she said to her husband, "Something has happened to our grocery boy, I don't know what it is but he looks different." When he came she said, "What is the matter with you, Yamaguchi?" He replied, "God saved me and put a great joy in my heart last night at the Moore's home." It was wonderful to see him saved when he had been so deeply dyed in sin and in Buddhism.

We moved to Yokohama and built a chapel in a thickly populated residence section. (It was later destroyed by the earthquake.) Here we saw the power of God fall on thirty-five at one time when they rose right up from their seats, with hands raised toward heaven, and began singing in something that was not Japanese. And such healings! A lady came who had a cancer on her left breast, saying, "Teacher, can God heal this?" "Yes," we replied, "He can heal that if you will believe." She said, "I do believe." We said, "Will you believe that God will heal you now?" "Yes," she answered, "because the doctor has just told me that within four days this will eat into the vital parts of my heart and I must die." We called for the congregation to pray, the power of God fell upon her and she was filled with the Holy Spirit. She sat down on a front seat and began speaking in another language, and all through the service she was softly speaking in tongues, though not loud enough to disturb us at all. When the meeting was over she bowed and went out. Reaching home she rolled back her kimono and the old cancer dropped out. About three nights later she came back to the meeting with the tears of joy rolling down her cheeks. She went around to everyone, saying, "See what God has done for me." Even the hole where the cancer had dropped out was healed, only a little scar was left.

We were called to Isamagahara, a wilderness section of Japan, and conducted services throughout that part. In the first section where we held our meetings there were six chiefs, or heads of small tribes from the old feudal regime. These would not associate with other Japanese people, and the government did not collect any taxes from them. God started to work in a remarkable way. One morning a man left the meeting and went back about fifteen miles, telling the people as he went along that a man from America who represented the living God, and come to his village and was preaching a joyful salvation. He said, "My countrymen are receiving the joy of heaven in their hearts and the sick people are being healed." Filled with enthusiasm, and running at a dog-trot, he went along shouting out the good news.

A man from a village about fifteen miles distant stopped and listened to him; then calling his wife and son and daughter, he said, "I have heard a rumor that sounds like a miracle. Take off your kimonos." Placing his family in a row, he got a tub of water which held about ten gallons; then pouring it over his wife he said, "In the name of the white man's God, who is blessing the people over there in that village and giving them joy and healing, I wash away your sins." He repeated the process with his son and daughter, and then poured a big tubful over his own head.

We heard of this but did not have a chance to visit him, so we sent him a Bible. He began to worship the Bible and pray to the God of that Book. When we heard this we could stay away no longer, and made arrangements to go there. We found them with shining faces, saying they were very happy and were trusting the heavenly God. We read to them from the Bible. My, how the tears streamed down their cheeks as they bowed to Jesus, the Son of the great heavenly God! We baptized them in the proper way, and the whole family received the baptism in the Spirit with the speaking in other tongues. The man and his son began to preach the gospel in the villages around about, and have been doing so ever since.

But the wife took seriously ill with dropsy, swelling to an abnormal size, and finally becoming unconscious. After several days of unconsciousness, in which some declared she was dead while others thought she still lived, the doctor cut a long gash in her face and another in her body to see whether there was life. She did not bleed, neither did water ooze out, so he pronounced her dead. At this her husband, who had been walking the floor wringing his hands, began to cry out, "O God, I cannot spare my wife, I must have her back to help me." Suddenly the wife sat right up, the swelling felt her body, and the wounds healed.

I went and talked with her myself, asking her about this experience. She said, "Teacher, I went up to the gate of heaven and looked in and saw Jesus and the apostles—Peter and John and the rest of them. Such great throngs of people were there. A message came to me, 'You cannot enter now but must go back and join your family, then you can come later.'" After receiving this message she said she got up and cooked supper for her family. The crowd that had been there fled; some ran through the rice fields, even getting their clothes wet as they ran, but they were so panic stricken they did not notice where they were going. When the earthquake came in 1923 this little family prayed for the safety of my wife and myself for three days and nights, until they heard we were alive.

This brother, (Pastor Soeno), who knew nothing of the coming of the Lord, never having been taught concerning it, had a vision in which he saw the saints being resurrected. He saw living people from England, America, China, Africa, the islands of the sea, and every country in the world, all going toward a wonderful light that was shining from the sky, and they met Jesus in the air.

Since the earthquake of 1923 in Japan the records show there has been at least one tremor a day. Earthquakes, revolutions, plagues and famines have become the order of the times which mark the closing days of the dispensation. We saw all we had swept away in fifteen seconds, proving that we must not trust in uncertain riches or in temporal things, but in the living and true God.

This is the testimony of a man who attended the services at Azusa Street, was touched there and continued in a lifetime of service to God. Moore and his wife became Assemblies of God missionaries. The testimony was published in The Penetecostal Evangel *on January 17, 1931. Used by permission* The Pentecosal Evangel.

En Route to Africa

G. W. and Daisy Batman

Bro. and Sister G. W. Batman who last wrote from New York on their way to Monrovia, Liberia, Africa, are tried and true workers and have the enduement of power from on high and the fitness of the gift of tongues. Their faith was severely tested as to their fare. A brother who paid the most of their fare was praying the night before they left that the Lord would give him some revelation. So that night the Lord showed him a lamb that was tied and told him to loose it and as he did so, a great Shekina glory shone in the room. The Lord showed him, later that it meant the missionaries he was to be the means of sending on their way. They started with faith in God though they were taking their three little children and their destination is called the "white man's graveyard." They did not have more than their fare to New York. They have the gift of healing and we believe God will wonderfully use them among those darkened souls.

Bro. G. W Batman's Testimony

I was converted nine years ago, and got a know-so salvation–no guess work about it. I repented of my sins and forsook them, accepting the Lord as my Savior. Praise God. A few years later, I fasted and prayed for about three days and during that time I put off the old man Adam in the form of inbred sin and God came in and destroyed the devil's workshop by casting his tools on the outside. Praise God I got a real evidence that I was sanctified and the Blood applied. After that, I received the baptism with the Holy Ghost and fire and now I feel the presence of the Holy Ghost, not only in my heart but in my lungs, my hands, my arms and all through my body and at times I am shaken up like a locomotive steamed up and prepared for a long journey. O it is blessed to let the Lord have His way with you. I also speak in six foreign tongues given me at God's command. God has called me to Africa as a missionary, and told me to go to Monrovia Liberia. He showed the town which is on the west coast. I described the town and country to Bro. Mead, a missionary that had been there and he said it was a perfect description. Saints, pray much. Fast and pray.

Mrs. Daisy L. Batman's Testimony

At the age of fourteen the Lord saved me from my sins. Last April He sanctified my soul, took all inbred sin out and gave me a clean heart fit for the Lord's use.

Hallelujah! But still I hunger for more, so when the Pentecost came to Los Angeles, I found that was just what I wanted. But I was working every day and could not be at the meeting much. One day the Lord told me to stop everything and go to the meeting. I said, Lord, I have three small children and, no way to support them. He said, I will supply your needs. Glory to God, He has supplied all our needs. We have never needed for anything and have never asked anybody but the blessed Lord for a penny. Three years ago last April, the Lord gave us the call to Africa. At first I thought I would stay and let my husband go, but He said, "No, you must go too." I thought He wanted us to go right away, but when He saw I was willing to spend my life in Africa for precious souls, He revealed to us that He would tell us when to go. And three months after we received our baptism, He said, "Now go to Africa." O glory to God, I am so glad I got to the place where the blessed Lord's will is my will.

These testimonies appeared in the December 1906 edition of The Apostolic Faith. *G. W. Batman was introduced to* The Apostolic Faith *readers in October 1906, when a testimony is given of him praying for a twenty-one year old epileptic who was instantly set free from demons and healed of seizures.*

The Batman family stopped in Topeka, Kansas and ministered on the way to New York. Their testimony of what God was doing in Los Angeles made the congregation "real hungry for more of God." (The Apostolic Faith, *Feb-March 1907).*

The January 1907 issue reports that the team had sailed from England to Monrovia late in December. The paper reported, "We must not forget these dear ones that are one with us and a part of the body in dark Africa."

This precious family arrived in Liberia with Julia Huchens, her husband and Lucy Farrar, but soon after their arrival in Africa they contracted a deadly fever and the entire family of five perished. Their sacrifice was great. Surely their bodies planted in the cold earth were seed that have grown into a great Spirit-filled revival in Africa today.

Sister Hutchins' Testimony

Julia W. Hutchins

I was justified on the 4th of July, 1901, and at that time, I felt that the Lord wanted me in Africa, but I was not then at all willing to go. But on the 28th of July, 1903, the Lord sanctified me. Before He sanctified me, He asked me if I would go to Africa. I promised Him I would. From that time on, I have felt the call to Africa, and have been willing to go at any moment, but not knowing just when the Lord would have me leave.

On the sixth of last month, while out in my back yard one afternoon, I heard a voice speaking to me these words: "On the 15th day of September, take your husband and baby and start out for Africa." And I looked around about me to see if there was not someone speaking to me, but I did not see anyone, and I soon recognized that it was the voice of God. I looked up into the heavens and said: "Lord, I will obey." Since then I have had many tests and temptations from the devil. He has at times told me that I would not even live to see the 15th of September, but I never once doubted God. I knew that He was able to bring everything to pass that He told me to do.

After hearing the voice telling me to leave Los Angeles on the 15th, I went to one of my neighbors and testified to her that the Lord had told me to leave for Africa on the 15th of September. She looked at me with a smile. I asked her what she was smiling about. She said: "Because you have not got street car fare to go to Azusa Street Mission tonight, and talking about going to Africa." But I told her I was trusting in a God that could bring all things to pass that He wanted us to go. He has really supplied all my needs in every way, for the work where He has called me.

I want to testify also about my husband. He was a back-slider, and how the devil did test me, saying: "You are going out to cast the devil out of others, and going to take a devil with you." My husband was not saved, but I held on to God and said: "Lord, I will obey."

I continued to testify and to make preparations to leave on the 15th. The Lord reclaimed my husband and sanctified him wholly and put the glory and shout in him. So now it is my time to laugh. The devil has oppressed and mocked me; but praise the Lord, now I can mock him. Glory to God! It is now ten minutes to four o'clock in the afternoon on the 15th day of September. I am all ready and down to the Mission with my ticket and everything prepared, waiting to have hands laid on and the prayers of the saints, and expect to leave at eight o'clock from the Santa Fe station en route for Africa. We expect to go to Mt. Coffee, Monrovia, Liberia.

Feeling the need of a real companion in the Gospel that was out and out for God, I prayed to God that He might give me one to go with me. I had my eyes upon one that I wanted to go, but in prayer and humility before God, I found out it was not the one the Lord wanted to go. So I said: "Any one, Lord, that you would have to go will be pleasing to me." And, to my surprise, He gave me my niece–a girl that I had raised from a child. Now she is nineteen years of age, is saved, sanctified and baptized with the Holy Ghost, and is going with me out into the work of the Lord. So instead of giving me one companion, He gave me two–my niece and my husband.

Our first stop will be Chattanooga, Tennessee, Harge Row. I want the prayers of the saints that I may stay humble.

When William Seymour travelled to Los Angeles it was to preach in Julia Hutchins' Holiness mission. Because Seymour preached the baptism in the Holy Ghost, an experience he had not yet received, the Southern California Holiness Association closed his meeting. This testimony demonstrates that Hutchins not only received the Holy Spirit baptism, but was one of the first Azusa missionaires to Africa.

This article was published in the Apostolic Faith *in October 1906. According to the newspaper, Hutchins had "received the baptism with the Holy Ghost and the gift of the Uganda language, the language of the people to whom she is sent."*

T. C. McConnell

Larry Martin Collection

Courtesy of John McConnell

Experience in Trusting God for Needs

T. C. McConnell

The first time I was out of wood after the Lord had shown me to trust Him, I asked the Lord for wood and the wood did not come. The Lord had shown me that I could not ask for what I already had. If there was flour in the barrel, I could not ask for flour till it was gone. I went down into the basement that morning and found some hard knots that had been laid aside and had enough wood for that day. The next morning I asked the Lord for wood. The wood did not come. I picked up enough chunks and chips to do that day.

The next morning, I went to the Lord and said, "Father, there are no more chunks and chips, we are out of wood. Send the wood." I went down to the city and forgot all about it. Did not think of it, until I returned home, and my daughter said, "Papa, who brought the wood?" I told her that "she need not trouble, the Lord would send it. But she said, "Some man brought wood, who was he that you sent it by!" I thought she was joking, but she said, "Look in the box and in the basement." I went down and found a large load of wood already for the stove and just the length that we used in our stove.

I did not know for some time who brought the wood; but one day when holding meetings in South Seattle, a man invited me home with him and while at dinner he said, "I want to tell you something that happened to me. I was crossing the bridge with a load of wood. My wife had written out a bill of some things that we had to have, and I needed feed for my horses. I was taking this load of wood in to get the groceries and feed. While out on the bridge and no one near me, an audible voice said behind me and just above me, 'Take this wood to McConnell.' I looked around me and there was no one near me. I said, 'I cannot take this wood to McConnell, I have got to have the groceries and feed,' and drove on. The voice said again, 'Take this wood to T. W. McConnell.' I said, 'How can I take this wood to McConnell; I must have these groceries and feed for my horses.' And the third time the voice spoke, and so strong that it scared me, and I answered, 'Well, I will,' for I believed it was the Lord talking. There was no one about.

"I went and made inquiry, finally looked in the directory and found where you lived. I drove to the house and unloaded the wood, then drove back home as quickly as I could, loaded up some wood that I had and drove back to town, sold my wood as soon as I reached town, got my feed and groceries, and from that time I have prospered as never before."

This testimony was published in the September 1906 edition of The Apostolic Faith. *The same issue carried this testimony of McConnel's conversion and Holy Ghost baptism:*

> *About 28 years ago, I went into a meeting to break it up, and the Lord broke me up. My conversion I never could doubt. I was called to preach and refused, and went on for a number of years trying to got away from the call. Finally I obeyed the Lord, and started in to work for Him, but not to preach. The Lord sanctified my soul. Then I commenced to try to preach. About two years after, the Lord appeared to me in a dream. He so filled me with His Spirit that people were not able to stand up before me, for a time. A few days after, He told me to give up my business, and make my wants known to Him, and not to man. I obeyed. The Lord supplied my every need, and was with me in revival meetings and in healing many that I prayed for. But I heard of people receiving the Holy Ghost and speaking with tongues. I came to Los Angeles to investigate, and found it was a fact, and earnestly commenced to seek the Lord for the baptism with the Holy Ghost. And the Lord, knowing my heart, came and took possession of me and spoke with my tongue. I want to say to every person, test God and you will never deny the baptism with the Holy Ghost.*

Maggie and William Bowdan

Courtesy of Lisa Rollerson

Personal Testimony

Frank R. Bowdan, Sr.

A great revival had swept the Pacific Coast, stirring up all sorts of creeds and provoking comment far and wide. It had first begun in Topeka, Kansas and spread to Los Angeles, California. Ministers, Missionaries, laymen, and men of all walks of life visited the little church on Azusa Street either to approve or criticize the services which were being held, for the Holy Spirit was being manifested in great power as it was at Pentecost centuries ago.

A little woman interested in these meetings later voiced her desire to get the Holy Ghost. Her husband greatly objected and even threatened to leave her if she got "mixed up" in that strange "new" religion. However, the lady with a determined mind set out to get the thing she desired–the Holy Ghost. She visited the meetings once or twice and finally came home shouting and praising God for the real baptism of the Holy

Ghost. When her husband heard her speak with tongues and magnify God, he changed his mind about leaving her and their two sons, but rather prayed that he too might be endowed with the same power.

A few nights later when all the congregation was assembled together and everyone had bowed to pray, they heard a sound as a high wind sweeping around the building and suddenly they all began to speak in tongues and glorify God. Her husband was in the room that evening too with tears streaming down his cheeks, he had yielded himself to God. So with the manifestation of the Spirit, he too felt a Divine touch as the joy ran into his heart as a river, filled him to overflowing and spake out of him in a language he did not understand.

That night two souls which had already been blessed knew for the first time much more the joys of eternal salvation were than that which they had claimed in their former church life. Before they had done well, now everything was better. New things in the household began to displace the old. They began hanging mottos on the walls. The husband who always asserted his manhood in governing all things of the home, one evening brought in a motto which read, "Christ is the head of this house"; and the wife who always was a blessing to all she met began searching too until she brought a motto which read, "With Thy blessings let the house of Thy servant be blessed forever." The Lord honored them both and let them enjoy His favors as he added daily to their joys and kept their little family in good health.

Four years had passed since their last child and now they longed for another to grace their home. They sought the Lord and promised him, "Lord, if you will give *us another child, let it be a son. If it is, we will give him back to you to preach your gospel."* The prayer was answered. I am that son, "Frank" Rueben Bowdan, born March 16th, 1910. Although I was always called by my nickname Frank, my real name is Rueben Bowdan.

Frank Bowdan was a child at the Azusa Street Mission. His parents, William S. and Maggie A. Bowdan received the baptism of the Holy Ghost at the mission. The Bowdans embraced the Jesus Only movement after the Arroyo Seco Campmeeting in 1913, became members of The Belvedere Mission led by Frank Ewart and later founding members of both the Pentecostal Assemblies of the World, Inc. and the Apostolic Faith Home Assembly church in Los Angeles, CA. Frank would later become the pastor of the Home Assembly church and the Assistant Presiding Bishop of the Pentecostal Assemblies of the World.

Frank's testimony was written in 1924 and was published in Like A Rose: Life, Times and Messages of the Late Bishop Frank R. Bowdan, D.D., 1910-1976 *and is used with the permission of the Apostolic Heritage Foundation, directed by Lisa LeBlanc Rollerson, eldest granddaughter of Frank R. Bowdan, and great-granddaughter of William and Maggie Bowdan.*

For further information contact the Apostolic Heritage Foundation at apostolicheritagefoundation.org

Azusa Street Credentials Committee

Courtesy of James Corum
(Digitally Enhanced)

A Holiness Preacher Who Received Pentecost

W. A. Love

I know when I really repented of my sins and turned away from them that God did for Christ's sake forgive me. He gave me the blessed evidence that the work was done. "We know that we have passed from death unto life because we love the brethren," and "If any man be In Christ Jesus he is a new creature, old things are passed away; behold, all things are become new." He has a new life Implanted in his heart. God gives us all the evidence we need for everything He does for us.

After I was really converted to God, and wonderfully blessed of the Lord, I heard the Holiness people teaching that the Lord would sanctify our souls, but I did not see how it was that the Lord did not sanctify us when we were converted. So, I went to studying the Word of God, and soon found that I did not get sanctified when I was converted. Not only by reading the Word, but from the testimonies of others that had the experience. But you know,

Satan was on hand to tell me that I could grow into it, so I tried to grow into the experience, and made a complete failure of it. But when I made a complete sacrifice to God—all on the altar—bless God, He really did sanctify my soul, and gave me the real evidence; the witness of the Holy Ghost that the work was done, and the carnal mind was destroyed; and, oh, what a sweet peace did flood my soul. I was wonderfully anointed time and again for the work of the Lord, and when I heard of the baptism with the Holy Ghost that some claimed they had received since they were sanctified, I said they never had been sanctified, or they would know better. But I went down to investigate the matter. And when I first went to Azusa Mission, I heard Brother Seymour preach the Word. He said that the disciples were sanctified before the day of Pentecost, and of course, I could not swallow that, because that was not in harmony with the rules and teachings of the Holiness church of which I was a member. He told us to search the Word, and so I began to do this, and the Word made it clear to my mind that his statement was true, and I became hungry for more of God. But the tongue business was a hard problem for me, and I took the 2nd chapter of Acts, and tried to harmonize my sanctified experience with the experience the people got on the day of Pentecost but I could not get them to harmonize so I came to the conclusion that they got something that I did not get. I then began to tarry and pray night and day, and did not stop until I was wonderfully baptized with the Holy Ghost, and He gave me the blessed evidence which always follows, which is the speaking in tongues.

The Holy Ghost has spoken five different languages through me since I got my Pentecost, some of which has been interpreted. I am glad the Lord knows all the languages of the nations.

From The Apostolic Faith, *February-March 1907.*

Called and Baptized

E. S. Hanson

"Ye have heard of the patience of Job, and have seen the end of the Lord; that the Lord is very pitiful, and of tender mercy." I, in a great measure, realize the meaning of the above words, although those who have never experienced the loving and tender mercies of our God cannot understand these things.

Dear friends, as far back in my life as I have any remembrance I have felt the call of God upon me to preach his gospel, but there has been much in this world to hinder me in giving myself up to His service. The first thing to contend with was, I didn't know how to preach, didn't have any education. My folks were poor and couldn't afford to send me to college, so I concluded I would learn some trade and make enough money to get an education. But God's hand was upon me, and I could not be silenced, for just when I began to get a little money then God would permit sickness to lay hold of me, so it would all go for doctors and drug bills. And this continued for the last few years of my life. I little realized that this was God's way and God's theological school He was taking me through, for God spoke to me in many ways before He could get me to understand that my ways were not his ways.

During this time I gave my heart to God, and found rest from the condemnation of sin, and God was still calling me to preach, but I couldn't, for I didn't know how. I would try it, but would fail. Everything I would say would be contrary, so I told the Lord I just couldn't preach; I didn't know how, and that I would do anything else that He wanted me to; but that didn't satisfy God, for His calling is without repentance, so He permitted Satan to get a hold on me. I was afflicted with some large abdominal abscesses that took me to death's door, and while lying on my bed the Lord said: "Though you have trusted me many times before for healing of your body, and I have healed you, because you put all your trust in me, but this time are you willing to die?"

That was a hard question, so I studied a little before I answered, for I had a great desire to live and help in the salvation of souls, and I said, yes. I had a most earnest desire to go home to glory, but God willed it not to be so, for He said, "You shall recover and be of service to me." Then I was made to pass through awful suffering, but I knew God was true, so I just pleaded to Him, and had requested most all the Christian people in reach of me to pray for me, so God delivered me and gave me the victory in the name of Jesus, teaching me how to preach His glorious gospel, giving me the baptism of the Holy Ghost, making me a witness of those things I have heard and seen, and of those things which He will allow me to all the nations. Glory to His name.

My Experience in Receiving of the Holy Ghost

A few weeks ago after having had the prayers of many, I heard through a dear brother about the wonderful works of God in Los Angeles, and He sent my name in for a paper, and when I had received and carefully read it, the Spirit testified with my spirit that it was the true teaching of the gospel, and that was the reason the Holiness movement has fallen short of the full power of God, and I immediately examined all the passages of scripture bearing on sanctification being the baptism of the Holy Ghost and fire, and found none to support that teaching, and began immediately to seek God that I might have this gift.

Well, the outcome has been this, that my old experience of sanctification was cleaned up wonderfully, and I got healing for my body and began immediately to recover, and in a few days, by the leading of the Spirit and the power of the precious blood, was able to come to Salem from my home, seventeen miles west, and attend the meeting. God had given me a wonderful anointing of His Spirit witnessing to my entire sanctification and the second evening the workers came into my room and laid hands on me and prayed, and I received the gift of speaking in tongues. The Spirit just took possession of my face and jaws and began moving them sideways back and forth, and I began to speak in other tongues, as the Spirit gave utterance, saying only a few words in each, and then began to chant in the Spirit. There was wonderful thrilling of joy sweeping all over me of such a sweetness of love that it is impossible for tongue to describe it, and the next morning, while I was sitting by the stove praying, I spoke a complete language for about five minutes. I just thank God for this gift, and prize the leadings of the Holy Ghost more than anything in life. Glory to our God forever and ever. Amen.

E. S. Hanson lived in Dallas, Oregon. His testimony appreared in the November 19, 1906 issue of the Apostolic Light, *published in Salem, Oregon. This is a good example of the thousands who received the baptism in the Holy Ghost after reading* The Apostolic Faith *newspaper from the Azusa Street Mission.*

A Short History of the Pentecostal Movement

Max Wood Moorhead

In the city of Los Angeles, California, U.S.A. in April, 1906 in a private house where a little group were gathered together to wait on God for the outpouring of the Holy Ghost, a woman received the baptism and began to speak in new tongues as did the disciples on the day of Pentecost (Acts 2). The news spread like fire, and the numbers of seekers increased rapidly. Meetings were held in Azusa Street in a disused church which had been used latterly for stabling purposes. Very many of this company were Negroes, poor, lowly, ignorant, and despised. Less than 50 years ago Negroes were owned by white people in the United States as slaves. No one but an American can rightly understand how despised the Negro is. The twentieth century Pentecostal Movement had its birth in a despised place amongst a despised people; because there was no room for it in the modern church.

Many different races live in Los Angeles, and multitudes came long distances to seek their Pentecost, and to see and to hear the wonderful works of God. This crowd included beside Negroes, Mexicans, English, Spanish, Germans, French, Russians, Chinese, Scandinavians, and North American Indians. Hundreds have received their Pentecost in Los Angeles as at the beginning; for Africans, Germans, Frenchmen, Mexicans, Scandinavians, and Russians have all heard, in their own tongues, Spirit-filled believers proclaiming the mighty works of God.

One day a little group of long bearded Russians not one of whom understood English, came into the meeting, where in the Russian language, they heard Jesus exalted; and suddenly they felt at home and with tear bedewed eyes embraced the speaker, thinking that he too must have come from their fatherland.

People living hundreds of miles away send handkerchiefs to be prayed over. On some mornings the post has brought so many handkerchiefs that owing to lack of time it has not been possible to pray singly for each; and so three or four Christian workers would kneel around the pile forty or fifty deep; and touching it with their fingers, would pray in Jesus' Name, remembering the various requests. Then the handkerchiefs would each one be returned to the senders. One woman slipped one of these into the pillow case of her demon possessed husband, who rolled about his bed as if irked by needles. At midnight he awakened, saying, "Wife, pray for me," and he got saved. In this way men have been delivered from the drink habit and the tobacco habit, and insane people have through the power of the Holy Ghost recovered their senses.

A resident of Los Angeles, Cal., who frequently attended the Los Angeles meeting noticed these five good points:

1. They always honored the Blood of Jesus;

2. They honored the Holy Ghost, giving Him room to work;

3. They had a burning desire to spread the Gospel—the true missionary spirit;

4. They were earnestly looking for Jesus' Second Coming;

5. They did not take collections, nor throw out hints for money.

It has been repeatedly stated that there are now in the United States, 50,000 men, women, and children who are praising and magnifying God in new tongues. We do not know a single state without witnesses to Pentecost. In the city of Chicago it is said there are 1,000 persons who are in Pentecostal blessing; out of which number a few scores are simple Italian peasants, some of whom have returned to Italy to tell the story of the Cross in the power of the Holy Ghost.

How many thousands of souls have been won to Jesus during these days of the Latter Rain, no one knows exactly. In the southern states multitudes have been saved.

This article appeared in the periodical, Cloud of Witnesses to Pentecost in India, *published by the author in Bombay, India. It was released in November 1908. Moorhead was a Presbyterian missionary. The article continued to describe Pentecostal movements in other places around the world.*

Carrie Judd Montgomery

Courtesy of Tony Cauchi

Letter from Los Angeles

Carrie Judd Montgomery

We print the following extracts from a remarkable letter from Mr. F. Bartleman, of Los Angeles, published recently in the *Way of Faith.*

My husband has recently visited Los Angeles and attended some of these meetings. He felt at times great power of the Holy Spirit in the meetings, and is convinced that the work is of God, even though there be counterfeits of the enemy. Let us all bow down before God, and be as humble and simple as little children, that we may miss nothing of the blessing God wants to pour upon His children in these last days.

What has impressed us most of all in the Oakland meetings is the great work of grace in several children, one little girl only nine years old, being so baptized with the Holy Spirit, that her face seemed, to look like an angel's, and the wisdom and sweetness which she displayed in dealing with another child to lead her to Christ, we have never seen surpassed.

Frank Bartleman

Photo Used by Permission
Flower Pentecostal Heritage Center

Letter from Los Angeles

Frank Bartleman

I believe the Lord would have me mention a few facts, especially in regard to the feature of the "tongues" in our meetings. It may be helpful to some, inspire confidence in faltering, troubled ones. I will be brief, simply state facts.

At first many said, "There is nothing in the 'tongues,' all a delusion of the devil." but this was the voice of unbelief. To be sure the enemy has moved hell to counterfeit and bring reproach, but he saw something worth imitating. The "tongues" at least have created an interest and proven the miracle-working power of God still with us as of old.

Hitherto I have been led to say but little regarding the "tongues," for there is always danger at such a time as this of diverting the attention from the great Giver to the gift, nor do I intend now to unduly exalt them. A few statements will suffice.

Let me say just this, that we are living in an intensely materialistic age, while about everything supernatural is being attributed to the devil. There possibly never was a time of such danger of committing the sin against the Holy Ghost. Many think the great sin of the end of this age will be just that.

But is it reasonable to suppose that God would forsake the field, leaving it and us to the devil in such a time of need? Oh, no, a thousand times no. And we are realizing His faithfulness today. Aaron's rod is again turning to a serpent and swallowing up the rods of the magicians. But after the "tongues" had been satisfactorily proven to be genuine, in many instances at least, unbelief must make another shift, and now said: "Well, what of it? Of what practical use?" Oh, accursed unbelief! What subtle subterfuges. Beware you tempt your God. Why should we be so eager to discover wrong? "Rejoicing in iniquity?" Oh, give God a chance. If you ask for bread will He give you a stone? But now the facts. It has not yet been proven of just what practical value the present gift of tongues will be in foreign fields. We have not had time. There have been a few cases where they have worked salvation among foreigners within our own borders. But I will speak more particularly just now of their benefit to the Christians. In a general way they have proven a very great blessing and impetus to the meeting. The congregations have been awed into silence, subdued into reverence, by their exercise. Sometimes the speaker has understood the message spoken, through him, oftimes not. Foreigners have been converted directly through such messages.

At one time Sister Prince, a colored lady well known and reverenced among us, a very ordinary woman, as natural talents go, but intensely pious and of childlike faith (of great quality, however), spoke in the most perfect German, of which she knew absolutely nothing in the natural. Two of the brethren who were German born, in different parts of the house, interpreted to those around them, and a few minutes afterwards notes were compared and it was proven genuine to the extreme satisfaction of all present. Let me say; the messages as far as I have interpreted, have always been proper messages, praises to God, exhortations, warnings, etc. Never anything of a foolish or irreverent character, but very often of a very highly exalted and intensely practical import, often of tremendous meaning, especially for the individual for whom the message was intended. Instances could be multiplied in the narration. But we simply seek to satisfy us as to the genuineness at this time. Many through blank and deceptive prejudice, listening to hearsay, and satisfied with the same, gathered from the enemies of the cause, have denied the whole and reported it of the devil. This has been caused by failure to impartially investigate, or unwillingness to be convinced, or possibly from both. Such have done great harm to the faith of many, retarded the work greatly from spreading widely, as it should, hindered the coming of His glory, besides running fearful personal risks in their relation to God. Many are suffering from this great mistake today, perhaps unconsciously as yet, but doomed with Samson ultimately to realize their strength departed from them. Oh, I warn such solemnly once more, beware!

Another instance I might mention of a young colored lady, very ordinary, with no knowledge whatever of the language, speaking at length, in my hearing at a meeting in "tongues." God is being pleased to use the people we would least expect it from. All that no flesh might glory. "The things that are not most glorify Him at this time."

Immediately she had spoken, Rev. S. J. Mead, well known in church circles and highly respected, lately returned from Africa, where, while actively engaged in the mission field, God spoke to him and bade him come at once to Los Angeles, for what reason he did not then understand, arose to his feet and readily interpreted the message just spoken by the girl, giving the name and dialect of the tribe in Africa to which the language belonged, and then immediately proceeded to speak the very same message in the very same tongue which he himself had become familiar with while in the field in Africa. Nothing could have been more satisfactorily proven.

Dear Brother Mead is now on his way back to his field in Africa with other workers called to go with him from these meetings. Glory!

Another instance I might mention, which I can vouch for, in fact they are too numerous to take space to mention all here.

Brother Burt, well known in the churches here, a returned missionary from India, while at the altar seeking power from on high, and rather doubting, was spoken to by a white man who was all unconscious of the language in which he was speaking, that of Gujarat. The message was so assuring to our brother that he opened his heart wide, without reserve, and the fire went through him in a most wonderful way, to hear him tell the story. He now longs to get back to dear India, especially to tell the good news to his fellow-missionaries, whom he declares must have just this experience. A few days later he interpreted for me a "tongue" in which a white sister was speaking, who had just received her Pentecost. It was another language spoken in India with which he was familiar. And so these things are happening every day to convince those who will be convinced. What more can God do? Also people are being healed by scores, as of old. God is trying to attract our attention, prove His compassion for us. Oh, shall it be spurned, refused, rejected?

One more and interesting instance of the "tongues" and I am done for this time. Rev. Joseph H. Kelley, ex-soldier from the Philippines, was converted later in St. Louis, and returned for missionary work in the land of Mindanao. Lately he felt called to return to this country to gather up a band of workers to return with him. After making strenuous efforts in that direction, he seemed only to fail, and finally became discouraged. The devil so taunted him that, pressed beyond endurance, he finally declared to himself that if God did not care for the Philippines, he need not either, and determined to return without making any further effort toward interesting anyone else in that direction. He has spoken in many churches in this country on the subject. Having heard of the work in Los Angeles, however, and of the "tongue" business, he, like Saul of old, began to breathe out threatenings, and headed this way declaring that before he returned to his field he would do the Lord one more good turn and expose the tongue deception proper. By the time he reached the place he was just about furious, as so many others have been. In fact, as he confesses freely he was simply an unvarnished backslider. But God had mercy on his soul. The saints realized his condition quickly and began to pray for him openly. This he resented. The Irish got the better of him and he confesses he even harbored a desire to whip the preacher soundly. But soon after, while sitting in his chair, a delicate, quiet little white sister spoke to him in a "tongue" which he understood—that of a hostile tribe in the interior, where he had been laboring. He knew that language was altogether unknown in this part of the world, and he nearly fell off his chair. There was something more than "n----- religion" in this. He went upstairs to the private room, quite in serious trouble, but still resisting. But there the Lord slew him properly–stretched him on the floor until he was glad to ask for quarters. The next day, after having been forgiven, he knelt at the "old plank" and sought his pentecost. And then another precious white sister, just as ignorant as the Filipinos spoke a message to him in another tongue he had become familiar with in those islands, and assured him "this is that." It was sufficient, and he swept into the experience. And now the Lord is giving him his band of workers to go with him after all. But, best of all, instead of going back a plain, backslidden preacher, he goes filled with the Holy Ghost. Oh, glory! And the "tongues" have played their part already.

After all our judgment is far from perfect, and we do well to walk softly at such a time as this. There may be many things we have yet to learn. At any rate, the "government is on His shoulders," and the ark perhaps will ride safer without our steadying. Pray about it anyway.

The "heavenly choir" is another feature of this work of the Spirit which deserves especial mention, but I have consumed my time and space. The voice of this song is a direct gift of the Spirit, given to many.

Sometimes it is expressed without words, sometimes in praises to God. Often it is a chant by one or two, or more. But the greatest effect seems to be produced when suddenly in the meeting a dozen, or perhaps a score, will burst forth in the most beautiful chords, all in harmony, and all pitches of voice. This will sometimes continue for as much as half an hour, though generally a shorter time. It is under direct inspiration of the Spirit, and can in nowise be produced at any other time. None can take part in this but those who have received their gift. They treasure it most sacredly. It is one of the most effective exercises of the Spirit in the present work. It simply cannot be described, hence little has been said about it but it seems at such times indeed to calm the most savage heart. It surpasses and defies the best trained choir of our land for harmony and feeling. This has been declared by most competent judges of voice culture. Besides this, the rapture the performer undergoes especially when a number are singing in unison of spirit, is beyond description. I speak this most humbly from personal experience. It is the very foretaste of the rapture that we soon shall realize when he shall call for us, I believe the blessed Christ is coming soon. It must be so. I anticipate it in my spirit, especially at such times, in a way beyond my powers to describe. Oh, be ready!

Yours for Jesus at His coming,

F. Bartleman

Frank Bartleman is best known for his book How Pentecost came to Los Angeles. *Bartleman was a prolific writer and an eye witness to the events in Los Angeles. The letter was republished by Carrie Judd Montgomery in her periodical,* Triumphs of Faith *in December 1906.*

Mrs. Montgomery whose introduction to this article is on page 137 was one of the most significant female voices in the early Pentecostal revival. Montgromery was a teacher, writer, editor, social worker and managed "faith homes."

Lucy Leatherman

Larry Martin Collection
Courtesy of *Grace and Glory*

From Sister Leatherman

Lucy Leatherman

We have had two good letters from Sister Leatherman this month, and the best news in them is that the Lord has once more touched her with his healing hand and after months of suffering she is well again. In her letter of August 10th from Yokonama, Japan this heroic woman says amongst other things:

"Dear Old Egypt, they are writing for me to come back there: but God's will be done. Sometimes I get weary and can say with Paul 'To me to live is Christ, but to die would be gain.' When the body staggers as I walk, the spirit is willing but the flesh is weak.

"My three months in Egypt almost finished me. I worked day and night, and lived in a house alone with rats, which kept me awake till four in the morning; and then I would sleep late until some great overgrown boy or Egyptian man would knock on my door. When I would look out of the window asking who was down there, I would see some of the flock who had come to be prayed with. Often I found when I got downstairs more than one who were seeking salvation. They would say 'Praise God' when they started to seek the Lord and never quit until they got the witness of the Spirit that their names were on the Lamb's Book of Life!"

Sept. 10th–"Hallelujah to God and the Lamb! I do praise God this afternoon for victory in my soul and body. You will never know how I have suffered with my spine and head for two months or more. But God, our God is able to do exceeding abundantly above all we ask or think. My sight was so bad I could scarcely see to read at all and I had a talk with a oculist. He said the nerves in my eyes were in a dreadful condition and that I was a nervous wreck. But I had no money to get glasses, so I took my poor body to God, and He healed me without price. Truly He is the poor man's (and woman's) friend. I sought Him with my whole heart for I was aware that something must be done very soon.

I am truly thankful to have found a friend like Miss Cummings–when I came to her house I wanted to start some meetings, but she made me rest–and when I relaxed I slept three days and nights except for meals. The only thing that broke my sleep (or stupor) was wet towels on my head and prayers of others. I could not pray myself. But when I would get awake a desire would come for God to heal me and finally I became desperately in earnest and touched the hem of His garment, and He has made me whole again. Ever since I left Egypt, my blood had been congested, while at Assiont [Egypt. Ed.] we had to take our crowds out in the courtyard of nights; and our pulpit was a hard, cold stone; one night I chilled and my feet were numb. After that my circulation never seemed to be the same, and my right lung seemed almost to close up and get heavy as lead, and my suffering was great. But all things work together for good to them that love God and He has now healed me.

I heard of some souls seeking the baptism in the interior of China. Do pray that messengers may be sent to them, also to the Philippines. Pray too, for Persia, Arabia, Armenia, Palestine and Egypt. And please pray for me that I may be used as He pleases and my will always be His will. Amen.

Love to all the saints in Los Angeles; and to the saints abroad greetings in His dear Name.

This report was published in The Upper Room *in January 1910. Leatherman left the Azusa Mission in the Summer of 1906 with several other missionaries. She began her missions service in Jerusalem, but served many years as a missionary in various places in Africa and Asia. The report was followed by a note, "Sister Leatherman has now gone on to Manila and asks a special interest in our prayers."*

Geoge B. Studd

Photo Used by Permission
Flower Pentecostal Heritage Center

America

George B. Studd

In April, 1906, the Holy Spirit fell on a company of humble Negro Christians, who were met together in a small house in the City of Los Angeles, California, U.S.A., and as they one by one yielded to the divine power, they spoke with other tongues, as the Spirit gave them utterance. The news of this wonderful manifestation of Pentecostal power soon spread far and wide, and large numbers of earnest Christians came to Los Angeles seeking to be baptized with the Holy Ghost in the same manner. Los Angeles has a cosmopolitan population and people of almost every nationality heard messages in their own language, and many remarkable conversions can be told of foreigners, who heard the Gospel in their own tongues. Let one, told by Mr. George Studd in a letter published in *Confidence*, suffice.

"Last Sunday night we had a truly wonderful meeting, and amongst other beautiful features in it was the following: A young Spaniard, or Mexican, of good appearance and address, arose after the message had been given and said, "I have been here before and have laughed at you people, and did not believe in you; but I will never do so again. My wife is by my side and cannot speak or understand a word of English, but that young lady who gave her testimony a little time ago turned round and looking towards my wife with outstretched arms said in Spanish under the Spirit's power, 'Oh, come to Him, do come to Him now!' My wife is broken down in tears, and wants you to pray for her that she may become a Christian; pray for me also. Later on, at the penitent form, they both gave their hearts to the Lord and were saved, as far as I could judge. Praise God."

The fire has spread rapidly through the United States and Canada, and today, at a low computation, there are in America 50,000 people baptized in the Holy Spirit, speaking in new tongues. Bands of missionaries have gone out from different Pentecostal centers, carrying the glorious Gospel of Christ to all parts of the world, trusting the Lord to supply all their needs. There are 16 Pentecostal papers, most of them free publications, that we ourselves know of published in America all of which testify of the great things our wonder-working God is doing in these last days. Two of the best of these, and both free papers are: The *Apostolic Faith* of Portland, Oregon and *Trust*, published at Elim House, Rochester, New York.

George Studd was from a weathy family in England. He was well-known as a crickett player. His brother C.T. Studd made his fame as one of the Cambridge Seven missionaries. This article appeared in Victory! *in April 1909.*

Wonderful Times Coming

A. S. Worrell

That the present is the season of "the latter rain," when the Spirit is to be manifested in mighty power, can scarcely be doubted by any one of ordinary spiritual discernment. The wonderful revival in Wales, and the very remarkable work in India—especially in connection with the work of Ramabai—and the Pentecostal movement in the United States—all go to indicate that the Lord is about ready to put His mighty power upon those who are ready to receive it. Happy, thrice happy, the people who discern the signs of the times, fall in with the divine purpose, and get the best possible equipment for service. Those who have the wisdom to distinguish between the true and the false, and have the practical common sense not to reject the whole movement because of the Satanic counterfeits that are intermingled with the genuine Pentecostal coin, those who take the good and reject the spurious, have great possibilities of usefulness before them in this movement. Jer. 15:19.

Those, however, who are suspicious and critical, and are looking for perfection in human instruments, will be likely to let the present opportunity go by unimproved; and, all unconsciously to themselves, will, most likely, enter the realm of spiritual deterioration, and find themselves losers, rather than gainers, because they have not made the most of their opportunities.

Some men are vain enough to suppose that, if God should wish to introduce any great movement designed to elevate the cause of Christ, He would certainly select themselves as chief instruments in the pushing forward of such an enterprise; whereas, God would be most likely to choose humble, obscure men, who would never think of themselves in connection with anything great or noble. Self-sufficiency, a sense of self-worthiness, a high estimate of one's self–then are the very things that show one's unfitness for any exalted position in the cause of God. "He that exalts himself shall be abased," is ever an active principle in the government of Jesus Christ.

Yet the work of God is moving on; and some of His people, of humble; lowly type, are receiving as genuine "baptisms in the Holy Spirit," as were ever received; and, through Spirit-filled, Spirit-gifted disciples of Christ, the cause of Christianity will be rapidly pushed forward to its consummation, when the fullness of the Gentiles will have been brought in, and the number of full overcomers–composing the ruling force with Christ in the age to follow–will have been completed. Then Jesus Christ will return to the earth, to establish His Millennial reign, Hallelujah!

We have studied this Pentecostal movement in the light of a number of concrete examples among our beloved friends; and, while none of them with whom we have mingled are faultless; yet it is plain to be seen that a mighty uplifting power has come into their lives; differing, in some respects, from the receiving of the Holy Ghost for character-development. It should be remembered, that the Holy Savlor never did any mighty works, until the Holy Spirit came upon Him; and, what He did in His official capacity, He seems to have done in the power of the Holy Spirit (see Acts 10:38). And, if this was true of Jesus, surely His disciples can hope to do efficient work for Him only as they are imbued with power by the same Spirit.

Of course, there is more or less in every Pentecostal meeting we have attended, that could be referred to Satan or to "the flesh;" but this is exactly what was to be expected; for where the Holy Spirit works, Satan works. It is to be hoped, however, that, as the gift of discerning spirits, and the power to cast them out, are, bestowed upon God's true, Pentecostal people, they will be able to separate the false from the true; that so the genuine Pentecostal power and blessed fruits will show forth in the lives of God's fully equipped people.

Worrell was one of the most notable worshippers at Azusa Street. He was a Civil War chaplain, educator, Baptist evangelist, author, publisher and Bible translator. Worrell's endorsement appeared in The Household of God *in May 1907.*

Conrad Dottin

Larry Martin Collection
Courtesy of Abundant Life Church
Cambridge, MA

How Pentecost Came to Cambridge, Mass

Conrad Dottin

In the year 1909, the Lord spoke to Bro. and Sister Edward Vinton, of Somerville, Massachusetts, who had been to Los Angeles, California, and been baptized in the Holy Ghost, and told them to come to this city and open a mission. After much prayer and looking about, a vision of a place was given to Sister Vinton, and several visits were made to find the place shown her before it was found because they were not looking in the right locality. After prayer one morning, they were assured of God that if they would go forth in faith and praise, they would find the place that day. Going to the right and left as the Holy Spirit led, in a short time they came to an unoccupied meeting house, on Hampshire Street, formerly used by a Presbyterian assembly. It was secured without delay and everything within was ready for occupancy.

Not long after the opening of this house of worship the Lord led a few of the West Indian brethren there to hear the different ones sent there to preach on the baptism of the Holy Ghost and fire when we were led to search God's Word to know if these people were preaching truth or error. To our surprise, we learned that it was truth and we were short of the promises and power of God. Our rest was broken and we seemed as we were in the beginning, and under deep conviction and hunger, so that night after night we got before the Lord in prayer and He revealed unto us that the promise was for us and to our children, and to all who are afar off, even to as many as the Lord our God should call. The place where we had worshipped and where we had heard much truth no longer satisfied us and what they tried to give as a full and free salvation for soul, body and spirit came far short of meeting the hungry cry of our hearts, and though they declared they had the truth and the people at Hampshire Street were in great error, we were obliged to leave them, fall into line with the despised ones and tarry for the promise of the Father as we read in Luke 24:49.

In a few weeks, after meeting all God's requirements and continually waiting on Him, we and many who had believed our report and had come, heard and searched and found it all was in full accord with God's will and word, were baptized with signs following. Since then hundreds have been baptized in the Spirit with the Bible evidence, speaking in other tongues, as the Spirit gives utterance. After we had received the Holy Spirit in His fullness, a very strong crying came into our souls that the West Indies might be visited by the Holy Spirit and believers there might be baptized according to the Scriptures. Giving ourselves to prayer for them as we had for ourselves, in a short time the news reached us that several of the Indians were receiving the Holy Spirit with the same signs as had we. In our home town and parish, the Christian Mission, Barbados, the spirit broke out with the same manifestations when the elders had a meeting called, when they investigated these matters, put all who had given the Scriptural evidence of the Baptism out of fellowship.

O, that believers would go by the word of God if it is beyond their experience and be honest and seek the fulfilling of Acts 1:8 and 14, then would the Lord show Himself as in Apostolic times. Men were saved but Jesus knew they needed more, far beyond what they had and through yielding all to Him the Lord Jesus sent the promise of the Father upon them.

Have ye received the Holy Spirit since ye believed? God is no respecter of persons. The promise is to all. Meet the conditions and you will be met by a mighty incoming and outflowing of the Holy Spirit.

This is an example of the many, many church planters who left Azusa Street and spread the Pentecostal message to Massachusetts and also all across the United States and even the world. Dottin was a minister with the United Pentecostal Council of the Assemblies of God. This testimony was in the Apostolic Messenger *in December 1920.*

Wesley Steelberg and Ruth Fisher on their wedding day.

Photo Used by Permission
Flower Pentecostal Heritage Center

I Remember

Ruth Fisher Steelberg Carter

Pentecost–How the memories come flooding in at the mention of that word which has become almost synonymous in these last days with a supernatural power of the Holy Spirit which imparts vision and blessing to all who hunger and thirst after righteousness.

It is a privilege to be able to look back and say "I remember" when considering the mighty works of Him who is the same yesterday and forever.

When I was very young my father [Elmer Fisher, Ed.] was pastor of the First Baptist Church in Glendale, California. He became very hungry for more of God and especially for a move of the Holy Spirit. He spent all nights in prayer. He gave a series of messages in his church on the work of the Holy Spirit. When a man named Joseph Smale returned from the revival in Wales and opened a hall he called the New Testament Church in the heart of Los Angeles, my father joined with him, with other pastors, to seek for an outpouring of the Holy Spirit.

On Easter Mrs. Seymour came over and told them that Baptists had received the Pentecostal Baptism also. The second time that Elmer Fisher went to Azusa Street he received the baptism. That was in June 1906.

I remember a great camp-meeting in the Arroyo Seco, in Los Angeles in 1907. It was convened by two Canadian men, named Scott and Webster. The people from Azusa Street (colored) were there and also the white people and they lived in separate tents but they all worshiped together.* The most vivid memory is of the colored people, singing–as only Spirit-filled colored people could–

Oh, have you stayed your mind on him?
In peace, in perfect peace, I'll keep him
whose mind is stayed on Him.

I remember standing on a seat (because I was so small) to testify in an afternoon testimony meeting in old building in Azusa Street. I stood for such a long time awaiting my turn, as so many who had so much to tell of God's blessings, gave their testimony. When the leader finally said, "All right little girl," I became frightened and sat down, as my courage failed.

I remember, after my father had opened the Upper Room Mission on South Spring Street, the continuous revival for years. Five days a week there were at least two services a day. George Studd, a brother of C. T. Studd, the well-known missionary, had a Bible study in the mornings. My father gave himself so continuously to the work of the Lord, going out to pray for the sick and often staying to intercede until victory came. He only came home

---

**This language may be offensive to some today, but was very acceptable when this was written. No offence is intended.*

on Mondays and Saturdays. Many thanked God for his prayers. There was Rex Qualls, who later became a minister, whose blind eyes had been opened; and Charlie Rosenfeld, ever rejoicing after his dumb tongue had been loosed and his deaf ears opened; and Gertrude Levander, who had been violently insane and delivered after fasting and prayer had been made continuously for her. There were hosts of others healed of almost every kind of sickness and disease in answer to prayer.

There were all day services on Thursdays, when, while listening to testimonies of others of God's wondrous works, people fell off their chairs into the aisles at times, as they too were filled with the Spirit.

I remember going out on special trains–chartered for the occasion, and filled with happy, singing, crowds, to a place called Terminal Island. Here great baptismal services were held, as many were immersed in the sea as they followed their Lord in the symbol of confession by burial in a watery grave and resurrection.

I remember folk leaving to take the gospel to the ends of the earth. The Cooks, with their little daughter Blossom, at the altar in a great dedication service before they left for India. The McLains going to China, and John Lake in my father's study before he left to take the message of Pentecost to South Africa.

I remember–how could I forget–a glorious day in November 1913. The Upper Room Mission had moved to a small street, now an arcade between Spring and Broadway, and Fifth and Sixth Streets in Los Angeles, to a large hall, formerly a dance hall. In a Sunday afternoon meeting with several hundred people present, the Shekinah Glory seemed to fill the place. People were singing in the Spirit and one by one had stood to their feet, with eyes closed and hands upraised, to join in the heavenly choir. Such harmony, as the chorus increased in volume, in cadences almost indescribable. As a young girl, sitting beside mother on the front seat, I longed to join in the paeans of praise, but being very timid, was fearful. But as I saw every one with eyes closed, I felt I, too, could stand and worship him, whom my soul loved. I stood to my feet with the thought I could sit down before anyone else did and no one would know I had stood. I became so lost in the Spirit, they told me I stood for two hours singing in the languages of heaven as I was baptized in the Spirit that afternoon.

In 1917, when my father had a burden to see a work opened in Modesto, California; a thriving little town up in the San Joaquin Valley, a caravan was formed of four families and some other young men, to go to Modesto. A tent was erected to take the message of Pentecost to that town. It was not without persecution that the message went forth. They cut the tent ropes, tried to burn the tent, threw rotten eggs and tomatoes; but today there are several Pentecostal churches in Modesto.

Upon returning to Los Angeles, we found a meeting with Mrs. Woodworth-Etter in progress. Such meetings! The power of God was manifest in so many ways. There was dancing in the Spirit. People had visions. My brother was one among many filled with the Spirit there.

In 1918, just before my father passed away, we attended the Old Victoria Hall Mission where Warren Fisher [No relation. Ed.] was pastor and my future husband Wesley Steelberg was assistant pastor. We had a great band of young people aflame for God; going out to help the works in towns around Los Angeles on great interurban electric cars. We sang and testified in the cars as we went. We held great street meetings on the busiest corner in the heart of Los Angeles–where a big burly policeman knelt in the street in penitence. Many of that group became ministers or missionaries, among them Clarence Radley who gave his life in service for the Lord in Nicaragua in 1927.

It was then Mrs. McPherson [Aimee Semple. Ed.] arrived after driving clear across the country with her small children and her mother. How could we forget the wonderful works of God as the blessings increased. It was real revival as Mrs. McPherson walked in a large prayer room, packed with hungry, seeking people; as she touched all she could reach they were filled with the Spirit.

I remember the great camp-meeting in 1924 convened by Brothers R. J. Craig and M. R. Tatman in Berkeley, California, Uldine Utleys the eleven year old girl preacher was an evangelist together with Smith Wigglesworth from England and Dr. Shreve, a Spirit-filled Methodist pastor from D.C. One day Mr. Wigglesworth prayed for a man whose people had brought him to be prayed for requesting that he be very gentle with him as he was a very sick man. Mr. Wigglesworth, in his characteristic fury against the devil, struck him a terrific blow in the stomach as he commanded the illness to go. The man lost consciousness. His people were indignant, declaring he had killed him. They even called the police to bring charges against him; when the man regained consciousness and was perfectly healed.

This testimony is compiled and condensed from two documents "I Remember or What Pentecost Means to Me" and "Notes by Ruth Fisher Steelberg Carter (Mrs. Howard Carter) 1961." Both documents are in the Flower Pentecostal Heritage Center. Mrs. Carter was the daughter of Elmer Fisher one of the early Pentecostal adherents in Los Angeles. She was married to an Assemblies of God General Superintendent Wesley Steelberg and after his death to the British Pentecostal leader, Howard Carter.

Kelso R. Glover

Larry Martin Collrection
Courtesy of Jeanne Flournoy

God Is in Pentecost!

Kelso R. Glover

Thirty-five years ago, on the twenty-second of February, 1911, I received the Baptism of the Holy Ghost. I encountered people who had received the Holy Ghost in August of 1910, but not until the following February did the glory come into my soul. But it came! I want to testify to you that I am thoroughly convinced that God is in the Pentecostal Movement.

I wish also to bring to you the truth that Divine Healing and the Baptism of the Holy Ghost are inseparable. These are the foundation stones of the church of Jesus Christ. I bring to you the Gospel, as found in Acts 19. There we find Paul speaking to certain disciples in Ephesus, and asking that all-important question: "Have ye received the Holy Ghost since ye believed?" Their answer was: "We have not so much as heard whether there be any Holy Ghost." We, together with Paul, want you to know there is a Holy Ghost. There is a Holy Ghost for believers

With this miraculous Baptism goes the other great miracle of Divine Healing. We find that "God wrought special miracles by the hands of Paul: so that from his body were brought unto the sick handkerchiefs or aprons, and the diseases departed from them, and the evil spirits went out of them" (Acts 19:11-12).

The Baptism with the Holy Ghost, Healing and a Separated Life unto God go together.

I was studying for the ministry, attending the University of California, and my church theological seminary when, in 1910, I ran across people who believed in the Baptism in the Holy Ghost, Divine Healing, and real Holiness–things my church did not believe in. My church said the days of miracles are over; that holiness is not possible at all in this life, and that we already had all the Holy Ghost we would ever have.

I left my church, bidding them good-bye and came down to Los Angles, came to tell one, a friend whose mother had died–whose mother was a friend of my mother that there was a Comforter of all who sorrowed. I went down to tell the one who, later, became my darling wife, who has stood by me and who stands by me today that there is a Comforter who can heal the broken heart and who can bind up every wound. And God came into that broken heart, dried her tears, and I watched her saddened countenance changed by a mighty power to ecstasy. I watched Him change her mourning into laughter! The Holy Ghost came in! Before my very eyes she received the blessed Baptism of the Spirit. Then I cried out, "But, Lord, what are you going to do about me? I have been seeking for a year and you have not given the Baptism to me! Yet she who has not sought receives before me!"

Then the sweetheart God gave me began to help me. We went down to old Azusa Street. But why should I go down there? Was not my grandfather a Virginian and my grandmother from Kentucky and my very own mother raised with black slaves? Why should I go down to the black folks to get the Baptism of the Holy Ghost? But they had it and I wanted it. I went.

You had better go also my friends, if they have it and you do not! I had not received my Baptism, my sweetheart now had–others had–every one, it seemed–but not I. I must have it. I got it–got it in old Azusa Street. The first night I received a blessing and the second night I received more blessing, and on the third night, in that old Azusa mission, the glory came down. I had to get behind the piano, such was the crowd, to have a private conference with the Lord. I wanted this settled. And there the Holy Ghost came and found me behind the piano.

"Hiding?" you say. No, I was hiding from man that I might find God. I found Him. Flowing from my innermost being came a flood of ecstatic utterance–whether in tongues of men or of angels, I know not–nor cared. My first words that I could at last utter in English were –"It is finished, It is finished!" Then at a quiet moment I heard some one say, "He could go on like that all night." Opening my eyes reluctantly, I discovered the place to be empty and the janitor and his wife discussing what disposition to make of me. I found I had been able to stop the great flowing fountain, but I had too long waited for this moment to endanger the loss of so great a glory so I closed my eyes and gazed again upon the Lord and praised and thanked Him and asked Him if it would start again. It did. And also stopped again. So I arose and bidding a brief good night I stepped outside. But not one step further would I go till I knew for sure whether this fountain would start again. Looking up into the starry midnight sky I found voice again in those heavenly words. Satisfied, I walked toward home enjoying the fresh–flowing of this stream as I went along. But upon seeing a man approaching, I wondered if the fountain would stop till he passed. It did. I wondered then would it begin again. It did.

So has it been all these lovely 35 years that his wonderous soul satisfying Fountain has been stopping and starting in this most proper and heavenly manner.

God is in Pentecost! Are you?

This testimony was excerpted from God Is in Pentecost, *a sermon preached at Angelus Temple and published in 1946. Glover served as an associate to the Temple pastor, Aimee Semple McPherson.*

Before taking the position at the Temple, Glover preached around the world and served a tenure as lead pastor at the Stone Church in Chicago.

This rare booklet was found after an extended search by Glover's niece, Jeanne Flournoy. The editor deeply appreciates Ms Flournoy's sacrificial efforts.

Epilogue

Today in downtown Los Angeles.

312 Azusa Street is now part of a plaza adjoining the Japanese Cultural Center.

A plaque marks the site of the history making revival.

The Larry Martin Collection

Opportunity once passed is lost forever. There is a time when the tide is sweeping by our door. We may then plunge in and be carried to glorious blessing, success and victory. To stand shivering on the bank, timid or paralyzed with stupor, at such a time, is to miss all, and most miserably fail, both for time and for eternity. Oh, our responsibility! The mighty tide of God's grace and favor is even now sweeping by us, in its prayer-directed course. There is a river (of salvation) the streams whereof make glad the city of God (Psalm 46:4). It is time to "get together," and plunge in, individually and collectively. We are baptized "in one Spirit, into one body" (1 Cor. 12:13). Let us lay aside all carnal contentions and divisions, that separate us from each other and from God. If we are of His body, we are "one body." The opportunity of a lifetime, of centuries, is at our door, to be eternally gained or lost. There is no time to hesitate. Act quickly, lest another take thy crown. Oh, church of Christ, awake! Be baptized with power. Then fly to rescue others. And to meet your Lord.

Frank Bartleman
Gospel Tract
June, 1906

Once again America stands on the verge of a great spiritual awakening. The river is rising across the nation. Let us not let this mighty torrent pass us by. Pray, church, pray! May the same Spirit that flooded Azusa Street now flood every street from Pennsylvania Avenue to Wall Street to Main Street to your street. Please, God, send revival to the United States of America.

Larry Martin
2010

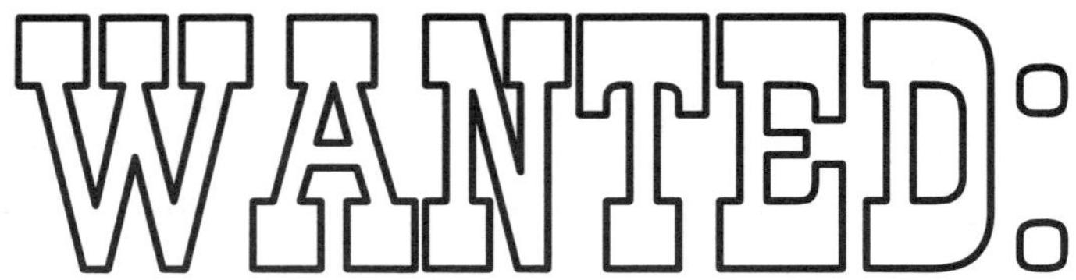

More Information on the Azusa Street Revival

Did any of your ancestors attend or participate at Azusa Street?

If so, I would love to hear from you. Please send me:

- ☑ *Names*
- ☑ *Photos (or copies)*
- ☑ *Stories*
- ☑ *Printed Materials*

With your help, we can preserve and record the Azusa story for future generations.

CHRISTIAN LIFE BOOKS

www.azusastreet.org

P.O. BOX 36355

PENSACOLA, FLORIDA 32516

email: info@azusastreet.org